Mabel Gray

and the Wizard Who Swallowed the Sun

For Lillyanna,
who has the makings
of a very good
wizard.

Printed in the United States of America

First Printing, 2015

ISBN 978-0-9898068-8-6

Cover art and design by Steven Luna

For Bailee,
who could teach Mabel a thing or two about good behavior.

Mabel Gray

and the Wizard Who Swallowed the Sun

Clayton Smith

A Prologue
That You Would Do Well to Read

Most people will tell you that all fairy tales must start with Once Upon a Time. I'm certainly not one to balk in the face of such a grand and long-standing tradition. However, as your faithful narrator, I am duty-bound by the Guild of Storytellers, Fairy Tale and Folklore Division, to tell the full and honest tale of Mabel Gray and the Wizard Who Swallowed the Sun, and the simple truth is, sometimes events happen *before* Once Upon a Time that directly relate to the story at hand.

This is one of those times.

Therefore, in as succinct a manner as I am able without betraying the sacred duty of the narrative voice, I shall relay to you the events that immediately preceded ours.

Six hours, seven minutes, and forty-three seconds before our story begins, Elder Alder was sitting at his desk, staring at nothing in particular. There was plenty he *could* have been staring at, mind you; the office of a Brightsbane elder was a stately and impressive room, and Elder Alder's office contained pillars of polished marble, ornately carved tables of iron oak, and floors of petrified gold leaf. The walls, of course, were positively beset by bookshelves, so full of carefully-bound knowledge that the room itself appeared to actually be made of books (though we can safely assume that it was not, for a wall of books would be rather unsturdy, and an elder's office must first and foremost be a haven of relaxation and safety).

But despite all the books, and all the polished marble, and all the ornately carved iron oak, and all the petrified gold leaf, and all the carefully bound books that he could have been looking at, Elder Alder stared at nothing in particular instead. He was thinking, you see, and when one is lost in a good think, one has little time for ocular focus.

The night had grown quite late, and the fire in the elder's hearth was whittling itself down to embers. Elder Alder swirled the glass of anteberry wine in his hand, and his thoughts tumbled over themselves, causing quite a row in his head.

Then the window on the far end of the room was flung open, and a mighty wind burst through the office.

"Good heavens!" Elder Alder cried, spilling his wine as he leapt from his chair and hurried to the window. It took a great bit of strength to shut it, so insistent was the wind on being let in. The elder threw his entire weight against the frame and finally succeeded in latching the window closed. He stood before the glass, panting and shaking spilt wine from his hand. The moon was bright that evening and cast a luminous white glow on the world beyond his quarters. The southern edge of the Briarbranch Woods loomed on the horizon, but despite the strength of the wind that had exploded into his room, not a single leaf on a single branch from a single trunk of a single tree so much as fluttered. The night appeared to be quite still.

That's odd, the elder thought.

"Not so odd as all that," said a gruff voice behind him.

Elder Alder yelped in surprise and turned to face the intruder, holding his wine glass above his head and preparing to hurl it like a flash pot grenade. "Who's there?" he cried.

A figure melted forth from behind one of the pillars. He was tall, made taller by a conical hat that sagged at the very top. He had a long white beard, and a longer midnight blue robe that was illuminated with little pinpoints of light, so that he seemed to be cloaked in the night sky. In one hand, he grasped a gnarled, wooden staff topped with a glowing, bright blue jewel; in the other, he held a glass of the elder's wine.

Elder Alder gasped. "The wizard!"

"Well, *a* wizard, anyway," the old man said. "Emerys Croup.

Pleased enough to meet you." He sniffed the drink in his hand and made a sour face. "Is this anteberry?" he asked. He tossed the whole thing, wine and glass, into the dying fire. The embers blazed and grew to healthy flames once more, though now they took on a strange, pinkish hue. "I hate anteberry."

"How did you get in here?" the elder demanded. He clutched the front of his dark brown dressing gown and held it tightly, as if he could sprout armor by drawing into himself. "The Elderary is protected by powerful magic. Magic to keep *you* away, specifically."

"Not in its entirety," the wizard said with a little huffing snarl. "As it turns out, each office is protected by a spell that has been placed by its owner. When your predecessor—or should I say when *your father*—passed on, his protection spell passed with him. It seems you haven't managed to replace it yet. A stroke of luck, wouldn't you say?"

"No, I wouldn't." The elder eyed the door and wondered if he could make it to the latch before the wizard turned him into a scrumpton.

"You'll want to weave some sort of spell or other after I'm gone, then. Something to keep the rabble out. I'm sure you can find a passable one within these handsome volumes." The wizard clasped his hands behind his back and stalked about the room, exploring the spines of the hundreds of books that lined the walls. "Do you think anyone has actually ready any of these?" he asked.

"What do you want?" the elder demanded, adding more courage to his voice than he felt.

"I want to introduce myself," said the wizard as he continued to peruse the shelves.

"You've done it. Now please leave."

The wizard's shoulders shook with silent laughter. "I sense a tension in you. Has your first day on the job been stressful?" He plucked a book from the wall and read the title aloud. "*The Self-Digestion Habits of the Housebroken Grubbabout.* How fascinating." He opened the book and flipped through the pages.

"I'll call the guard," the elder said. He inched his way around the wall, moving toward the door. "They'll bind you in iron chains and toss you into the lake."

"Now what cause would they have for that?" The wizard snapped the book closed and slipped it back into its place on the shelf. "Seems like a harsh punishment for a simple drop-in."

"It's better than you deserve." With the wizard wandering along the bookshelves, not seeming to pay particular mind to the elder's movements, Alder began to feel something very like the beginning of bravery. "If I had my way, you'd be lashed to a post in Parchrock's field and left for the crows."

The wizard snorted softly. "That's quite a sentence. What is it that I've done to deserve such a cruel demise?"

"You mean *aside* from swallowing the sun?" the elder asked. He tiptoed around a pillar and continued his slow slide toward the door.

"Ah. That." He lifted a hand and ran it along a row of books. Clouds of dust puffed up from their spines. "I knew your grandfather, you know. The original Elder Alder. I knew him quite well."

"Funny…he never spoke of you," Alder said, nearing the door.

"He was a good man. Lots of potential there. Until he disappeared, of course." The wizard took another book from the shelf. "*Mother Crabnoodle's Improbable Tales for Parlor Room Entertainment.*" He smiled as he slid the book back into place. "Now we're getting close."

Elder Alder chanced a look to his left. The door was close now, just three more steps away. If he could just keep the wizard talking…

"Did you know my father too, then?" he asked, taking another step. The gold leaf creaked under his foot. He winced. But the wizard did not turn.

"Unfortunately, I did," the old man said sourly. "A brutish creature, your father. Did you know that you're the youngest elder in the history of Brightsbane?"

"So the other elders enjoy reminding me," Alder sighed. He slid one step closer. *Just one step more...*

"Ah!" The wizard stopped walking, and the elder's blood froze in his veins. Still, the old man did not turn. "Perhaps that's the source of your tension?" The wizard resumed his easy pace. Elder Alder took the last step and reached for the door handle. As he did, the wizard said, "I've locked the door, you know."

Alder's heart sank. He gripped the latch and pulled, but it didn't budge. "I don't expect there would be much point in calling for help," he sighed.

The wizard snorted. "Try it if you want. I find that shouting can be quite cathartic. Perhaps we can work through some of that stress. Go on and scream yourself silly. I brought ear plugs." He opened his palm, and two shapeless white blobs of wax bubbled into existence. He stuffed them into his ears and motioned for the elder to begin. "Whenever you're ready."

Alder frowned. "Fine. Let's get this over with. What do you want? What do you *really* want?"

"Eh?" the Wizard said, cupping his ears with his hands.

"Oh, for sun's sake, take the plugs out of your ears," the elder said, making the proper hand motions.

The wizard plucked the wax from his ear canals and threw them into the roaring fire. "Sorry. What were you saying?"

"Tell me what you're doing here. It's late, and since I can't escape, if you're going to spit me and roast me, I'd rather get it over with." He crossed his arms in what he hoped was a convincing show of determination.

"I don't eat elders," the wizard mumbled, turning his attention back to the shelves. "They're all either too spindly or too fleshy." He shuffled toward the last case of books. "I truly did want to meet you, young elder. To get a sense of you."

"You didn't risk entering the Elderary to say hello," Alder insisted. "What else are you after?"

A book on the last shelf caught the wizard's attention, a slim little volume with three horizontal iron bands striping its spine. He walked up to the book and read the title. "Ah," he breathed, pulling the tome from the shelf. "*The Boneyard Compendium.*"

The elder stiffened. *That's it,* he thought, suddenly alarmed. *Of course that's what he's after.* "Put it back," he said, his voice faltering.

"I think I'd like to borrow it," the wizard said with a wicked grin.

"Put it back!" Elder Alder said again. He rushed forward, his panic swallowing up his fear. "Leave it!"

The wizard waved his staff, and a shimmering field of light appeared between himself and the elder. Elder Alder skidded on the gold leaf floor and slammed into the barrier. It knocked him flat on his back.

"You really should install some magic in this place," the wizard said with an amused little smile. "Any number of witches and spell-casters could find their way in here and wreak all manners of havoc. I'd make it my first order of business if I were you, younger Elder Alder." He tucked the book under his arm and tipped the sagging peak of his hat. "Do try to have better wine next time." Then he stamped his staff on the floor, and in a puff of smoke, he was gone—hat, book, and all.

Elder Alder struggled to his knees. His head swam, and he felt as if he might become sick. He pressed his forehead against the cool golden floor and waited for the nausea to pass.

His first day as a Brightsbane elder, and he'd already lost the single most powerful book left to his care.

Stupid, stupid, stupid, he cursed himself. When Elder Whip found out that he'd lost the compendium, Elder Alder would be the one lashed to a post in Parchrock's field. The very thought of the crows with their razor-sharp talons sent shivers through his shoulders.

He heaved himself to his feet and lurched over to his desk. He rummaged through his drawers with shaking hands and pulled out a piece of parchment and a quill. There was only one way to get the book back without drawing the attention of the other elders…and he *had* to get the book back. *The Boneyard Compendium* was a book filled with terribly powerful spells, and whatever the wizard had planned, it would make swallowing the sun look like a parlor trick. He scratched out a brief letter and ran forth from his chambers to find his steward before the ink even had a chance to dry.

And now, dear reader, our story may begin.

CHAPTER 1
A SINGULAR SORT OF WAIF

Once upon a time, in a land far away, there was a village called Brightsbane, where it was always nighttime, even at the height of day. Brightsbane did have a sun once, but it was swallowed by an evil wizard named Emerys Croup, one of a covey of seven Brightsbane wizards who delighted in trickery, depravity, and making a general mess of things. Croup gobbled it right up, plunging the world into eternal night, where it would never again bask in the light of day.

The moon, to its great credit, began to pull double duty, rising once in the evening, as it had always done, and then rising again in the morning, to provide what light it could. The stars chimed in as well, when the clouds allowed it. Those ancient people of Brightsbane who witnessed the loss of their sun wailed and grieved and bemoaned their misfortune, rending their clothing and coating themselves in appropriate amounts of ash. The elders did their best to banish the evil wizards from the village, and over the course of a generation, they managed to banish six of them. But try as they might, they could not wield power over Emerys Croup himself. The evilest wizard remained at large, hiding in his caves beneath the earth and staunchly refusing to regurgitate the sun.

Eventually, the villagers resigned themselves to a life spent in eternal nighttime. So life carried on in Brightsbane, and eventually, everyone who could remember a world with the sun died away. Everyone, that is, except for the wizard himself, who used his dark powers to extend his life to an extraordinary length, as evil wizards are wont to do.

He dwelt still among the people of Brightsbane, though he was rarely seen. He kept largely to himself in his hidden lair deep within the caverns of Gallows Hill. Through the generations, many had sought out the wizard's cave in foolhardy attempts to achieve some sort of justice for his many nefarious deeds, but its entrance was cloaked in powerful magic that not even the three Brightsbane witches were able to breach. And so the wizard lurked underground, biding his time, lying in wait, ever hungry for his next chance to throw the village into chaos.

This was the story that every Brightsbane child knew, no matter how high or how low their station. "History must be remembered," the good and kind Elders of Brightsbane said, "and every child born should well know the treachery of the wizard." It was the first lesson given in schools, and it was the story parents whispered to their children before bed. It was heralded once a year in the town square with a rousing reenactment directed by Mayor Poppet and performed with puppets on strings. The tale was even told in St. Crippleback's Home for Waifs and Strays, where the sour-faced matrons recited the words once each month, in accordance with the Elders' law.

And that was how even a friendless orphan like little Mabel Gray came to know the history of Brightsbane.

Mabel was more of a waif than a stray. Her parents had perished in a horrible pumpkin accident long before Mabel was of a straying age. In order to stray, one needs strong legs and the ability to use them in a walkabout manner, and Mabel was hardly old enough to crawl when the accident happened. With no other family in Brightsbane, the young girl was scooped up by servants of the general welfare and deposited into an open crib at St. Crippleback's. She had been a ward of the village ever since.

The fact that she had never been adopted had very little to do with Mabel's disposition, though her quiet nature did allow her to come across as sullen, in most people's opinions. But the true reason she had never been adopted is that no child was *ever* adopted in Brightsbane. In the long history of St. Crippleback's, not a single child had ever been claimed by happy parents and incorporated into a standing home. None of the villagers wanted a waif, or a stray. Once you went into St. Crippleback's, you didn't come back out until you were a respectable age of sixteen. And that's just how it was.

One of the few benefits of spending her entire young life at the orphanage was that Mabel had been there longer than any of the other girls on her floor, and over time, as others aged out of the home, Mabel was able to claim better and better mattress assignments, until eventually she found herself with the most coveted mattress of all: the one near the window that overlooked the town's moon pool.

Day after day, young Mabel sat on her mattress with her head pressed against the cool glass, watching with a churning mixture of envy and delight as the well-to-do of Brightsbane came to the pool, the gentlemen in their tall hats, the ladies in their bustles and bonnets. They plunked their golden coins into the money box and were admitted into the fountain, where they would dip their hands into the water, cup them around the reflection of the moon, and draw them back out...and the moon's reflection would come out with them, a small, grey-dappled sphere of softly glowing moonlight. All day long, and all night, too, Brightsbane's wealthy came to the pool, drew out Luna Lamps, and returned to their carriages, holding the moon in their hands.

The bewitched fountain was breathtaking in its beauty. Magic was banned within the walls of St. Crippleback's, and though Mabel knew sorcery was a part of daily life for most people in Brightsbane, she had never seen it firsthand until she peered out the window and beheld the moon pool that very first time. Now witnessing magic was part of her daily ritual. It was a thrill to watch, each and every time. She always tried to pinpoint the exact moment the reflection of the moon transformed into a three-dimensional facsimile. She thought that if she could catch the metamorphosis—if she could actually *see* the magic—then perhaps she would understand it enough to make a bit of magic herself. If a pool of water could turn a reflection into a moon, then maybe a young girl could transform herself from a friendless waif into someone's daughter.

Magic can do wonderful things, you know.

Mabel was so consumed with this idea of siphoning off a bit of magical prowess that whenever someone approached the moon pool, everything else faded away into blackness of a sort. That was why, on this particular morning, she sat staring with her nose pressed against the glass, so entranced by the sight of a young debutante giddily drawing out her first ever Luna Lamp from the pool that she almost didn't notice the excitement in her own sleeping quarters. She might have missed it altogether if another young girl hadn't bumped into her mattress in her haste to reach the door. Mabel was jolted back into herself as the last few waifs and strays stampeded into the hallway.

"What's going on?" Mabel called, scrambling to her feet and chasing after the horde. "Where's everyone going?"

"*Shhh!*" a younger girl silenced her, really quite rudely, in Mabel's opinion.

"Where's everyone going?" she asked more quietly.

"There's a new errand from the Underground," the girl hissed. She pointed at a scrap of paper that had been tossed aside amidst the furious exodus. Mabel skidded to a stop and trotted back to where the paper lay on the floor. It was a letter, written in a breathless scrawl, in ink that had been smeared with haste. The words were legible enough, though, and this is what they said:

I seek to employ a ragamuffin child, be he waif or stray, for the purpose of carrying out a matter with a need for urgency matched only by a demand of secrecy. The wizard of Brightsbane has stolen a book from the Elderary that absolutely must be returned with the utmost haste.

Please appoint a brave, competent, and trustworthy child to take on the task of quietly tracking down the wizard, retrieving the stolen text, and returning it, unblemished, to the office of Elder Alder. The successful ragamuffin will be rewarded with an official Letter of High

Station.

Mabel gasped. She clapped a hand over her mouth, embarrassed at the outburst, but there was no one left in the room to hear it. *A Letter of High Station*, she thought. *No wonder they were in such a hurry.* She folded the letter, tucked it into her pocket, and ran back to her window. But this time, she was not looking for the moon pool.

Just as she suspected, she spied a little boy, a fellow waif, stealing through the shadows of the market square. And there, over by the bowery, a girl, a portly stray, squeezing through the wood slat fence and out into the field beyond. Another boy here, another girl there…the orphans of St. Crippleback's were escaping, one by one, and they were all headed toward Gallows Hill.

It may seem odd, this sudden and hasty evacuation that was sure to result in severe punishment by the matrons of St. Crippleback's, but you must believe me when I tell you, dear reader, that there is nothing a young ragamuffin would not do to obtain a Letter of High Station.

Mabel grabbed her tattered shoes and squeezed them onto her feet. She hurried across the bunkroom and peered out into the hallway. It was empty. The matrons hadn't yet realized that their charges were spiriting themselves away through any nook, cranny, crack, or crevice they could find.

She hurried down the hall and ducked into the laundry room when she heard footsteps echoing down the corridor. She pressed herself against the wall and held her breath, silently pleading for the nurse or the matron or whomever it was coming down the hall to turn around and go back the way she'd come. But the approaching shadow fell over the laundry room door, and Mabel exhaled with relief, for it was neither a matron nor a nurse, but Bartilus Plug, the blind groundskeeper who was not very good at his job, and who made an awful mess of the topiaries, but who was a very dear man. He shuffled down the hall, pushing a mop bucket on wavering wheels, a contraption of his own design. Every few steps, the bucket banged into the wall, and Bartilus righted his course and carried on.

When he had banged and bungled his way down the hall and around the corner, Mabel slipped back out of the laundry room and hurried across to the lavatory. She crept inside and closed the door behind her, then locked it, just for good measure. She entered the fourth stall and clamored atop the toilet seat so she was standing facing the wall. She worked her fingertips into the thin space between the wooden slats and pried away one of the pieces. She set it carefully on the floor, leaning it against the stall door. Then she rolled up her sleeves, grabbed the iron pipe that ran vertically behind the lavatory, and pulled herself into the wall.

If you're surprised that young Mabel had such a daring and complex escape plan so readily accessible in her mind, you needn't be. Every child at St. Crippleback's knew how to slip past the matrons and venture out into the world, and all for various reasons. The most popular reason for excusing oneself from an orphanage is that it is a distasteful place to spend one's life, and it becomes necessary to escape every now and again in order to maintain an acceptable level of personal sanity. This was true for Mabel, as it was for most of the children in St. Crippleback's, but it was not her primary motivation. As I have already stated, Mabel knew that her parents were dead, but she did not entirely *believe* it, and she slipped out of the orphanage every now and again to look for them, just in case there'd been an embarrassing mix-up.

Mabel was a bit advanced in the field of escapology and actually had four separate escape routes: one through the lavatory; one through the library's coal chute; one through a secret passage behind a large painting of Elder Whip that she discovered quite by accident one day while looking for a hiding spot for her favorite napkin (yes, napkin….it is a very long story); and one through the kitchen's floor drains. The route through the lavatory was the quickest and most easily accessible from the bunkroom, so it was the one she used most frequently.

She shimmied down the iron pipe and dropped onto a larger, horizontal pipe several feet below. She crept along the metal support, slipping here and there and pressing her hands against the inside of the orphanage's walls for support. Below this pipe was a twenty-foot free fall straight down onto the burning hot steam tables of the sanitarium in the cellar.

It may be worth mentioning that the lavatory escape route was also the most dangerous.

But her feet were practiced, and her steps were true, and soon she made a left turn that took her behind the matrons' sitting lounge. She stepped more quietly here, holding her breath and listening for movement from the other side of the wall. But this morning, the room was blessedly silent. Mabel crept along the pipe until it came to an abrupt halt just past the sitting lounge and turned downward. The pipe disappeared down a huge, dark hole far below her feet. Mabel took a deep breath. This was her least favorite part of the escape. She crouched down and wrapped her arms around the cool, wet pipe. Then she spun out over the edge of the drop and, clutching the iron tightly, she spiraled down, down, down into the sewer beneath the building.

At this point in Mabel's liberation process, she was forced to go through a few unpleasant steps in order to wade through the various debris and blockages that one would expect to find in a large and primitive underground sewer system. I hope you'll excuse me if I refrain from sharing specifics about this stage in her journey, for I find them unsavory and inappropriate for polite story time conversation. Suffice it to say, young Mabel charged ahead with admirable aplomb, and before long, she emerged more or less unsullied (well…perhaps less unsullied than more) from the sewer grate set into the cobblestone Spectre Road some half-mile south of St. Crippleback's Home for Waifs and Strays.

Mabel replaced the grate and stole away into an alley between the cobbler's and the cooper's. She brushed what filth she could from her clothes and wrung the sewer water from the cuffs of her dark red bramble-cotton pants. Her shirt, an oversized, rough-spun shift that had started out white once upon an earlier time, was stained and sooty and generally shabby, and the escape through the sewers hadn't changed that one bit. She shook out the wrinkles as best she could. With her clothes thusly restored (if you'll forgive such a fast and loose definition of "restored"), she crept forward, closer to the edge of the alley, and peered out into the darkness. The moon was in waxing crescent this morning, and its light was sparse, but even so, Mabel's sharp eyes could pick out a smattering of children creeping down the cobblestones heading toward the path that would take them to Gallows Hill and the wizard's cave.

"Move it," hissed a voice behind her. A younger boy who Mabel knew by sight and whose name she thought might be Caverdish (or perhaps Davenwish) ran out of the shadows of the alleyway and elbowed past. "And don't follow me," he added as he ran.

"I don't *need* to follow you…everyone knows where you're going," Mabel pointed out. "It's where *everybody's* going."

The young boy slowed at the end of the alley. He pulled off his cap and peeked out at the street. "But don't *follow* me," he hissed. "You'll get us both caught."

Mabel thought about pointing out that his bright blue cap was more likely to get him caught than a whole herd of Mabels, but she decided against it. Better for him to learn that one for himself. Instead, she asked, "How are you planning on finding the wizard's cave when you get there?"

"By *looking*," the boy said, rolling his eyes.

"People have been *looking* for the entrance to the wizard's cave for hundreds of years," she said, giving her eyes a little roll. "It's cloaked in magic. I'm not sure you'll have much luck."

The boy snorted. "You got a better plan?" Then, with the coast clear, he darted out into the street, not bothering to wait for an answer.

But Mabel answered anyway. "As a matter of fact, I do." She pulled the letter from her pocket. It bore no signature, but its author was apparent enough; the letter was fixed with an official Elderary seal, and since the letter demanded both secrecy and the return of the book to Elder Alder, that same elder was certainly responsible for the words on the paper. She tucked the letter away once more, peered around the corner to make sure the constabulary was not about, and hurried away to the west, toward the Elderary.

To find the wizard, she knew she needed something more powerful than magic.

She needed a little bit of knowledge.

Chapter 2
A Frightfully Delicate Errand

Mabel stood outside the Elderary and could think of nothing else to do but whisper, "Oh, goodness." She'd seen the towers from afar, but she'd never been right up against the walls. It was an impressive structure, all dark grey stone with iron fencing that glowed blue with protection magic. The magic was clearly designed to keep out someone—or something—very specific, and she hoped it wasn't little girls. Otherwise, she was liable to end up fried to a crisp.

She closed her eyes, held her breath, and took a step through the main gate.

She opened her eyes.

She had not been fried to a crisp.

"Whew," she said aloud. She hurried up the path toward the building.

"Who what?" a voice asked. Mabel raised her eyes to the great double door that led into the Elderary. Standing before it was a very tall, very thin man, made even taller by his high black hat and even thinner by the black pinstripes on his red suit. He held a sceptre in one hand and twirled away at his heavily waxed moustache with the other.

"I'm sorry?" Mabel said.

"Why be sorry? Did you say something wrong?" the man asked.

Mabel shook her head. "I don't think so. But when you don't understand what someone says, you're supposed to say, 'I'm sorry?'"

"Says who?"

"Says Matron Marble." Matron Marble was Head of Delicate

10

Manners at St. Crippleback's, a position that included both teaching politeness and handling sensitive and private issues around the orphanage. Mabel wasn't ordinarily concerned with proper decorum, but if she was going to become a Person of High Station, she was going to need to practice her manners. "She says we're supposed to say 'I'm sorry,' 'Excuse me,' 'Pardon me,' 'Thank you,' and 'I suppose that's none of my business.'"

"This Matron Marble sounds like quite the blockhead," the man said, stifling a yawn. His fingers continued to twirl the end of his moustache. "What you should say when you don't understand something is, 'What do you mean by that?'"

Mabel wasn't sure she agreed, but the man was standing between her and the door she needed to walk through, so she decided it was best to placate him. "What do you mean by that?" she asked.

"What do I mean by telling you to say 'What do you mean by that?'" the tall man asked.

"No," Mabel said. *What a confusing person!* she thought. "What I mean to say is, what do you mean by saying, 'Who what?'"

"Ah! Now you're asking the proper question!" the thin man said, delighted. "So I shall give you a proper answer. You said, 'Who?' And so I responded, 'Who what?'"

"I didn't say, 'Who?'" Mabel said. "I said, 'Whew.'"

"Are you quite sure?" the man asked, bending down to inspect the girl as if trying to seek her out for lies.

Mabel forced herself to look up and lock eyes with the man, even though he towered high above her and she had to strain her neck something awful to do it. "Yes."

"Hmm...I see." The man straightened up once more and tapped the sceptre against his chin. "Why did you say 'whew' when you walked through the gate? Do you think it is an impressive feat to walk through a gate?"

"I thought it might sizzle me up," Mabel answered. "It's glowing a very bright blue."

The tall man shook his head sadly. "Young lady, don't you know anything? Blue magic keeps out *other* magics. And green magic keeps out Devilden monsters; pink magic keeps out water sprites; orange magic keeps out witches, if it's done properly; umber magic keeps out sentient trees; and red magic is something that everyone should stay away from, no matter what their biology. It's *yellow* magic that keeps out little girls. Where do you go to school?" he demanded.

If Mabel told the truth, that she attended classes within the walls of St. Crippleback's, the man would be legally bound to send her back to the orphanage. So she tried changing the subject. "Are you the doorman?" she asked. "I need to speak with Elder Alder."

The man narrowed his eyes. "Yes, I am the doorman, and it's a lucky thing for you. Your second question gave away too much. It gave away everything! If I were *not* the doorman, I would know your goal, and then I would have absolute power over you, for if I know what you aim to do, I am empowered to either help or hinder your progress. Do you see? But since I *am* the doorman, I am duty-bound to follow a strict set of steps and ask you a strict set of questions, and the first one happens to be: Who are you here to see? So you have saved us both a bit of time by answering that one already."

Mabel thought that perhaps the doorman's explanation actually took *more* time, but once again, she decided to say nothing. Sometimes, silence is prudent.

"The second question," the doorman continued, "is do you have an appointment? Do you?" The man stopped twirling his moustache and grasped his sceptre with both hands. "I can see by the look in your eyes that you are trying to decide whether or not you should lie. Let me make the choice simple for you: If you tell a lie, this sceptre will know it, and it will turn from a beautiful gold staff into a fanged swampsnake that will bite you directly between the eyes and fill you with its venom, which will turn you slowly to a log over the course of three agonizing days. So I would opt to tell the truth, if I were you."

Mabel bit her lip. She didn't see any issue with telling the truth, especially in the face of such a persuasive sceptre. But the truth wasn't exactly a *yes* or a *no*. It was something a little muddier.

"I don't have an appointment, exactly," she said, speaking slowly, measuring her words, "but he should be expecting me. Sort of."

The doorman placed his hands on his hips and leaned forward again. "That," he declared, "is not a very good answer."

"But it's the most truthful," Mabel said.

"Hmm," said the doorman. "That may be so. Well, let me ask the third question, which is optional, so I am not duty-bound to ask it unless the answer to the second question is no. You didn't say no, but I think it may settle a thing or two anyway, so I shall ask it. Do you have a formal invitation?"

"Oh!" Mabel said, brightening up. She pulled the letter from her pocket and presented it to the doorman. "Will this do?"

The doorman plucked a monocle from his breast pocket and stuck it in his left eye. He peered down at the letter. "It's the Elderary seal, all right," he said, sounding somewhat relieved. "And the sceptre hasn't turned into a snake, so I suppose it's all on the up-and-up. Very well, young lady. You may see the elder." He stamped the ground twice with the sceptre, and the double doors behind him opened. "Follow the runner," he instructed. He bent down and cupped a hand around his mouth. "Lead her to Elder Alder's chambers," he hollered down at the rug inside the door, as if the poor thing were deaf. It sluggishly wriggled awake, then began to lopsidedly unroll itself into the depths of the castle. "Gadabout," the doorman said shortly.

Mabel curtseyed slightly and hurried through the doors as the runner unfurled down the main hall and to the left. The rug led her past a slew of rooms with open doors that she would have loved to look in and explore, for the Elderary was a building of great mystery, and she didn't know if she'd ever be back inside its walls again. But the runner was in a hurry, and it was rolling itself up behind her. If she didn't hurry along with it, she was liable to get rolled up and delivered to Elder Alder like a sausage.

The rug came to an abrupt end at a heavy oak door near the castle's western wall. Mabel, quite out of breath, placed her hands on her knees and took a moment to catch her wind. The runner rolled behind her and nudged her heels. "Oh, I'm sorry," Mabel said, though she was unsure if it was necessary to be polite to a runner. Matron Marble had never covered that particular lesson. Still, better safe than sorry. She stepped off the rug, and it rolled itself up with a little fluttering *hmpf*. Then it spun around and rolled all the way back to the front of the castle.

Mabel turned and took a deep breath. She straightened her shift and patted down her increasingly wild black hair. Then she raised her fist and knocked gently on the door.

"Who is it?" The voice inside the room was frantic and tired. If it were a living thing, it would have been decorated with dark circles under bloodshot eyes, Mabel decided.

"Mabel Gray," she answered. Then, realizing her name would mean nothing to an elder of Brightsbane, she added, "With the ragamuffin Underground."

After a few moments of silence, the chamber door creaked open. An eyeball pressed itself into the crack. "Are you a waif or a stray?" the man behind the door asked suspiciously.

"A waif, mostly," she shrugged. "I read your letter, and—"

"*Shh!*" Elder Alder threw open the door, grabbed Mabel by the arm, and yanked her inside, slamming the door shut behind her. "Good gracious, child, if you've read the letter, than you know this is a matter of utmost secrecy!" he hissed. "Have you no propriety?"

Mabel didn't know what propriety was, and was therefore not at all certain that she did. "I suspect I will have some, once I have a Letter of High Station." There was almost no limit to the things one could have with an official letter in one's portfolio.

The elder straightened up and frowned down at the little girl. "Yes," he said. "I suppose that's true." He crossed over to his desk and motioned for Mabel to follow. "Have a seat."

A Luna Lamp sat on the corner of the desk. Mabel marveled at it as she sat down. This was the closest she'd ever been to one, since she could not afford one of her own. They were even more beautiful up close. This particular lamp had been drawn from the pool when there was a half-moon, which is a wonderful time to draw a lamp, for the flat edge allows it to rest comfortably on a flat surface. But the light it gave off was soft and low, barely enough to illuminate the whole desktop, much less the entire room. Mabel was about to inquire as to whether the lamp had been scooped out of the water on a night when the moon was partially covered by clouds when Elder Alder picked up a pitcher from a tray behind the desk and splashed a bit of water over the little half-orb. Its glow intensified, and it bathed the whole office in its cool, white light.

"I didn't know they did that," Mabel whispered, her voice filled with awe.

"A nice parlor trick," the elder said with a frown. "Makes them somewhat useless in the desert, though."

"You've been to the desert?" Mabel asked. She'd never met anyone who'd been to the Desert of a Thousand Steps. The sands were so off limits that they were hardly ever talked about, even in stories. "What was it like?"

"Well, no, I haven't been there personally, per se," Elder Alder said. His cheeks took on a rosy pink hue. "But if one *were* to go into the desert, a Luna Lamp would be quite useless, I'm sure of it." In the brighter light, Mabel had a better view of her host. He was old, of course, but not quite as old as she'd expected with him being an elder and all. He, like his voice, had dark shadows under his eyes; his skin bunched and sagged, and he looked quite a bit wearier than was healthy for a man of his age and position. And he had grey hairs, though not *all* of his hairs were grey; many were still clinging to a reddish-brown sort of youth. "So you're the one the Underground chose, are you?" he said, changing the subject.

Mabel shrugged. "The Underground doesn't really choose anyone," she said. "More like it just makes an announcement."

Elder Alder hesitated. "And...*you're* the one who was brave enough to answer the call?"

"What?" Mabel asked, confused. A thought crossed her mind then. She decided to go ahead and give it a voice. "Do you know how the Underground works, sir?"

"Yes, of course," the elder blustered. "I draft a Letter of Need and drop it into the alley drain near the masonry. Then some young guttersnipe or other delivers it to the orphanage, where it is distributed to the child most apt for the task." He crossed his arms and leaned back in his seat. "At least," he added quietly, "that was my understanding."

Mabel stifled her smile, which was no mean feat. Adults, she found, were often quite affably clueless. "The first part is right—about the letter and the grate and the guttersnipe. His name is Bailiwick, by the way. He's the Underground's postmaster."

"How organized you all are," the elder mumbled.

"Bailiwick brings the letter to the orphanage, and it's passed around from mattress to mattress until someone decides to take up the cause."

"And that was you?" Elder Alder asked.

"No, sir. It was *all* of us," Mabel said.

The elder froze. His hands suddenly seemed clammy. They left a streak of moist residue on the desk when he slid them into his lap. "What do you mean, 'all of us'?"

"*All* of us—all the children at St. Crippleback's. We *all* answered the call. We're *all* out looking for the wizard."

"All..." Elder Alder muttered helplessly, passing his hand over his jaw.

"What did you expect, offering a Letter of High Station?" Mabel asked, crossing her arms. "There's not an orphan in the world who'd pass up a chance to get one of those."

"How many of you are there?" he asked, his voice tight in this throat.

"I'd guess about fifty."

16

"Oh dear." Elder Alder rose from his desk and pulled a stone jug from a shelf on the far side of the room. He poured a dark red liquid into a little glass. "Oh dear, oh dear, oh dear. Where are they, then?" he asked, gulping down his anteberry wine. "All on Gallows Hill?"

"On their way, at least," Mabel nodded.

The elder poured himself a second glass, and he drained that one down, too. "They'll be swarming all over the mountain by mid-moonfall," he murmured, more to himself than to Mabel. "They'll draw an extraordinary amount of attention...they're sure to! I'm ruined!"

"Oh, I shouldn't think so," Mabel said.

"Really? And why is that?" Elder Alder replied hotly.

"In the first place, it's dark on Gallows Hill, awful dark, and orphans don't have Luna Lamps or firekindle. They'll blend right into the dark."

"That's true," muttered the elder, rubbing his chin. "And villagers only journey to Gallows Hill during hangings, and hangings only happen—"

"—on full moons," Mabel finished, quite proud of herself and her vast knowledge of the world. She'd learned all about hangings on one of her secret outings from the orphanage, when she decided to look for her probably-dead parents inside the undertaker's workshop. Oh, that had been a day positively rife with education. "The hill will be empty for days yet."

"Yes, yes," said the elder, returning to his seat. "All of that is true. But what about the matrons of St. Crippleback's? Surely they're bound to raise the alarm when they've noticed fifty children gone missing."

"Are they?" Mabel asked slyly.

The elder stared. "Are they not?"

"Would you?"

Elder Alder thought about that. If he were accountable for half a hundred children who were wards of the village, and every single one of them suddenly vanished, he wouldn't exactly shout it from the rooftops. More likely that he'd try to cover it up and buy time until he found them and returned them to their proper places without Elder Whip or Mayor Poppet catching wind. "No," he said. "I suppose not."

Mabel sat back in her chair and bounced a little on the cushion. "So we've got a little time before it's a problem. Plenty of time for me to find your book, I think."

"Yes, of course," said the elder, snapping back to the task at hand. "Which makes me wonder…why are you here instead of at the hill with the others, looking for the wizard?"

"They say his cave is hidden with magic. Is that true?"

Elder Alder nodded. "Quite true, I'm afraid. But you're wasting your time here. I can't point you in the right direction. I haven't the slightest clue where to find the entrance."

"But maybe you know some sort of revealing spell…or maybe you have a recipe for a reversing potion…or something." Mabel slid her eyes over the hundreds of books that lined the walls of his office. "Maybe there's something on one of your books."

The elder shook his head sadly. "The wizard's magic is far too great. Not even the Brightsbane witches have been able to counter it, I doubt there's much hope for the rest of us."

Mabel bunched up her lips and furrowed her brow and set her mind to work. "I read a book once about a bright-smart constable who solved mysteries with the smallest of clues. Maybe the wizard left something behind? Like a strand of hair that a witch could use in a seeking spell, or a footprint in mud that's only found in one place on Gallows Hill, or something just as telling but not really very obvious…"

The elder stared at her, his eyebrows knitted together most complexly. "What a clever girl," he mused. "But no, I'm afraid there's nothing. I've been over every inch of this room and every memory in my head, and I've come up short. There must be another way to find him. There simply must…" he said, losing himself deeply in thought. "Hmm…"

"Hmm," Mabel agreed, sinking into the chair.

They thought in silence for several long minutes, wracking their brains for ways to track down the evil sorcerer. Mabel had assumed that Elder Alder would be able to shed a bit of light on the matter, since he was an elder, and all elders were good, and kind, and somewhat magical, and extremely smart. Why, Elder Mulberry had once defeated a three-headed boar with nothing more than a kerchief and a jar of blubberberry sauce, and Elder Roble was well known for being an avid seeker—and finder!—of children who had gone missing in Slurptongue Swamp. And Elder Whip! Why, Elder Whip's accomplishments were so great, they were beyond measure or description. But this elder? Though he seemed to be good and kind, he appeared to be not at all magical, and not quite smart enough to solve this riddle. Mabel was about to suggest that they should ask another elder for help, perhaps Elder Maybe or Elder Hemsheth, or even Elder Whip himself, when Elder Alder clapped his hands together excitedly. "You know, there *is* one thing…" he said. He hopped up onto the corner of the desk on Mabel's side, sitting there like a puffy, brown-cloaked bird. "The compendium that the wizard has stolen is secured by three separate locks. In order to open it, you need the three Skeleton Keys. The wizard will need to track them down…he's got a head start on you, but with any luck, you might catch him along the way, if you can find where the keys are hidden. And if you managed to find a key before he does and spirit it away in a good, safe hiding spot? Why, *he* would have to come to *you*!"

Mabel considered this carefully. She wasn't particularly keen on the idea of being chased down by an evil wizard…but if she happened upon a key first, she could bring it back to Elder Alder, and then the sorcerer would be his problem instead of hers. "Couldn't the wizard just use a spell to break through the locks?" she asked.

Elder Alder shook his head. "Even a wizard as powerful as ours won't be able to bypass *that* particular bit of magic. *The Boneyard*

Compendium is old, much older than any of us. Older than the wizard, too. The locks would have been forged long, long ago, when magic was more primal. No, I think the locks will hold until the wizard has the keys."

"You think?" Mabel asked, raising an eyebrow.

Elder Alder frowned. "I…I'm sure of it," he decided. But he did not sound terribly sure. "The locks will hold without the three keys."

"And all I have to do is get them before he does."

"Yes, or even just one of them. He'll need all three."

Mabel nodded. That seemed reasonable. Surely she could find just one key. "Where are they kept?" she asked.

Elder Alder coughed politely into his sleeve. "Ah…well…you see…I'm not exactly sure."

Mabel's heart sank. This elder was worse than useless. She was never going to find the keys, and she was never going to track down the wizard, which meant she was never going to retrieve the elder's book, which meant she was never going to get her Letter of High Station. Without that piece of paper, she'd be a waif for the rest of her childhood, and then she'd be turned out to the streets on her sixteenth birthday, and she'd become a vagrant, or a drifter, or a transient, or a ruffian. She'd beg for meals and wear cast-off clothing and drink rotten water and never hold a Luna Lamp of her own.

But, oh! A Letter of High Station would change all that! A Letter of High Station would make her an instant debutante. With a Letter of High Station, she'd be able to part the lace curtain and be taken in by a Brightsbane aristocrat as a lady-in-waiting. With a Letter of High Station, she'd be able to show anyone and everyone that she, Mabel Gray, was more than a waif, more than a ragamuffin, more than a poor orphan girl destined for the gutter. She would be a young lady deserving of a finer lot.

It was her passport to a better life. A *real* life.

And it had almost been within her grasp. But now it was fluttering hopelessly out of reach.

"Well," she said, wholly unable to suppress the sadness in her voice. "I suppose I'll go scour the hill with the rest of the waifs and strays and see if I get lucky."

Elder Alder perked up, and so did his eyebrows; they knitted themselves together as if this idea were both surprising and offensive. "Good gracious, child, I do hope you prove to be more perseverant than that!" he said. "I doubt you'd survive an encounter with the wizard otherwise." He swallowed hard, as if it had just occurred to him for the first time that the death of a child was a possible outcome in this scenario. And perhaps it had. His voice was softer, more careful as he continued. "*I* don't know where the keys are hidden, but there is one who *does* know."

"Who?" Mabel asked. The Letter fluttered a little closer, and her heart fluttered with it.

"The Warden of the Boneyard. He is the one responsible for the Skeleton Keys. He will know where you can find them."

Mabel's eyes flashed with excitement. "Then there's a chance."

The elder nodded. "There's a chance." He pulled a bell rope near the door and whispered instructions to a footman who appeared in the hall. Soon, the footman was back, rolling in a cart of poppenberry sandwiches and jaderock greens. Mabel and Elder Alder ate a late-morning lunch, and the elder spent the better part of an hour cautioning the waif against the dangers of tracking a wizard, much less encountering and stealing a book from one, and he bade her to back out now if she had the slightest misgiving. But Mabel heard none of it, for she was relishing the rich meal and picturing the thousands of exquisite lunches that awaited her when she became a Lady of High Station.

She agreed to the danger, she swore to the secrecy, and before the moon reached its highest point in the noon sky, Mabel Gray shook Elder Alder's hand and promised to seek out the compendium.

Neither she nor the elder noticed the pair of eyes that watched them through the window as they ate.

Chapter 3
Graveyards, Dead Things, and Creatures of Bone

Mabel had never been to the Boneyard before, but that wasn't unusual. There were a few requirements for being granted entry.

Chief among them was that you had to be dead.

Of course, it wasn't enough *just* to be dead. Dead bodies were admitted to plenty of places: graveyards, mausoleums, tombs, heaps, piles, and the like. But dead bodies weren't allowed into the Boneyard unless their flesh had been stripped away, leaving behind a bare white skeleton of clicking, clacking bones. If you died in one of the old-fashioned ways, such as by hanging, or by falling down a very long drop, or by being shot with a musket ball, then you weren't allowed into the Boneyard for many years—not until your flesh had worked its way naturally off of your bones. If you were lucky, though, and met with a death that resulted in a clean skeleton—perhaps by becoming a meal for a predatory alligator, for example, or by tripping and falling into Boiling Lake, where your bones were boiled clean—then you were allowed to spend the rest of eternity in the Boneyard. Very few living people had ever gained admission to the place, for the obvious reason that most living folks don't go running around in just their skeletons. (It did happen once, some time ago, when someone made Brightsbane's Bad Witch extremely upset by accidentally running over her favorite cat with his apple cart. She dunked him in a potion that removed everything but his bones while keeping him very much alive, so by the general rule of things, that particular person could have taken a tour of the Boneyard, but I suppose he had too much on his mind, for he never even thought to take advantage. But I digress.)

A small handful of living creatures had ventured into the Bone-yard, usually under the influence of some powerful spell or other. But none of those who went in ever came back out. Residency in the Boneyard is permanent, you see, and once you step over its threshold, living or not, it is practically impossible to leave. I say *practically* impossible because it is *technically* possible, but it involves mountains and mountains of paperwork that must be filled out perfectly and without error on the first try, and you are only allowed to fill it out with a bewitched ink pen that purposefully misspells every fifth word. It takes great patience, and no one has ever bothered to try it.

But I have strayed from our story again. Let's get back to Mabel, shall we?

The Boneyard was flat, and quite large, and surrounded by a black wrought iron fence that stood taller than the trees in Briar-branch Forest. The gate was of an enormous size, and as she approached it, Mabel couldn't help but wonder what sort of creature had a skeleton that required such a large passage to accommodate it.

A low mist covered the ground inside the Boneyard, but it stopped abruptly at the fence, as if it buffeted up against an imaginary wall. Through the bluish brume, Mabel could make out the shapes of discarded bones cluttering the overgrown grass. Some of them were attached to other bones, forming full or partial skeletons on the ground. But many were solitary pieces, forever disjointed, displaced, and alone.

She stepped up to the gate and looked for some sort of bell or knocker, but found nothing by which to announce her arrival. So she cleared her throat and called out, "Hello?"

She waited. There was no answer but the gentle moan of the wind.

"Helloooo?" she tried again. She gripped the bars of the gate and gave it a good shake. It clattered and clanged, and the sound echoed across the bone field. Still, the Warden did not show his face. Mabel took a real chance and pushed open one of the gates. She pushed it only lightly, for she was afraid that if her arm extended into the Boneyard too far, that would be as good as taking a step into it, and she'd be stuck there forever. But she pushed too hard, and her hand *did* break the plane. Or, at least, it tried to break the plane. Because she was not bewitched, bepotioned, or under any sort of spell, her hand was stayed by an invisible force field that tingled a bit when she brushed against it, as if her fingers had fallen asleep and were beginning the pin-and-needle process of waking.

The gate creaked open. Mabel now had an unobstructed view of the field and its various bones and mists. "Hellooo!" she called a third time.

A heavy wind blew and whipped the fog into billowing clouds that rose and puffed and blossomed, but they still could not venture beyond the Boneyard's boundaries, and soon Mabel was staring at a solid wall of mist. The wind continued to blow, harder and harder, and the bones began to clatter and shake. A femur went skittering over the grass, followed by a finger joint, then a kneecap, then a half-broken skull. More and more bones leapt up from their spots in the grass and rolled toward Mabel and the gate. The wind blew harder still and picked up whole clusters of bones as it rushed the wrought iron fence. By the time the powerful gusts reached the edge of the Boneyard, there were hundreds of bones caught up in the little eddy, pushing aside the clouds as they swirled and spun through the air. They began to arrange themselves in a very particular manner: a clavicle connected to an occipital bone, which connected to a fibula, which connected to a metacarpus, which connected to a mandible. On and on the link of bones grew until it curved back in on itself and began to take the shape of a large beast made of bones with large holes for eyes, a staved-in nose, and a wide mouth set with scraggly bone teeth. The creature had short bone ears and long bone horns and four bone legs with sharp bone claws. He even had a tail made of bone that rattled as it twitched from side to side.

"Yes, yes, I hear you…what do you want?" demanded the creature. Mabel stepped back, aghast. She had never seen a creature assemble itself out of bones before. If you have ever seen it, you know it is quite a shock. "Well? You're the one who called me, let's have it. I don't have all day." The creature tapped his bony foot impatiently.

"I—I—I—" stammered Mabel.

"Oh, for sun's sake," moaned the creature. He gave himself a mighty shake, and half of his bones flew apart and went sprawling across the yard. The pieces that remained reformed and reset themselves so that he looked quite the same, but a fair amount smaller. "Better?" When he spoke, every syllable was a dry death rattle. His voice reminded her somehow of fall.

Mabel steeled herself and balled her hands into fists at her sides. *He can't eat me if I don't go in,* she reasoned, *and I can't go in, so there's nothing to be afraid of.* Of course, she didn't know for sure whether or not *he* could cross the threshold…

"I'm looking for the Warden of the Boneyard," she said, mustering up her courage. "Do you know where I can find him?"

"I do, and so do you, for found him, you have," said the creature with no small amount of irritation in his voice. "Why are you waking me up at this hour?"

"At this hour? But it's just after noon," Mabel said. "It's a common time to be awake."

"For you, maybe," the creature snorted. "We bones are nocturnal."

Mabel cocked her head suspiciously to the side. "But it's always nighttime," she said.

"Yes, obviously," the Warden said. "So?"

"So it's always a nocturnal creature's time."

"Oh, little girl, you know so little. Where do you go to school? What I mean is, we bones are *historically* nocturnal. When the sun was swallowed up, we didn't just magically gain the ability to stay up for all hours of the nighttime night and all hours of the nighttime day. What an absurd and, frankly, *insulting* notion! We have to stick to a regimented rest schedule, or else we become weary and begin to creak and pop and sound of a general malaise. When I say we are nocturnal, I mean we sleep during the hours that most consider day and we are awake and rather active during the hours that most consider night."

Mabel nodded slowly. "That would explain why I sometimes feel restless when I'm trying to sleep," she decided.

"It would, and it does," the creature nodded. He opened his mouth and let loose a yawn that smelled of rotted leaves. "Which is why I should be sleeping right now. But you called 'hello' three times, so I figured it was important."

"Oh, it is," Mabel assured him. "I need your help, please. I'm looking for the three Skeleton Keys."

The Warden bristled and sat up straight. Some of the bones he had shaken off now rose into the air and returned to his body, and he puffed up a bit in size. "You don't just show up and ask for the three Skeleton Keys," he scoffed, somewhat outraged. "Who on earth does such a thing?"

"I'm sorry," Mabel frowned, taking a cautious step backward. She gave a polite curtsey, in case it might help. "I don't know all the rules about things like this." Her various short-lived departures from St. Crippleback's had made her very worldly, but she had cause to be stealthy when she went on those little jaunts, and she had never had occasion to make a formal request of a magical creature before.

"That, my child, is quite obvious." The Warden lowered his head so that he was on Mabel's level with just the invisible Boneyard wall between them. "What do you want with the Skeleton Keys?"

"I need to get them before the wizard does, so he doesn't open *The Boneyard Compendium* and use its magic for evil."

The Warden barked a throaty laugh and settled his chin down on his hands. "What an absurd little quest you're on," he said. "It is so for three reasons. First of all, I would never betray the locations of the three keys, not to a wizard, not to a little girl, and not to anyone else. Second of all, the compendium will weave its magic wheresoever it will, with or without the help of a wizard. And third of all, the wizard doesn't have the book, the elders do. Now please go away."

"But the wizard *does* have the book!" Mabel blurted out. "He stole it last night from the Elderary!"

The Warden laughed again. "That, my little dear, is really quite impossible. The Elderary is protected by a great bit of magic that glows blue around the edges, so the wizard could not have magicked his way inside."

"I don't know how he did it, but he did. He got in, and he stole the book, and the new elder is in an awfully big hurry to get it back."

The Warden's ears perked up, and a few of the bones that made up his horns clattered downward and added themselves to his ears to make them bigger and more apt to hear properly. "Did you say the *new* elder?"

Mabel nodded. "Elder Alder. He's new."

"So," the Warden of the Boneyard considered, tapping his finger against his jaw, "the older Elder Alder has shuffled off his mortal coil, has he? Yes, hmm. A death would account for a break in the magic. All right, you have convinced me, small person. It may be that the wizard has had access to my compendium, and it is a matter which I shall take up with the elders at the next all-village meeting, for what is the point of giving a book to a person for safe keeping if that person cannot possibly be trusted to keep it safe? There is very little point indeed, I hope you see that." Mabel nodded that she did see it. "Yes, I think you must," agreed the Warden.

"Will you tell me where the keys are hidden?" the girl asked.

The Warden sighed, and if he'd had eyeballs in his bony sockets, Mabel felt sure he would have rolled them. "Absolutely not. I wouldn't have hidden them away if I wanted them to be found."

"But what if the wizard finds them first?" she asked, planting her hands on her hips. "He'll be able to open the book and do all sorts of horrible things!"

"Yes, he could do that, if he knew where to look for the keys.

But the wizard's magic is no match for the power of the Boneyard, for I am old and strong and in rather good physical condition, all things considered, and I weave great magic. Even the wizard Croup could not see the secret locations of the keys in his brewpot. No… he would have to come see me face-to-face and ask in person, and that, I assure you, he has not done. I would remember."

Mabel supposed that was true. Surely a creature as powerful and important as the Warden of the Boneyard could be trusted to remember events that had occurred less than 24 hours earlier. But then she thought about the wizard's power, and how he made it so that no one could see the entrance to his cave, as if it wasn't there, as if no tools or spells had ever cut their way into the stone at all. And then she wondered if the wizard could do that sort of magic to other things, as well; not just to walls of stone, but to more intangible things, like memories. Could he make it so that a memory looked patched over, as if nothing extraordinary had ever imposed upon it?

But if the Warden's memory had been erased, how would he know it?

"I didn't know bones were nocturnal," she said, the beginnings of a plan knitting themselves together in her brain.

The Warden waved the air with his bony claws. "Yes, yes, that's well-worn territory now. You've learned something, and I'm glad to have been of service."

"What is it that bones do in their waking hours? My own bones are wrapped up tight in my skin, so they can't do much of anything on their own. What do they do when they roam free? What do they do at night? What did you do last night, for example?"

"What a tremendously personal question!" the Warden gasped. His bones shifted to make his eyes bigger, showing how surprised he was by her effrontery. "But I'll answer you anyway, because some day, your skin will rot away, and your meat, too, and you'll be nothing but bones, and I shudder to think how they'd get on with their nights if they didn't know the proper way to behave. Now, let's see."

He tapped a bony claw thoughtfully against his chin. "I woke up just after second moonrise. I had a nice breakfast of squashed squirrel. Breakfast is a very important meal, you know, and squashed squirrel is quite a treat. Let's see…then I welcomed a new skeleton to the yard. He was burned to a crisp two days ago, and all that's left of him are charred bones, so he was a shoo-in for the Boneyard. Say hello, Jeroboam," the Warden commanded. Off to the right, a blackened set of hand bones rose above the grass and gave a little wave. "That took quite some doing," he continued. "The orientation process is extensive." He leaned in and gave Mabel a devious little wink. "One day you will find out for yourself. At any rate, that ate up quite a bit of the evening. After Jeroboam was settled, there was a knock at the gate, here, and I…I…" The Warden paused and scratched his upper vertebrae. "Now, let's see. There was a knock on the gate, and I'm sure I went to answer it…didn't I?" He frowned. "For the life of me, I can't seem to remember."

"A memory spell!" Mabel whispered excitedly. She was right! "What's the next thing you *do* remember?"

The Warden sat up on his haunches and tilted his head. "Hmm…eventually, I grew tired. I had roasted cream for dinner, and then I went in for a sleep. But that was much later…" His voice trailed off and belied his confusion.

"Listen, Warden, sir…do you think it's possible someone cast a memory spell on you?"

The Warden laughed uproariously. His rotted leaf breath gusted through the open gate, and Mabel covered her nose in her sleeve. "A memory spell? On me? Ridiculous!" he cried. "There is no magic that's a match for the Warden of the Boneyard, for I am old and strong and in rather good physical condition, all things considered. Have I not mentioned that?"

"You have," Mabel nodded, "but you also have a large gap in your memory. Is that normal?"

The Warden frowned. "No. It is highly irregular. My memory is often quite comprehensive, and it is also, if I may say, rather profound."

"Then I think we need to face the fact that you've been bewitched," Mabel said, taking a chance and stepping closer to the Warden and the gate. "The wizard was here, you had a conversation, and he glamoured you so you wouldn't remember and cause a ruckus. Mr. Warden, I think you told the wizard where to find the Skeleton Keys."

"Impossible!" the Warden cried, aghast. "Those keys are my sacred charge, I would never betray them." He seemed to relax a bit, and his teeth clacked together thoughtfully. "Still…the memory lapse is a curious thing. Well, better to be safe than sorry, I suppose. No sense in losing the kingdom for fear of losing face, I always say. There's one way we can be absolutely sure."

"Even without your memory?" Mabel asked.

"Oh yes. All conversations involving me, the Warden of the Boneyard, regarding the Skeleton Keys are recorded in the ledger." He made some clicking sounds with his tongue, and more bones rolled forward from the mist. They locked themselves together to form an immensely thick book with webs of finger bones for pages.

"It records your conversations automatically?" Mabel asked, thinking that it sounded a bit intrusive. She wondered if the matrons in the orphanage ever secretly recorded *her* conversations.

"Yes, indeed. Checks and balances, you know—checks and balances. Everyone is accountable to someone." Mabel shuddered to think what sort of creature someone as old and strong as the Warden of the Boneyard might be accountable to. He flipped open the book and found the last page with writing on it. "Oh dear," he frowned, running his finger down the page. "Yes, here it is, right here. 'The Warden of the Boneyard, Keeper of the Skeleton Keys, passed forth extremely detailed information about the locations of the three keys and instructions on how to use them to open the three locks in order to access the compendium that is the Boneyard Warden's charge.'" Maybe it was just a shift in moonlight, but suddenly, the Warden's bones seemed much paler. He closed the book, and the various bones that formed it broke apart and scattered back across the yard. "It seems you are right, little girl. I was weak in the face of the evil magician." He began to cry tears of marrow. "I shall be stripped of my position if anything untoward happens because of this! I shall no longer be Warden of the Boneyard, or Keeper of the Keys, or Denizen of the Mist Fields, or Fire Marshall of the Rear Graveyard! Oh, I shall be ruined!" The Warden dropped his great head onto his hands and wept.

"But maybe I can help," Mabel said, creeping a bit closer. Her heart hurt for the crying beast, even though he was a little frightening. "If you tell *me* where the keys are hidden, I may be able to track down the wizard and steal back the book before he can open it. Wouldn't that be helpful?"

The Warden lifted his head. "It—it would be," he decided, sniffling back his tears. "You would do that for me?"

Mabel thought it a poor strategy to point out that this was precisely why she approached him in the first place, for she didn't want the Warden to feel manipulated. So instead, she nodded and said, "Yes. You seem like a dear creature, for a monster. I'd like to help you."

This brightened the Warden considerably. "Well, then! We have no time to waste! The wizard already has a head start on you. Come, let's not dawdle. Let's discuss the Skeleton Keys."

The little ledger bones rolled forward again, though more slowly now, annoyed at having to assemble themselves for the second time in one day. They came together, and the book opened itself to a fresh page and waited for the Warden to begin speaking. When he did, little red letters began to appear.

"Now, the instructions on where to find the keys are in rhyme, and that's how you know they're important and official. If something is told to you and it's not in rhyme, you must be careful, for it may be counterfeit, or at least incomplete. Are you ready to hear the first rhyme?" Mabel nodded. "All right, then. Here it is." And he read:

The first key is planted, but will never grow;
It's impossible to get if you are a crow.
Don't waste your time with every man you meet,
You'll find it beneath the boy with black feet.

"That's the first part," said the Warden. "Do you like it?"

Mabel nodded. "Very much," she said. "Did you write it?"

The Warden nodded proudly. "I did."

"It's very good. It's a rhyme, but also a bit of a riddle, isn't it?"

"Yes, yes, you've got it!" the Warden cried happily, clapping his huge, bony hands together. "It is a rhyme that you have to *solve!*"

"I think I've done it," Mabel said carefully. She ran through the verses in her mind. "It must be in a field where things are planted and usually grow…a field with scarecrows, I think, since crows can't get to it. I haven't figured out the bit about the boy with black feet, but the first key is buried somewhere in Farmer Parchrock's mud-root field. He has more scarecrows than anyone else in Brightsbane. Is that it?"

"My, my," the Warden said, clearly impressed. "You are a bright little girl, aren't you? I'm sorry I spoke poorly of your school. Are you ready for the second rhyme?" And he recited further:

The next key, I fear, is harder to take.
You'll find it in the middle of a fiery lake.
The heat of the place may have caused it to melt.
Spill common blood to operate the smelt.

"That one's a little harder, I'd wager," the Warden said, sounding pleased with himself.

Mabel agreed. The only thing she was able to glean from the second riddle is that she'd have to visit Boiling Lake. Other than that, she was coming up empty, and she didn't know how she could go about solving the riddle. She would have to think about that one.

"How about the third rhyme?" she asked. "Where do I find the last key?"

The Warden recited again:

To find the next key, you'll need a stout heart;
Witches and owls and Shimmers play a part.
You'll find many keys in the Grandfather Tree.
Speak the right answer, set the real one free.

Mabel gulped. "The witches of Brightsbane live in the Briarbranch Woods," she said, her voice barely louder than a whisper. "And Shimmers, too. The last key must be there."

Oh, dear reader, if you only knew! The dark, sprawling forest was absolutely rife with tricks and traps. Devious animals lurked in the shadows, and some people even said that the trees themselves were capable of gobbling up little children. The Briarbranch Woods was a dangerous place. Sometimes, when people went in, they never came back out.

And sometimes, they came back out a little bit different.

Mabel squeezed her eyes shut and pictured her Letter of High Station. She could quit now, give up and go back to St. Crippleback's, and maybe even curry favor with the matrons for returning on her own accord. She wouldn't have to deal with crows, or fields, or boiling lakes, or witches, or riddles, or magic, or anything of the sort. She would be safe…but her low station would latch itself to her back for the rest of her days. She wouldn't go to lavish parties or stately schools. She wouldn't taste rich desserts or drink bubbly Champagnes. She wouldn't ride horses or design bridges or become adequately equipped to tackle higher mathematical equations. She wouldn't wander through curious shops or talk with foreign kings or sail mighty ships. Without the Letter of High Station to unlock new doors, her path was set in the muck and mire of the lowborn orphan. But if she could steel herself against the dangers ahead, she just might be able to change all that and make something extraordinary out of her life.

"Are you sure you're up to the task?" the Warden asked, as if reading her mind.

Mabel opened her eyes. The Letter of High Station disappeared and was replaced by the curious construction of bones that comprised the Warden's face. "Yes," she said with absolute resolution. "I'll search out the keys and steal back the compendium, if I can."

"Excellent! Both my reputation and the future of Brightsbane may depend on it." The Warden shook his whole body, and bones began to pop themselves loose and roll away into the mist. "Go with luck, brave child. Come back some evening during a reasonable waking hour and inform me of your progress." All the femurs and vertebrae and tibiae and ulnae broke free of the Warden's form, and soon there was nothing left but a small pile of ruined, broken bones too feeble to skitter away. Even so, the Warden's voice rang through the fog:

"Be careful, girl. And be mindful. And for sun's sake, don't die."

Chapter 4
Birds of a Feather Slice Together

The journey to Farmer Parchrock's land was largely uneventful (which, I must admit, was a bit to Mabel's chagrin). Mabel knew the way by the constellations in the sky; if she followed the White Queen and stayed to the left of the Duplicitous Otter, her path would take her northeast, toward the mudroot fields. Of course, she did stumble and scrape her knees on the road a time or two, so consumed was she by her celestial navigation, but this was not uncommon; because of the lack of suitable light, the villagers of Brightsbane were always falling down.

Before long, she arrived at the farmer's fence with minimal injury. A shadowy legion of scarecrows stretched off beyond the fence and into the horizon.

Scarecrows aren't alive, Mabel reminded herself as she stood at the edge of the field. *Scarecrows aren't alive.*

But she didn't know for sure that this was true.

Farmer Parchrock's scarecrows filled the mudroot field like flakes of mold on month-old bread. They were staked so closely and so thickly into the earth, you couldn't see the mudroot stalks through the maze of straw legs, even though it was nearing harvest season. The scarecrows writhed with life in the afternoon breeze, their canvas faces and dull-painted eyes glistening in the moonlight. There were hundreds of straw men in the field. Maybe thousands.

And one of them was guarding a key.

"Here goes nothing," Mabel sighed. She squeezed through the rail fence and walked straight ahead between the rows. She was of a medium height for her age, which is to say that she was rather on the shorter end of things, and the straw men were fixed high on their crosses of wood, so their feet dangled just below her chin. This made it easy for her to see their feet and check them for black coloring, but it also made her feel as if she were being trampled on by a sea of itchy, scratchy scarecrows.

They don't have feet at all, she realized as she passed the first row of straw men. *Just straw sticking out of their cuffs.*

Mabel reached out and brushed her hand along a pant leg. "Ouch!" she shrieked, yanking her hand back. She stuck her finger into her mouth and tasted the metallic tang of blood. She drew the finger out and inspected it in the dim light. A long, thin line had been slashed into her fingertip. It trickled tiny drops of ruby red blood onto the dirt. "The canvas is made of glasswire," she realized miserably. And indeed, as she moved through the throng of straw men, their clothing glistened like sanding sugar when the moonlight caught it just so.

The scarecrows were more dangerous than she'd expected. She'd have to be more careful.

She turned to the side and eased her way down the row, trying to avoid crushing the mudroot where she could. The deeper she pushed into the field, the more the scarecrows choked out the light, and soon it was so dark that the straw men were little more than silhouettes. If it got much darker, *every* foot would look as if it were dipped in black ink. "I should have nicked the elder's Luna Lamp," she said aloud, and it was good to hear a friendly voice, even if it was her own.

She heard something then, a dry straw rattle of a whisper. *Beware the birds,* the whisper said.

But that was silly. She was alone in the field with only a legion of scarecrows for company. And scarecrows couldn't talk.

The crows are coming, came another rasping sigh.

The crows, more voices agreed, barely audible above the rustling of the mudroot leaves. *The crows are coming back.*

Beware the crows.

Mabel felt something brush against her hair. She jumped back with a little cry and looked up at the scarecrow looming above her. His patchwork shirt was shredded about the shoulders. Little scraps of fabric hung down his chest. One of his eyes had been scraped away from his canvas face, and straw poked out of little, ragged holes all over his body. He reached out with his straw hand and cradled her chin. He tilted his head down, and his sewn-on mouth struggled to work as he whispered, *Leave now, child. Save yourself.*

Mabel screamed.

Shhhh, the scarecrows urged her, lifting their fingers to their lips. *Quiet, or they'll hear you.* Mabel skittered backward, but she bumped into the scarecrow behind her, and the glasswire cut into her back. She twisted and turned and slipped between the rows, running back toward what she thought was the edge of the field, but she was hopelessly turned around, and she couldn't be sure. But she didn't want to stay in the field—not now, not with the whispering scarecrows—so she pushed on, because no matter which direction she was heading, surely she would come to the end of a row eventually.

As she tumbled past the straw men, she began to notice that they *all* bore rips and tears. Their shirts were shredded. Their torsos were in tatters. Their legs had been lacerated, and their heads had been hewn. They reached out to her, trying to herd her toward the edge of the field, but their clothes tore into her skin. She ducked under their arms and ran on, blindly, wanting the whispers to stop.

And then, they did.

The scarecrows straightened up and fell silent, as if listening for something on the wind. After a few moments of stillness, they turned their sad eyes back to young Mabel and said, *It's too late. They're here.*

A screeching caw echoed through the field. The air filled with the flutter of wings, and a murder of crows descended.

Hide! the scarecrows urged. *Hide!*

The straw men above her stretched their arms wide, trying to block Mabel from view. The crows rushed the field, cawing and cackling and shrieking with excitement. They dove at the scarecrows and attacked them with their talons, which were sharp— fearsomely sharp...*unnaturally* sharp. They used their claws to rip and rend the straw men from above.

"I thought scarecrows were meant to scare away the crows," Mabel whispered, even though common sense should have told her not to make a sound while being attacked by bloodthirsty crows. Poor Mabel was frightened beyond sense.

These are glass-footed crows, a scarecrow whispered back. *We're helpless against them, and so will you be.*

"What's down there?" a crow asked, flying above the field. "What are you scarecrows trying to hide?"

Nothing! Nothing! the scarecrows insisted.

"There's something," another crow agreed, landing atop a poor scarecrow's torn head and tearing it even more. "It has feet—I can see them!"

"And arms!" cried another bird.

"And a head!" shrieked a fourth. "It's a girl! It's a girl! It's a real live girl!"

"A girl in our field!" the crows squawked. "She's trampling our sweet mudroot! Get her! Rip her! Tear her in two!"

Mabel cried out in fear and cowered behind a scarecrow's post. The crows were diving and swooping down above her now, cutting into the scarecrows that so bravely protected her from their attacks.

Run! the scarecrows said.

Mabel turned and scrambled across the field. The glasswire canvas scratched her neck and her shoulders as she ran, but she pushed on, trying to escape the hovering cloud of crows. But their eyes were well trained, and they tracked her easily. The caws followed close behind, and the birds dove. Some of them made it through the wall of scarecrows, and she felt a rough claw slice through her shoulder blade, and another cut a line in her ear.

The birds overhead broke into two ranks. One curved around

to the left, the other curved around to the right. They met on the far end, and just like that, Mabel was surrounded.

The crows floated down and alighted on the shoulders of the scarecrows that towered above her. "A girl! A girl! It's really a girl!" they screeched, delighted. It had been so long since a human had wandered into their field.

"How shall we divide her up?" one crow asked.

"Let's draw lots!" said a second.

"First come, first served!" said a greedy third, snapping his beak.

A fat crow with silver streaks in its plumage settled down upon a scarecrow's arm, digging into the elbow with his sharp feet. The arm sagged under the bird's weight. The other crows fell silent as he held up his wing and began to speak. "We will be equitable, my friends. We shall serve her up in a mudroot hash, and everyone shall have a bite!" A raucous cheer went up among the birds. It cut right through Mabel's spine and sent shivers all the way down to her toes and back.

The birds closed in. Mabel grabbed a dirt clod and hurled it at the nearest one, smashing it right in the beak. "*Caw!*" it screeched, falling backward onto the field. "My eyes! My eyes!" Mabel threw more dirt, and her aim was true, but for every bird she knocked over, three more hopped down from their scarecrow perches and landed in the soil around her. The fat crow with the silvered feathers plopped down directly before her and rubbed its wings together greedily. "I think I'd like a piece of cheek," it said.

Then something caught the fat bird square in the chest and knocked it to the ground. "A mudroot!" a crow squawked. "Some-one threw a mudroot!"

More of the knobby roots came hurling through the air. They rained down on the crows and knocked them senseless. Off to her left, Mabel saw a shadow dart past the murder of crows and run deeper into the field, pulling out mudroots by the leaves as he went.

"Stop him! Stop him!" cried the crows. "He's stealing our precious mudroot!" They took to the air and charged the mysterious silhouette, which was moving fast and had gained quite a lead on them. Each and every bird that was still conscious took to the sky, and Mabel found herself more or less alone in the dirt.

Go, whispered the scarecrows. *Before they come back.*

But Mabel remembered the key, and she wouldn't leave without seeing if the wizard had snapped it up first. She *couldn't*. "I need to find a scarecrow with feet as black as ink. Can you help me?"

There was a heavy rustling sound as the scarecrows lifted their arms and pointed to the north. Mabel rose to her feet and ran in that direction, avoiding the glasswire canvas clothing as best she could. The straw men pointed the way.

There, they said with their dry straw voices. *He is the one.*

Mabel pushed into a little square clearing. At the center of it stood a small scarecrow, much smaller than all the rest, and more lifelike than the others, too. He wore the same clothes and had the same canvas face and the same straw-stuffed arms, but his shape was somehow more convincing. The way he rustled in the wind was less jerky, more controlled. When the wind whistled through his canvas, it made it sound as if he were actually crying. And he had feet—*real* feet, or close enough to real as to make no difference. They were fashioned out of wood, Mabel guessed. And they were painted black.

"Thank you," she whispered to the scarecrows.

Hurry, they replied.

She fell to her knees before the little straw boy and dug through the dirt with her hands. The ground was loose and easy to push aside. After only a few inches, her fingers scraped against something metal. She cleared the dirt off of it and pulled out a long, flat tin box. "The key!" she squealed triumphantly.

She flipped the latch and opened the lid. The box was lined with rags that bore the impression of a large key, but not the key itself.

It was too late. The wizard had beaten her to it.

Go, the scarecrows urged. *They are coming back.*

Mabel threw the box down in frustration. The wizard had a head start, and she would have to hurry if she was to reach one of the remaining keys first.

By the time the crows reached the straw boy with black feet, Mabel was already gone.

CHAPTER 5

THE SAGE ADVICE OF
IMPROPERLY SIZED COWARDS

Mabel was scraped, scratched, and scuffed after her ordeal in Farmer Parchrock's field, but she found herself free of any life-threatening injuries that required either immediate surgery or healing potions. The identity of the figure who had run through the field and drawn away the crows was quite a mystery, but she supposed she shouldn't wonder too much at her good fortune and should instead be thankful for his interference.

Still. It gnawed at her brain.

But there were more immediate matters that needed attention, chief among them: the search for the second Skeleton Key. Which should she go after next—the key at Boiling Lake, or the key in Briarbranch Woods? Both options filled her with dread. If the tales were true, only the worst and most troublesome sort of magical creatures roamed the forest, and the things that dwelled beneath the surface of the lake were old, and powerful, and not at all of this world. Mabel felt rather ill-equipped to deal with any of them, especially given the fact that she'd been unable to manage a simple flock of crows.

Witches and daemons and sprites and ghouls, if you didn't know, tend to be more troublesome than birds.

The chance of her surviving either pursuit on her own seemed very unlikely. At the beginning of her quest, she felt sure that she could overcome all odds, like the heroes and heroines of ancient lore, but her experience in the mudroot fields had squashed that confidence flat.

"I'll ask Elder Alder," she finally decided. "He's an elder, and he will know what to do."

The Elderary sat more or less directly between Boiling Lake and the Briarbranch Woods, so she wouldn't waste much time in stopping in for advice. As she walked, she tried very hard not to think about the many painful ways she could meet her demise if she took a wrong turn in the forest or slipped for a second beneath the waves of the lake. But it was difficult, for she was destined to face them quite soon, and by the time she reached the Elderary, she had quite unconsciously compiled a fairly long list of possible deaths. They included, but were not limited to, the following: death by charring; death by swallowing; death by binding, chopping, and scattering; death by hanging; death by drowning; death by boiling; death by falling; death by time travel; death by riddling; death by trans-dimensional misunderstanding; death by rich, delicious foods; death by spriggots, wiggots, and glouts; death by perfumery; death by steaming; death by leaf; death by limestone; death by alchemy; death by explosion; and death by Death.

She took only a small amount of satisfaction in the illumination that death by boredom did not present itself as a likely option.

"You look awfully familiar," said the Elderary doorman when she walked through the glowing blue gate.

"I was here earlier," Mabel said. "Don't you remember?"

"Hmm..." He tapped the sceptre against his chin and thought hard. "I remember a moderately well-groomed girl in a dirty but perfectly solid shift. But you are not that girl." He popped his monocle back onto his eye and examined her closely. "You are a disastrously ill-groomed girl in a dirty and mostly shredded shift. You've got scrapes and scratches and dirt of all sorts. No, the girl who came in this morning was a girl who knew very little of the world. You, on the other hand, seem to be in the midst of a great and dangerous adventure."

"I've had a difficult day," Mabel said wearily.

"I shall ask the sceptre if you are lying; if you are, your day will become even more difficult." The doorman whispered a question to the sceptre. The sceptre, in return, did nothing at all. It did not change into a snake, or into anything else, for that matter. "Hmm...I suppose you really must be that same girl after all," said the doorman, pocketing his monocle. "You may enter."

Now that the day had gotten on with itself, there was quite a bit more activity in the Elderary than there had been early in the morning, when Mabel first visited. As the rug unrolled itself toward Elder Alder's chambers, Mabel found herself hurrying past half a dozen men in elder's robes. She wished she could stop and introduce herself, for the elders were something of celebrities in Brightsbane, and even if Elder Whip *was* reputed to be something of a taskmaster, it was only because he cared so deeply for the village and its people that he had to work diligently for their benefit. The songs the people sang about the elders' benevolence were lovely and stirring, and now the heroes of those songs were within arm's reach, glancing curiously at the young girl who ran by on her way to meet with the newest of their order. But Mabel had no time, for surely the wizard was not stopping along *his* way for polite conversation, and his lead was already so great. And besides, the rug was in a hurry, too. So Mabel rushed along and satisfied herself with the hope that she would be allowed to make personal appointments with the each of the other elders in turn when she received her Letter of High Station.

"Good gracious, child!" Elder Alder exclaimed upon opening the door. "What happened to you? Come in, come in!"

"I had a run-in with some crows," Mabel said, hopping into her chair on the far side of the elder's desk. There was a dish of sweets on the corner of the desk now, and she popped one into her mouth. It tasted of banana jam and butterscotch.

"Glass-foot crows, from the looks of it. But in the Boneyard?" the elder asked. He opened a cabinet below one of his bookshelves and pulled out an apothecary jar filled with a greenish-yellow liquid and a fabric napkin. He set about to work dabbing her scrapes with the healing tonic. Her skin went tingly where the liquid was pressed into her wounds. "I've never heard of glass-foot crows venturing so far south."

"Not in the Boneyard," Mabel said, flinching more by instinct than because of pain. Truth be told, the elder's salve didn't hurt one bit, but one should always expect a healing tonic to offer a certain amount of burn. It is only prudent. "In Farmer Parchrock's mudroot field. There were plenty of crows there."

"Farmer Parchrock? Why on earth would you venture there? Even the scarecrows are scared of the crows in that field!"

"I was looking for the first Skeleton Key."

Elder Alder finished his dabbing and set the tonic on his desk. "The Warden confided in you, did he?"

Mabel nodded. "The wizard tricked him, then cast a memory spell, and I had to help him get it sorted. He told me where to find the three keys, but the first one's already gone."

"Where are the other two?" the elder asked. His fingers worked nervously at the thin rope cinched around his waist. "Somewhere less dangerous, I hope."

"One's in the Briarbranch; the other's in Boiling Lake." She proceeded to tell him the Warden's rhymes, and she told them exactly, for she had a good head for memorization.

The elder's face fell as she spoke. "Oh, Mabel," he said when she was finished, his voice hardly more than a whisper. "What have I gotten you into?"

"I don't suppose any of the other children found the wizard's cave by accident?" she asked. She didn't want to back out of her accord with the elder, but if the problem of the book had already been solved by someone else, then she would be forced to give up her errand, and it wouldn't be anything close to her own fault, and she could live with that, she supposed. But Elder Alder shook his head.

"I haven't heard a pip about the other children. They must still be on the hill."

"Well," Mabel said, casting her eyes downward.

"Mabel, you can call off this dangerous task. I'll write you a

Letter of High Station right now. You've already been through so much." He withdrew a plume and a clean sheet of creamy white paper from the desk drawer and laid it on the desk. "Thank you for your enthusiasm, but this has gone too far."

Mabel stared with an open mouth at the paper beneath the elder's plume. Just like that, with a few flicks of his wrist, he could write her a formal Letter, stamp it with the Elderary seal, and she would be a Better Class of Person. The gilded doors of society would open, and suddenly, her future would spread before her like a never-ending picnic blanket, boundless and full.

But what sort of society would be left if the wizard used *The Boneyard Compendium*'s horrible spells to destroy the village? The Letter of High Station was important, oh yes, but even the highest station meant nothing if there were no existence to serve as a platform. And just like that, the paper appeared a little duller before her eyes, a little less bright. A little less important.

"I can't," she said, shaking her head.

"Pardon?" The elder's ears perked up as he stayed his hand above the page.

"I can't. I can't quit now. If I don't find the wizard, who will?"

Elder Alder looked for all the world as if he might cry. "I should do it myself," he said.

"You wouldn't have hidden very well in the mudroot field," Mabel pointed out. "You would have stood as tall as the scarecrows, and the crows would have gotten you for sure. Who knows what other adventures you might be improperly sized for?"

"Yes, I suppose that's true," the elder frowned. "But the larger truth is, I'm also a coward. I'm afraid that if I leave the Elderary, I'll draw attention to myself, and the other elders will begin to ask themselves where I've gone, and my failure to protect the book will be found out. I'm afraid that I will be cast out if all of this comes to light. I am afraid I will lose my station, and that I will sully the name of my father and my grandfather, both of whom were highly respected elders in their days. I am afraid that I'm sending a young girl to her death in my stead, but I am also afraid of facing the wizard Croup again…and because of all this, I am afraid that I shall be responsible for the demise of the entire world." He buried his head shamefully in his hands. "You see? I am a coward of the worst sort."

Mabel drew her knees up to her chin and thought for a moment. Finally, she said, "I read once that the worst sort of cowards are the cowards who pretend to be brave. So maybe you're just a regular sort of coward."

"I'm not sure that's a difference worth noting," sighed the elder.

Mabel thought a bit more. Elder Alder was afraid, but she had an inkling that maybe being afraid and being terrible weren't the same thing. "I think some people are cowards just by their nature," she said slowly, testing the words as they rolled off her tongue, "and some people are brave because they're born that way or manage to become that way, and if you're the sort of person who's brave, then you ought to help the people who are cowards, and maybe show them how to be brave. And I think there's plenty of things a lot of people who are brave can't do, and I think sometimes there are cowards who can help them do those things." She paused and chewed at her bottom lip, trying to gnaw a bit of reason from it. "And I think that I might be brave, at least a little bit. And if I am, then I think I should help you, even if you are a coward, or maybe especially because you're a coward, because maybe it will help you become brave."

Elder Alder whimpered a little then. It was the sound of a heart breaking, but in a soft way. "Mabel," he said, taking the girl's face gently in his hands. "You are extraordinarily brave. And I think there is much I could learn from you. If you're agreeable to the adventure ahead, then I'll do everything in my power to help you. And you've already proven that you'll do everything in your power to help me. But you must promise me that if things get too dangerous, or if you get too scared, or if your heart tells you that you can go no further, then you'll stop and return here at once, even if the job isn't done. We'll sort out what needs sorting then. It's not worth your life. Do we agree?" He offered Mabel his hand. She held her hand out in turn and shook. She couldn't help but feel that it was a very adult thing to do, and that made her very proud.

"We agree," she said. "Which key do you think I should go after next?"

"As I see it, there's only one option, for now." The elder moved to a shelf near the fireplace and skimmed the books residing there. He picked out a dusty tome from near the end and blew a layer of dust from its cover. He brought it back to the desk and plopped it down. Mabel read the title upside-down: *The Survivor's Guide to Briarbranch Woods*.

"The forest first?" Mabel said, trying to sound courageous for the sake of the elder.

"The other key likely rests on Steamsoak Island, near the center of Boiling Lake. There's only one way I know to cross the water without being boiled alive, and it will take some preparation. I can manage that part while you're hunting through Briarbranch." He opened the book and leafed through its many pages. Mabel caught glimpses of a few illustrations. One of them was a drawing of a witch sitting next to a cauldron filled with a stew of some sort. It was made of carrots, parsnips, mushrooms, broth, and one very confused-looking man with only his head and shoulders poking out above the soup. Another drawing showed a short, portly gnome with a full beard and a conical hat. His mouth was open frighteningly wide, and a horde of wasps spilled forth from it. A third picture showed something that appeared to be a small star shining among the scraggly trees. That, Mabel knew, was a Shimmer of Time and Place.

Finally, the elder settled on a two-page spread with a map etched onto the paper. It was a crude map, and not very detailed, but it showed where the Grandfather Tree stood in relation to the rest of the woods. Mabel was dismayed to see that it grew very deep in the heart of the forest.

"See, now," the elder said, pointing to a small, colored drawing in the bottom right corner of the spread. "This is the Grandfather Tree."

Mabel didn't think it looked so grandfatherly, though of course she didn't have a grandfather of her own, so it was difficult to draw a respectable comparison. The tree had a huge tuft of white leaves so fine and billowy that they seemed to be made of cotton. The same white fluff ringed the trunk about halfway up the tree, giving it a passable beard. The trunk itself was a deep, rich jade color. "I don't see any keys," Mabel pointed out.

The elder nodded. "It could be that this drawing was made before the Warden of the Boneyard hid the key there. It is a very old book." He turned the map so Mabel could see it properly, and at the angle from which she'd be entering the woods. "Mark the map well, Mabel. Memorize the path."

The girl nodded. The tip of her tongue poked itself out of the corner of her mouth as she studied the markings on the map. "I don't think it should be too hard," she decided.

But Elder Alder shook his head. "That is only because there is much that is missing from this particular map. The path looks easy, but there are bound to be many obstacles in the way." He took Mabel's hands in his own and locked eyes with her. "Listen to me, and listen well: If you meet a witch in the woods, well…there's not much to be done there. Be polite, and mind your manners, and keep your wits about you. The same goes for most forest creatures; they're not very easily magicked away, though I think you have the brains to get past them all. But it's the Shimmers I truly fear. Do you know about the Shimmers?" he asked.

"I know a little," Mabel replied. "They're like ripples of wind, and if you step into one, you'll go to a different time, or to a different place."

"Or a different time *and* a different place, depending on the Shimmer," the elder nodded. "But that's just the core of it. I've seen Shimmers strong enough to suck you in from twenty yards away. I've even heard tales of a Shimmer out beyond the desert that can draw men in over the span of a full league. Once you're through, there's no telling where you'll end up, or if you'll make it home. There's not always a Shimmer on the other end to bring you back to where you started. In fact, there *usually* isn't. Do you understand? If you're taken by a Shimmer, you should consider yourself gone from this world forever."

Mabel swallowed hard. "I will," she said.

"No," said the elder. "You won't. I'm determined to see to that. Before you go into the Briarbranch, I want you to go to Devilden. Do you know it?"

Mabel started. "Devilden? Where the monsters live?"

"The very same. There's a creature there named Abernathy. He's something of an alderman; his official title is Viceroy. A small yellow monster, with a penchant for fine clothes. He's in possession of a certain reflectoken, a pin that has the power to take a Shimmer's shine and reflect it back upon itself. Go to Devilden, obtain the reflectoken from the monster, and wear it the entire time you walk the Briarbranch Woods. Do you understand?"

"But Devilden is on the opposite end of the village," Mabel complained. She'd already walked so much today, and it wasn't the normal kind of walking, either. It was the kind of walking where you had to stick to the shadows so adults wouldn't see you and ask why you weren't tucked up behind the walls of St. Crippleback's where you belong. And besides, she was already so far behind the wizard...

"It's the only sure protection from Shimmers I know of. Go to Devilden—promise me you will, or I'll pop you back into the orphanage."

Mabel crossed her arms. "All right," she said, although she said it with a little scowl. "I promise."

"We must hurry," Elder Alder said. "I'll have some sandwiches brought up, and then you must be on your way. It will be second moonrise soon, and you have much ground to cover. I hope that when you return, I'll have the Boiling Lake problem all sorted out."

"I hope so too," Mabel said. "I should hate to be boiled alive."

Chapter 6
Clobbered with Shovels and Picks

At this point in our tale, a brief discussion of the Brightsbane geography may be prudent. We have plenty of time to explore it while Mabel busies herself with the long trek to Devilden.

You see, Mabel traveled to Devilden from the Elderary, which is in the Brightsbane town proper, an area we have not yet had much opportunity to explore, since Mabel's adventure has been taking us to the farther reaches of the village, and since she spent her time actively avoiding people who might recognize her as a waif. The town square is an intriguing place, to be sure, but we shall have to wait and see if Mabel's tale brings us to a point where we can comfortably observe everything it has to offer. If not, perhaps we shall visit it another time.

On the whole, the village of Brightsbane was quite flat, and mostly dry. This was rather fortunate, as the ever-present nighttime made it difficult to see obstacles in one's path, geographic or otherwise. If the town were riddled with hillocks and canyons and marshes and cliffs, the accidental death and dismemberment rate among Brightsbanians would have been astronomical.

The one glaring exception to this rule of horizontal steadfastness was Gallows Hill, a high mountain of sorts composed of black stone and topped with a strangely curling peak. The people of Brightsbane were loath to let a good name go to waste, and so it was on this hill that the village hangings were done. Many a ne'er-do-well met his end atop Gallows Hill before being shuttled off to some pauper's grave or other. It was also beneath this hill, as you well know by now, that the wizard Emerys Croup made his home.

Gallows Hill rose on the southern end of the village. I cannot say with full confidence that it was very far from town proper, for the distance between any two points in Brightsbane was a matter of the village's mood at that particular moment. But Brightsbane liked to keep Gallows Hill at arm's length, and the land had very long arms.

The district of Devilden was nestled within the southeastern slopes of the hill, hidden from view of Brightsbane proper. (The hill also served to block out the light of the moon for much of the day, and Devilden was by far the darkest section of the very dark village.) The best way to approach that particular neighborhood was by circling the eastern edge of Gallows Hill.

Which brings us back to our brave little adventurer. Mabel would have much preferred to avoid Gallows Hill altogether, since it was positively crawling with orphans who might inquire into her doings. But circling too wide to the east would have brought her within spitting distance of Slurptongue Swamp, where she would have had to contend with all manner of muck misers and eel sharks; nor could she really have gone all the way around to the west, for she was losing enough time with her errand as it was.

Mabel decided she would have to take her chances with the orphans.

She was a little less than a league from the base of Gallows Hill when she began to hear a soft *tink-tink-tink* coming from the general direction of the mountain. It was the sound of metal chiseling against stone. It was a strange thing to be hearing, for no one ever mined Gallows Hill for fear of disturbing the wizard. The only people who would be chiseling away at the mountain, Mabel knew, were the orphans, if they were trying to crack their way into the wizard's lair. But that wasn't possible. Orphans weren't allowed to have chisels, for the same reason that they weren't allowed to have dry matches, oily rags, or fragile things. They simply couldn't be trusted with them.

A little farther down the road, she heard a new sound: the squeaking of wooden wheels struggling under a rickety cart. She stepped off the path and lowered herself down into a thicket of brandybushes, lest the approaching villager see her and send her back to St. Crippleback's.

The cart came around a bend in the road. It was a curious sort of cart, as it was not being pulled by a horse, but by a man…a rather old man, from the looks of him. He mumbled and grumbled to himself as he walked, shaking his head ruefully and taking short, sharp steps that stabbed at the dirt. The cart couldn't have been too heavy, for it was empty, and it was made of boards that appeared to be more holes than wood.

The man struggled to a stop not ten feet from where Mabel crouched. He let the cart down, and it hit the hard dirt with a thud. One of the weathered boards tumbled off the side and fell to the ground. The old man cursed and spat.

"Might as well come out," he called into the night. "No use ambushing me, you little highwayman, I've got nothing left to steal away."

Is he talking to me? Mabel wondered. She glanced furtively around. There was no one else in sight. But it didn't seem possible that the old man's eyes had picked her out in the dark.

"You, there—in the bushes," the old man said angrily, staring directly at her hiding spot. "Come out, or I'll drag you out and hitch you to the front of my cart and give my weary arms a rest."

Mabel stood up sheepishly in the bushes, but she didn't move out from behind them. "I'm not a highwayman," she offered.

"That's what all the highwaymen say," gruffed the old man.

"But I'm just a girl." Mabel sidled out of the bushes so the old man could see just how little she was.

"And what of that?" asked the old man. "All the best robbers are girls. They steal your thoughts, then they steal your words, then they steal your heart, then they steal your soul." He spat a huge, brown glob of something near her feet.

"I would never rob anyone," Mabel insisted, "and besides, I wouldn't have time even if I wanted to. I'm in an awfully big hurry."

"That's just as well, for I've nothing left to steal."

"Has it all been stolen already?" Mabel asked, approaching the old man in her curiosity. Despite his rude demeanor, he seemed harmless.

"Of course it's all been stolen already! If I hadn't been robbed, old Bessie here would be piled high with posts, picks, sledges, and shovels, all of a useless metal. But you don't see any of those things, do you?" Mabel shook her head. "No, you don't. And now I've got nothing to sell to the alchemist on Bobbleton Street! That was a whole month's wages for me, right down the drain."

"Are there highwaymen ahead, then?" Mabel asked nervously.

"Aye, a right gaggle of them. Small ones, like you, and every bit as vicious. You'll go around them, if you have a mind."

The other children from the orphanage, Mabel thought. *They stole the metal tools, and that's how they're chiseling into the mountain.* "Thank you for the warning," she said politely.

"You're probably in league with them. A lookout for travelers coming the other direction. If only alchemists could turn little girls into statues of quiet, harmless gold." The old man spat a final time, then he heaved up the cart and resumed his stabbing steps along the road.

Mabel continued on toward the hill. The *tink-tink-tink* was louder now, and it was starting to sound more like *clang-clang-clang.* The road wound itself right up against the base of the mountain and hugged it tightly as it curved around the eastern edge. As she got closer, Mabel could see little sparks popping all across the mountain's face. They were the sparks of metal against stone.

The activity was mostly contained to the middle part of the mountain. Mabel crept quietly along the base, keeping to the darkest shadows, and for a while, she thought perhaps she could slip past Gallows Hill undetected. But as she neared the spot where the road broke away toward Devilden, a sharp whistle pierced the air. The *clang-clang-clang*ing on the mountain stopped. There was an audible rustle as a whole mountain's worth of waifs and strays raised their heads and turned to see why the alarm had been raised.

"Mabel Gray," said a familiar voice. It echoed off the mountainside and bounced around so that after Mabel heard it in one ear, she had to hear it again in the other. It was a strange voice, squeaky yet burly, and there was only one person it could have possibly belonged to.

"Barnaby Whipleton." Mabel's heart sank as she said the name. Barnaby was the biggest, meanest boy in St. Crippleback's ledger. He stood a full head taller than the second tallest boy, and he was three times as wide. Mabel sometimes thought that if a person had a mind to, she could fit a large shirt and a pair of suspenders over a barrel saddled with two sacks of flour and make a passable facsimile of Barnaby Whipleton. No one knew whether the lad was a waif or a stray. The smart money was on stray, but there were whispers that he was technically a waif, because he had murdered his own parents. Surely, that was a rumor and a lie, Mabel thought. *Still...*

"Where've *you* been?" Barnaby leapt down from his perch on a low cliff and skidded down the base of the mountain, kicking up a puff of rock dust that got in Mabel's eyes and made her cough. He held a huge crowbar in his hands and leaned against it now as he spoke.

"I stayed behind at the orphanage," Mabel lied. She knew lying was wrong, but she had a suspicion, or perhaps just a very strong hope, that it was okay under certain circumstances. She thought one of those circumstances was staring her right in the face.

"Is that so?" Barnaby narrowed his eyes, and a cruel fire flashed behind them. "Nibbles! Come here."

A young boy with a hitched gait hobbled onto the road. His real name was Porticus Merriweather, but the other children called him Nibbles because he possessed a remarkably rat-like face, and also because he inexplicably tended to get his fingers and toes caught in many of the mousetraps the matrons set around the orphanage. "Yeah?"

"Tell Mabel what you told me before."

"About what?"

"About Mabel, you dope!" Barnaby swatted him on the back of the head. This seemed to jar Nibbles' memory.

"Oh yeah! I told Barnaby before—because, see, back in the home, he told me, 'Stay here, Nibbles…see who stays and see who goes, you little rat,' because sometimes he calls me a rat, but he means it in a good way, not a hurtful way, like he does, you know." Barnaby cleared his throat. Nibbles got back on track. "Anyway, I said, 'Sure thing, Barnaby, I'll see who stays and see who goes,' and I saw a lot of people go, I saw almost everybody go, and I only saw a few people stay, but I saw you, Mabel. You went. I told Barnaby, 'I saw Mabel go, is she not here?' And Barnaby said, 'Why, no, she isn't,' and I said, 'That's downright strange, Barnaby, because I saw her go,' and I did, Mabel, I saw you go. I saw you sneak out of your bunkroom and slip out your lavatory passageway that you think is so secret but really isn't very secret at all…everyone knows about it. And that was hours ago, lots of hours. It was early in the morning, and now it's early in the evening." Nibbles suddenly flushed a deep crimson, as if this much talking was an embarrassing exertion for him. "Anyway, that's what I told Barnaby."

Barnaby rolled his eyes. "That's fine, Nibbles." The little rat-faced boy gave a nervous little bow, then he limped back over to the side of the road, where a large crowd of waifs and strays was gathering. Barnaby turned his cruel eyes back on the girl. "Care to twist a new fable, Mabel?"

"Oh…I went to the library," she blurted. This new lie came easily, because Elder Alder's office was something very like a library, with all the books stacked all the way to the ceiling. "I was looking for a grimoire with an uncloaking spell that would show us the entrance to the wizard's cave."

Barnaby's eyes narrowed themselves even further, so that they were little more than suspicious slits. He leaned in close to Mabel, so close that she could feel his breath on the tip of her nose as he hissed, "That's a lie. Everyone knows uncloaking spells are useless against the wizard's magic; they've been tried hundreds of times. And you *know* they've been tried hundreds of times. You know it'd be useless to search for a spell in a grimoire…because you're a dumb girl, are you, Mabel?"

"Um…yes?" she tried.

Barnaby's mouth pressed itself into a hard, straight line. "No," he said through clenched lips, "I don't think you are." He lifted a finger at a pair of orphans who had been standing behind Mabel, off to the side. At Barnaby's signal, they rushed forward and seized her by the elbows.

"Let go!" Mabel cried, but the boys held her fast. The other waifs and strays watching from the hill were as quiet as the Boneyard. If they disagreed with Barnaby's treatment of her, they were far too frightened of him to make it known.

"Know what I think?" the leader of the ragamuffins said, hefting the crowbar as if he'd just remembered that it was in his hand. "I think you read the letter and knew you didn't stand a chance of finding the wizard's cave. But you knew if you stayed, the matrons would pull their straps off the walls and flog you until you told them where the rest of us went, and then they'd flog you some more for letting us go. So you snuck out, too, but instead of making for the hill, you went to the constabulary. You told them we escaped and that you knew where to find us, and if they wanted to know, they'd have to give you something in return. Maybe a Day of Freedom, or maybe an Unquestioning Favor." He lowered his voice into something like a death rattle. "Or maybe they promised you a Letter of High Station."

The other children gasped. "No!" Mabel cried, struggling against the hands that held her fast. "I'm not a rat!" She looked pointedly at Nibbles, but if he was offended by her terminology, he didn't let it show. He'd been the target of such slurs before.

"And I say you *are*," Barnaby growled.

"If I did that, why would I be here? There'd be a cartload of constables instead of one little Mabel!"

Barnaby frowned. Mabel could see her logic squirming into his brain and laying eggs of doubt there. But the frown melted upward into a smile, and Mabel's ray of hope darkened. "I think they'd want to give us a chance to find the cave. No one else has done it, so they might as well let the orphans have a shot. If we find it, the whole town benefits. If we don't, there's no harm done. And if orphans run into trouble with the wizard, well, there aren't many who will care, is there?" he asked bitterly. "They sent you to spy and make sure none of us gives up and runs for the desert. I bet they'll be along in a few hours to round us up."

Mabel allowed herself a moment to actually be impressed that a goon like Barnaby had cobbled together such a reasonable, if wholly inaccurate, plan. She opened her mouth to refute his charge, but Barnaby silenced her by raising the crowbar over his shoulder. "Show her what we do with spies, boys," he said.

The two orphans holding her elbows looked at each other questioningly. One of them raised an eyebrow. The other one shrugged. He leaned forward and whispered, "What *do* we do with spies?"

Barnaby closed his eyes and rubbed the bridge of his nose. "We tie them to the mountain and clobber them with shovels and picks. You hear that?" Barnaby asked loudly, addressing all the boys and girls on the hill. "Everyone gets a swing!" Some of the children cheered. The boys, mostly.

"No!" Mabel wailed as her guards dragged her up the slope of the mountain. "I'm not a spy! I'm *not!*"

"Well," said Barnaby, following a few steps behind and giving the crowbar a practice swing, "better safe than sorry."

Just then, a bright green light exploded to life on the road in front of the mountain. Actually, to describe it as green is to do the light a great disservice. It was the color that chartreuse would be if it realized that someone had set it to "dim" many eons ago, and it flipped the switch to "exceedingly high." And to say that the light was bright is a grave understatement. It was so intense that it bathed the entire mountainside. Mabel could even see the gallows at the top of the hill as plain as if it were day (which was really a guess on her part, since she'd never actually experienced day, but we'll allow it, for there are only so many cruelties a girl in her position should be asked to withstand).

The light blinded the host of children. Even when they raised their hands to shield their eyes, the light was too great, for it shone through the skin, exposing the shadow of the skeleton within.

"Hello, children," said a voice behind the light.

"It's the constabulary!" shrieked a little boy off to Mabel's left.

"They've come to clap us in the stocks!" shouted a little girl to her right.

"Everyone! To the desert!" Barnaby bellowed. He stumbled blindly, caught his toe on a loose stone, and went pitching down the side of the mountain. The other children followed in precisely as successful a manner. For a few moments, the entire hill was alive with a landslide of falling, skidding children. (It may be a distasteful thing to say, but as an ever-dutiful narrator, I feel I must be completely honest on this point: it was quite an entertaining sight.)

Only one child among them did not try to run to the desert. Mabel stood petrified partway up the mountain. The rest of the children tumbled down, but Mabel, who was caught between submitting to the mysterious stranger behind the light and following her would-be clobberers into the terrifying Desert of a Thousand Steps, stood as straight and indecisive and scared as a board.

Boards are easily frightened, you know. And they are often uncertain when it comes to important decisions.

She did not know what to do. She did not know who the man behind the light was, or even if it was just one man standing behind it. It could have been the constabulary, or Mayor Poppet's men, or highwaymen, or bounty hunters sent in secret by the matrons of St. Crippleback's. That last one was the most likely, to be sure. The matrons were just the right sort to hire cutthroats to slip into the shadows and steal back the children by whatever means necessary before their flight became public knowledge. The bright light hurt her eyes and made it hard to think. She put the gears of her brain to work, but they creaked and groaned and made quite an objection. There was only one idea that surfaced clearly: *I have to get to Devilden.*

But oh, how to make an escape?

Fortunately, the person holding the green light was very obliging. At just that moment, he accidentally touched his finger to the lamp, and his skin sizzled against the extremely bright, extremely green, and extremely hot light.

"*Aieee!*" he screamed. The light snuffed out as the man dropped the lamp and howled in the darkness. Mabel still could not see, for the light had left a pinkish-red afterimage in her eyes that blotted out absolutely everything. But she was by no means a dull-witted child, and she knew that this could be her only opportunity to escape. She dropped to her knees and slid slowly down the hill, feeling her way with her hands and feet and trying to avoid the rocks and thistle with what a generous person might call a bit of success. But a few scrapes were a fair trade for freedom, and when she reached the base of the mountain, the mysterious man was still groaning in pain somewhere off to her left. Her vision began to clear, and she stumbled back onto the road and hurried around the corner, leaving Gallows Hill, the other orphans, and the mysterious person with the green light behind.

Devilden loomed in the darkness ahead.

Chapter 7

The Persuasive Abilities
of Toothaches

I feel it is only fair to give you a word of comfort as we enter this particular chapter in Mabel's adventure, because I imagine that you may be reading this while tucked into the safety of your bed. Perhaps you have just switched on your reading lamp, and you're settling in to read a bit while you nibble at a chocolate biscuit and try to keep the crumbs from falling into the sheets. Or perhaps you are a much smaller person, and the story is being read to you by a larger person, and you feel quite secure, because your life has been riddled with evidence that adults will not let harm come to you. Or perhaps you are not in a bed at all, but out in the world, going about your daily duties, and you're catching a short reading break on the train, or in the waiting room, or under your desk where you hope your responsibilities won't find you. Even if this latter scenario is the case, I feel comfortable assuming that eventually, you *will* find yourself near your bedroom closet, tucked away beneath your sheets, and you will feel quite safe there.

"Why do I need a word of comfort?" you may ask. And it is a good question, and a fair question, because surely there are few places in the world where we feel safer than in our own beds. But as you read on, you may feel a bit *less* safe, because you will learn that the neighborhood of Devilden was surrounded by a high wall of doors taken from dark closets. The doors were lashed together with belts and sashes and single socks whose partners had mysteriously disappeared in the wash. They were doors that looked very much like your bedroom closet door. In fact, if I were to show you the Devilden wall, you would surely find a door there that matched your closet door exactly. And then you would begin to wonder, "*Is* that my bedroom closet door? If I opened it, would I step through a magical gateway into my room?" And that question would inevitably lead to a much larger question; namely, "Can the Devilden monsters enter my bedroom whilst I am fast asleep?"

Therefore, I should like to bestow on you this bit of comfort: Even though the door to your closet may *look* like a Devilden door, it most certainly is not. Put that thought out of your mind right now. Do not wonder about the very darkest time of night, when the moon is hidden behind clouds, and barometric conditions are just so, and time and space get a little wishy-washy. Do not think about an entire assemblage of monsters having access to your room during this magical time of night. No, do not think about what creatures may lurk within it. Do not think about the tentacles that might slither under the door when you are fast asleep and helpless. Do not think about the great, horned beasts that might pad across the floor and stand over you while you rest, dribbling their drool down onto your cheek. (Oh? You awoke with saliva on your cheek this very morning? Well, I am sure it was your own, and not a great, horned beast's.) Don't dwell on any of these things.

For I am here to tell you, your closet door is *not* a Devilden door.

At least, I don't think it is. And I am usually right about this sort of thing.

Usually.

But ah, I digress! Let us return to Mabel, who has just spied the Devilden wall for the very first time.

There must have been over a thousand doors smashed together to form the wall, but only one of them opened into the district of monsters; the others opened into various worlds that spanned quite an impressive expanse of place and era. There were even whispers that some of the doors opened to villages where the sun shone all day long, and all night, too, but of course, that was folly. The sun was gone forever, and that was that.

Mabel had never been to this particular neighborhood before. Because it was a place of monsters, it was not considered a topic for proper conversation in polite society, and the only people she heard even mention it were the elders, who took care to warn the good people of Brighsbane away from it. But she wasn't as frightened as you might think, for she had seen plenty of monsters wandering about in Brightsbane proper. Monsters were not imprisoned within the Devilden walls, you understand. They were free to walk about as they pleased, so long as they took care to follow the rules about not biting, maiming, or tasting the other citizens. Mabel had even spoken to a monster once, a furry orange beast with propellers for hands and a bathtub plug stuck right into his belly. His name was Dr. Grublub, and he was a professor of geography who had come to St. Crippleback's to lecture the children on the particulars of the lands beyond Brightsbane. He discussed the north and the east at great length, and Mabel had asked him a question about the fabled fairy pits beyond Statue's Garden. The monster had promised to address the fairies after the lunch period, at which time he would discuss the lands to the south. But when they broke for lunch, the monster removed a live goat from his large lunch sack and began to devour it whole, right in the dinner hall, before the horrified faces of the children. He was asked to leave, and Mabel never got to learn about the pits.

She still didn't know what the world was like to the south or to the west of Brightsbane.

But she did have a rather progressive view of monsters, for the professor had equipped her with a goodly bit of knowledge before being escorted out. And though the goat incident was disquieting, she had never seen a Devilden monster attack a human being. They seemed happy to keep to themselves. So, unlike many adults in Brightsbane, the idea of monsters was to her no more frightening than the idea of goblins or witches or swamp water barnacles that nibbled off your toes.

Even so, her stomach fluttered a bit as she came around the

bend and saw the wall of doors stretching high above her. There is something ominous about walls, and something portentous about doors, and when you combine the two things into one, the result is rather unsettling.

Mabel hadn't the first clue which door might lead her into Devilden or which doors might whisk her away to places and times unknown. But luck was on our young heroine's side, for as she approached the wall, one of the doors—a rickety olive green thing of knotted pine—swung open at the base, and two monsters stepped out, having quite a row.

"We're not prohibited from eating children in *other* worlds, just from eating children in *Brightsbane*," said the first monster, a slimy green thing with ropes of seaweed draped about its shoulders. It slithered rather than walked, leaving a trail of mucous behind it.

"We oughtn't eat a child of *any* sort," insisted the other, a tall, slender blue monster with three dozen eyes. "It most certainly *is* outlawed, and it's bad for the digestion besides."

"I suppose we should carry on eating livestock all our days, then?" fussed the slimy one.

"There are worse things to eat."

"And better. Like children."

"Have you ever even eaten a child before?" the blue one asked.

The green one hesitated. "No," it finally said, its cheeks growing deep purple. "But some of them smell like cotton candy, and I want to try one."

This discussion continued as the monsters walked off along the wall, heading in the general direction of Slurptongue Swamp. When they had rounded the corner, Mabel slipped down across the grass to the knobby green door and turned the handle. The door creaked open, and Mabel peeked into the monsters' domain.

The first thing she noticed was the excessive destruction. Every single thing was in an advanced state of disarray. Giant holes had been smashed into most of the buildings. The cobblestone streets were stamped with deep craters in the shape of clawed feet. Most of the doors had been pushed out of their jambs, and there were no windows anywhere, only piles of shattered glass on the ground. Monsters lumbered through the streets, growling and snarling and rasping and roaring. There were big monsters, small monsters, furry monsters, scaly monsters, monsters with horns, monsters with snouts, monsters with no skin, monsters with too much skin, and monsters with a surprising abundance of limbs.

Mabel braced herself and slipped inside. The door slammed shut behind her.

"Well, well, well," rumbled a deep voice from above. Mabel cried out and pressed herself flat against the wall, willing the shadows to swallow her up. The shadows politely declined. A monster with the head of a tiger, the body of a caterpillar, and the wings and talons of a bird perched on a lamppost that had a big crease in the middle and was bent downward at an awkward angle. It hopped to the edge of the post to get a better look at the human girl. "It's not so very often we get a visitor of your ilk," the creature purred.

"I-I-I'm looking for Abernathy," Mabel stammered. She wished she'd had the foresight to pick up one of Barnaby's crowbars before leaving the mountain. "Do you know where I can find him?"

The tigerpillar bird squinted at her through one eye and said, "Hmmm…" A blue forked tongue escaped through its lips and curled back on itself, licking at the creature's snout. "Everyone knows where to find Abernathy," the monster grinned.

"I don't," Mabel said quietly. "Could you show me where he is?" She took a careful step to her side, sliding along the wall a bit and making some space between herself and the tigerpillar bird. But the monster leapt off the lamppost and crashed to the cobblestones before her. He smelled of salt and dirt.

"What would a bony sprout like you want with a monster like him?" the tigerpillar asked suspiciously.

Mabel wondered how much truth would be prudent. She was well aware that Abernathy might not approve of her request to borrow his reflectoken, and she was afraid that if she told this creature of her errand, he might think she was a thief bent on stealing something that did not belong to her. So she said simply, "I have an appointment," because it seemed a very grown-up thing to say, and it was a phrase that never seemed to draw further question among other grown-ups. But even as she said it, there was a tremble in her voice, for now that she was in such close proximity to a Devilden monster that was not orphanage-approved, she was starting to think maybe she wasn't so unafraid of them after all.

"Is that so?" the monster asked, fluttering its wings. "Then I shouldn't stand in the way. You'll find Abernathy right where he belongs, in the statehouse." He nodded toward a very tall, very formal looking building that rose high above all the others. It had a dome on top, with two massive horns twisting out from both sides. Of all the buildings in Devilden, this one alone appeared to be in good repair. Mabel mumbled a polite thank you to the monster, then ducked under his wing and ran for the statehouse.

As Mabel ran through the monster town, she couldn't help notice the similarities between Devilden and Brightsbane proper. The monsters had their own town square, slightly demolished though it was, ringed about with little shops and stalls manned—or monstered?—by creatures going about their vocational duties. There was a horn grinder with a long metal board wrapped in sandpaper, sawing away at a yellow monster's twisting, curling horns. To the left of that stood a furniture maker's shop. The big pink and red monster inside picked up a log and stuck it into his mouth, which was lined with rotating saws of various sizes. After a carefully plotted series of chews and jaw gyrations, he pulled the log out again. It had become a finely-carved table leg.

"Goodness!" Mabel said. "Human carpenters are at quite a disadvantage."

Next to the carpenter was a blacksmith, a massive, purplish-grey monster with a metal grate set into his chest, his heart a fiery ember locked safely behind the grate. As the monster pushed the bit of metal on which he was working through the grate, his ember-heart heated and softened it. Then he pulled it back out and began to whack it into shape with his hammer. Mabel couldn't help but wonder how much a blacksmith with a built-in forge might save each year on coal.

Then there was a baker's shop, filled with pastries of all sizes, sweets that would only appeal to creatures that lived in Devilden. Little bright-red cubes of raw meat were sprinkled over the tops, and many of them were iced with something rather blackish that Mabel wasn't sure she would ever like to taste.

There was even a furrier's shop, just like in Mabel's part of town, although the purpose of this one was to style fur while it was still on the monsters, not to peel it from their flesh and form it into fashionable hats.

In the center of the square stood a fountain, as was only proper. However, unlike the Brightsbane moon fountain, this one did not appear to contain any magical properties. What it *did* contain was a large water monster, with thick green tentacles that uncoiled themselves from the water as Mabel passed and plopped over the rim of the pool, their suckers *pop-pop-pop*ping against the marble fountain walls. They spilled out all sides of the large pool, and Mabel shuddered to think what size the creature beneath the waters must be. One thing was sure: the Devilden fountain was surely much, *much* deeper than the Brightsbane fountain.

The monsters that milled about through the square gave Mabel curious looks, but they did not accost her, for just as monsters were free to wander through Brightsbane proper, so too were little girls free to visit Devilden. It just didn't happen very often; most little girls are afraid of monsters, and most little boys, too. And most adults as well, come to think of it. So it was a very rare thing to see a human in the Devilden square, but even so, the monsters did not stop her from going on her way, although some of the shopkeepers did try to market their wares to the little waif. "Seaweed and pepper candied grouse!" called a kindly looking old monster from the sweets shop. "Half price for small humans! Or sugar cane pickled in eel shark saliva? Perhaps the young miss would care for a taste of sugarcoated worm crowns?"

Mabel pinched up her face. "Do all monsters eat that sort of thing?" she asked.

"Oh, my, yes," the old monster said, straightening his half-moon spectacles on the bridge of his nose. "Why? Do humans not?"

"We don't eat worms," Mabel said. "They're more pests than snacks."

"Pests!" the old monster cried. "Why, young lady, have you ever *tried* a sugarcoated worm crown? Or a bit of beetle brittle? Or even a honeyed leech?" Mabel admitted that she had not. "Not even a honeyed leech? Well, then, you must! Here," he said, dipping his hand into a barrel and pulling out a small piece of yellowish orange candy wrapped in cellophane. "Have one as a gift."

"Oh…thank you," Mabel said, quite uncertainly. She took the candy from the old monster and eyed it doubtfully.

"This is my most popular variety," the monster said proudly. He leaned in and whispered, "The secret is the tentacle glaze."

"Tentacle glaze?" Mabel said. She peeled open the cellophane wrapper and stared down at the honey-and-tentacle-glaze-covered leech in her hand. She could just make out the pale shape of the plump little worm through the amber coating. "Are you sure this is a sweet and not a trick?" she asked suspiciously.

"Quite sure!" the old monster smiled. To prove it, he unwrapped a honeyed leech of his own and popped it into his mouth. Mabel blenched and looked back down at her own little candy.

"Well," she reasoned, "the matrons don't serve them, so I don't know that I *don't* like honeyed leech. I suppose there's only one way to know for sure." And she closed her eyes, held her breath, and popped the whole candy into her mouth.

She tasted three things at once just then; a sharp, fishy tang; a sweet, lemony honey; and the unmistakable, unforgettable, unpalatable bite of fat, juicy, freshwater leech.

The flavors that filled her mouth were so vile, so horrid, so absolutely repulsive that her stomach lurched and begged her to spit the awful candy right out onto the cobblestones. But she did not want to insult the confectioner, who seemed like a very kind old monster, so she did something very brave and very, very ill-advised. She swallowed.

"What do you think?" the old monster asked, rubbing his hands together excitedly. Mabel tried to speak, but the instant she began to open her mouth, she knew that her stomach would upend its contents if she did. So instead, she just nodded and tried her best to smile. Then, before he could ask her anymore questions, she turned and hurried to the nearest rain barrel and washed the awful taste away.

"Well," she said after her taste buds had regained their neutrality. "Now I know."

She shook the water from her hands, left the town square, turned a corner, and found herself on the marble statehouse steps. They were crooked and uneven, due to a series of cracks and heavy impressions that split them here and there…as sturdy as marble is, it was no match for the larger Devilden monsters. There were ragged, gaping holes between some of the steps, but Mabel was a persistent child, and though she had to hop and leap from one step to the next and only narrowly avoided a handful of severe kneecap injuries, she eventually reached the top of the staircase, bedraggled, rumpled, and quite out of breath. She smoothed her shift and pushed back her hair and did her best to make herself as presentable as possible.

One must always try to look one's best when approaching a Viceroy, you know.

If there had ever been double doors in the entryway to the statehouse, they had long since been torn away. Mabel stepped through the gargantuan opening, feeling much smaller than usual. She felt no larger as she stepped forward into the open foyer and approached the receptionist's tall desk. Behind it sat a purple monster with roughly matted fur and eight spindly arms sprouting from her back. "Can I help you?" the monster asked, eyeing her suspiciously.

Mabel cleared her throat hard, hoping to dislodge a bit of courage. "I'm here to see Abernathy," she said, as clearly as she was able. "The Viceroy," she added, in case that was helpful.

The monster leaned forward and peered down at her over the edge of the counter. "Is that so?" she asked. "And what sort of business would a human girl have with Squamous Abernathy?"

"The elders sent me," Mabel said. It was only partly true, of course, as just one elder had sent her. But Alder was a brand new elder, and Mabel didn't know if his name would carry much weight. Even if it did, the full coterie of seven elders would certainly be much more impressive. Mabel knew that telling a half-truth was the same as telling a half-lie, and she felt a little guilty, but the clock was ticking, and it was better to be safe than sorry. "They instructed me to speak with him."

The monster raised a tuft of fur near its forehead, which Mabel decided must be an eyebrow. "Pretty young to be an emissary of the elders, aren't you? Have you got a Letter of Introduction?" Mabel fished the Underground letter from her pocket and held out the seal before the receptionist. "Let me see it," said the monster, crooking one of her spindly spider legs.

Mabel held the letter close to her chest. "I'm not to show it to anyone but Viceroy Abernathy," she insisted.

The monster didn't exactly appear to be convinced, but she flipped open a book of appointments and scanned the page. "The Viceroy is *very* busy today. *Very* busy. You can go in and see him now, but he *only* has *five minutes*. Do you understand? One minute longer, and I'll have the haberdasher come right down here, pull you out of the office, and fashion you into a hat. A rather horrid hat, I should think." She turned up her nose and gripped the handle of a gear wheel on the top of her desk. She twisted it counterclockwise. As it turned, a door to her left creaked open.

"Thank you very much," Mabel said with a curtsy.

She hurried across the foyer and peeked her head through the door. She peered through the darkness at Squamous Abernathy's office. It reminded her of Elder Alder's, but with a few key differences. Instead of marble columns, the roof was held up with piles of stones carved into blocks. Instead of a fire in the corner, there was a stone pit filled with glowing orange lava. And instead of bookshelves, the walls were lined with monster skeletons of every shape, size, and color. One of them perked up its head and waved to her as she entered.

"Who's that?" said a voice from behind a desk. "Who's there?"

The light of the lava flickered against the wooden desk, but Mabel couldn't make out the monster sitting behind it. "My name's Mabel," she called to the gloom. "I'm looking for Viceroy Abernathy."

"Well, I'm sorry to disappoint you, small miss, but I am that self-same Viceroy Abernathy—Squamous Abernathy, though I insist you call me plain Abernathy, minus the 'plain.'" Mabel heard the scuff of a chair's legs against the stone, as if someone were pushing it back. Two feet hit the floor and clopped around the side of the desk. Abernathy came into view, and Mabel realized why she couldn't see him when he was sitting in the chair. It wasn't because the darkness was too great, but because the monster was too short. Even standing, the top of his head didn't quite come level to the top of the desk. Mabel herself was a good twelve inches taller, at least.

He wasn't simply short; he was small in every way. He had small hands, small feet, small shoulders, and small facial features. Even the yellow scales that covered his body were small. He was well-dressed if garishly so, in green pants, a stiff white shirt, and a bright purple vest over a lime green tie. The tie was fastened in the center with a brilliant yellow pin that matched his scales. The crown of the pin was a tiny glass orb, inside of which a miniscule sea of gold seemed to roil and slosh. It was really rather beautiful, for such a small thing. On top of his head, the monster wore a cherry red bowler with a blue satin band. His hands were stuffed into matching red gloves with blue cuffs.

"What's your name, young lady?" the little monster asked, extending his hand. Mabel took it and shook carefully. His hand was light as a feather, and she was worried as she shook it that she might snap his finger bones like twigs.

"My name's Mabel," she said.

"Well, if you won't be forthcoming, I suppose I shall call you Scobald," Abernathy decided. "What can I do for you, Scobald?"

Mabel felt very confused. *What an odd little monster,* she thought. "I was sent by the elders. I'm supposed to ask you to borrow a reflectoken. One that wards off the power of Shimmers."

"Yes, yes…very good, very good," Abernathy muttered, rubbing his yellow chin. "Can I assume, then, that you are here to inquire about a vagabond's license?"

"A vagabond's license?" Mabel asked, thoroughly perplexed. "No, sir. I'm inquiring after a reflectoken," she repeated. "A pin to keep Shimmers at bay?" She eyed the skeletons on the wall nervously. She was suddenly starting to feel a bit uneasy.

"Ah! The skeletons," Abernathy mused, following Mabel's gaze with his own eyes. "My beautiful skeletons. Do you like them?"

"They're…numerous," she decided.

"That, my dear, is not a lie," Abernathy decided. "They are the bones of Viceroys past. When I am done with *my* tenure as Viceroy, my skeleton will be added to the wall, right over there." He pointed to a blank spot in the wall.

"Why are they all different colors?" Mabel asked, for even though she was in a hurry, children must always make time for curiosity. Otherwise, they are not children at all, but remarkably smooth-skinned goblins. "Are they dyed with vegetable pigments?"

"Certainly so! It is definitely *not* the case that monster skeletons are brightly colored of their own accord. It is certainly *not* true that we are born with our skeletons quite fluorescent. Do you see?"

This little monster was acting most curiously, and Mabel did not think she *saw* anything at all. But she nodded politely, because to say otherwise would be to encourage the Viceroy to explain, and the more he explained, the more confused she became. So instead of telling him the truth, she simply said, "Yes."

"Now, let us speak plainly." Abernathy gestured toward two chairs near the lava pit. "Shall we sit?"

Mabel glanced nervously at the lava. "Is it safe?" she asked.

"Oh, not at all, not at all," Abernathy said. "And it's frigid! This old statehouse is so warm, and there's nothing like a good pit of boiling lava to cool things down. Don't you agree?"

"I'm not sure I agree with anything you've said at all," Mabel admitted with a frown.

"Wonderful, wonderful! Please, sit."

"All right," Mabel sighed. "I will."

"Well, if you don't want to, that's fine," Abernathy said. "I know the proximity to lava is a worrisome thing to humans. We shall stand instead. Now, I'm afraid I have an appointment creeping around the clock, so while I'm always happy to oblige a child, I must ask that we get down to iron tacks, as some say. What is it that you would like from me?"

Mabel's cheeks grew warm with exasperation. "But I've already told you," she said. Her head was starting to feel as if it were being twisted into knots. "I'd like to borrow your reflectoken."

"Don't make me guess at your motives, child!" the Viceroy cried. "My secretary whispered to me through the interoffice communication mechanism that you've been sent by the elders. That sounds mightily important, indeed! Is it true?"

"Yes, sir."

Abernathy frowned. "Did you say yes, or did you say no?"

"I said *yes.*"

The Viceroy frowned harder. He frowned so hard, the two corners of his mouth almost touched in the center of his chin. "I'm afraid you have me at a loss," he admitted, "and I'm rather confused just now." *You're not alone in that,* Mabel thought. "Why would you tell my secretary one thing and tell me another? It's an odd way for a dignitary to behave."

"But I didn't tell your secretary one thing and you another!" Mabel cried. She had reached her wit's end. "I told you both that

I've come at the request of the elders, to retrieve a reflectoken that wards off Shimmers!"

"Yes, exactly!" Abernathy said. "And therein lies the confusion. Do you see?"

Mabel's eyes felt as if they might bulge right out of their sockets. "No!" she exploded.

Abernathy stroked his chin. "What an odd child. I'm beginning to think you're not a very good ambassador of state."

"I'm not an ambassador of state," Mabel said. "I'm a waif!"

Abernathy blinked. "A waif?"

"Yes, sir."

"Not an ambassador of state?"

"No, sir."

A wide grin spread across Abernathy's face. "Well, that explains it!" he exclaimed, clapping his hands together happily. "You must mean what you say!"

"I'm sorry, sir, but I don't understand what you're talking about."

"Of course not! Because you, my dear child, are not an ambassador of state!" Mabel frowned. "Ah…I see you're still a bit confused. You might not know any ambassadors, so allow me to explain. Ambassadors, you see, always say the exact opposite of what they mean. When I ask an ambassador of state to sit by the lava pit, and he wants to do it, then he'll say 'no.' But if he does *not* want to sit by the lava pit, he'll say 'yes.'"

"Why would he do that?" Mabel asked. "Shouldn't 'yes' mean yes and 'no' mean no?"

"Yes indeed! 'Yes' *should* mean yes, and 'no' *should* mean no. And for most people, they do. But for these officials, they do not. When an ambassador says he'd like to do something, it means he really *will not* do it. And when he says he would *not* like to do something, it really means that he *would like nothing better* than to do it."

"But why?" Mabel asked. The world of grown-ups was terribly confusing sometimes, even when those grown-ups were monsters.

"Because if an ambassador of state says what he means, he will never reach his stately goals. He must say exactly what he does *not* mean if he wants people to think he means what they *want* him to mean."

"Are there any ambassadors who tell the truth?" Mabel asked.

"Oh, goodness, no," Abernathy beamed. "Not a single one."

Mabel crossed her arms. "And is Viceroy a position of state?" she asked.

"Why, yes," he said. "Of course it is!"

"Then everything *you* say must be a lie," Mabel reasoned.

"Oh, no, child…I only lie when I talk to other elected representatives. It's why I lied to you about the lava pit being cold and about monster skeletons being dyed with vegetable pigment. You see, I'm not a politician anymore. I'm a Monster of High Political Position. There's a very distinct difference. Politicians are monsters who want to reach high political positions. Once a monster reaches the high political position, he is no longer a politician; he is something else entirely. He doesn't have to lie, because he's already reached the place he wants to be."

Mabel blinked. "But what if you want to be higher?"

At this, the Viceroy laughed, a strange, high-pitched titter. He adjusted his tie and smoothed his vest. "There is only one position in Devilden higher than that of Viceroy. That position is Fullroy… and *no one* wants to be Fullroy."

Mabel didn't know much about politics, but she was a bright girl, and she knew that if a political position existed, someone must be occupying it. "Surely the person who currently holds the office of Fullroy wants to be Fullroy…doesn't he?"

Abernathy giggled. "He wants to be Fullroy least of all! No, Viceroy is as high as you'd like to go—believe you me. Heavy are the horns that wear the crown!" Abernathy sat down in one of the chairs by the lava and patted the arm of the other chair. "Please, sit down. Now that we've got this political mess sorted out, perhaps we can have a real conversation!"

Mabel sat down in the chair, relieved. If she'd ever had an inkling to use her Letter of High Station to achieve the political brand of greatness, she was now cured of that particular disease. "It's very hot here," she noticed, scooting her chair back from the lava.

"Yes, of course! This is real lava, none of that synthetic stuff they brew in some parts. We pipe it straight in from the Black Flint Mountains far to the west. Do you know them?"

Mabel shook her head. "I only know the north and the east," she said.

"Ah! Well, we shall have to remedy that. Perhaps a tutoring session with Dr. Grublub, our resident geography expert would be in order. Whip-smart, he is. Very nice propellers for hands."

"Mr. Abernathy, I don't mean to be rude, but I'm in an awful hurry," Mabel said. "Elder Alder sent me to ask for a reflectoken... one that keeps Shimmers away."

"Ah! Yes, so you said, so you said." The Viceroy clapped his little hands together. "Dear me—you were being serious! Ha ha! I'm sorry for the confusion, dear girl."

"Do you have the reflectoken?"

"I do," the Viceroy said, fussing with his tie.

Mabel waited for more, but Abernathy said nothing more. She tapped the arms of her chair expectantly. "Might I be able to borrow it? Please?"

"Goodness, no!" Abernathy laughed. "The reflectoken is for monsters only. It's a sacred monstrosity artifact. I could no more give the pin to a human child than I could give water to a sleeping knibbet. It would be more than just a breach of monster etiquette... it would be an outrage!"

"But..."

"No. It simply isn't *done*. But I have so enjoyed your strange little visit! I do hope you'll return. Next time, give me a bit of notice, and we'll have blue squid ink tea and broken glass shard cookies."

Mabel rubbed her eyes. None of this was going as it should. *I'm wasting my time*, she thought miserably. *The wizard is probably unlocking the compendium with all three keys as we speak. The world will disintegrate any second now from one of his spells...I just know it.* "Please, Mr. Viceroy. The fate of the whole village may depend on it."

"Oh, I doubt that," Abernathy chuckled. "Do tell the elders hello for me, will you?" He got up from his chair and crossed back over to his desk, where he began shuffling papers about.

Mabel thought about the Devilden haberdasher bending and twisting her into a little Mabel hat, and she decided that perhaps she should give up this little portion of her quest. She didn't have time to browbeat this monster into changing his mind anyway. Besides, the reflectoken was Elder Alder's idea. She was confident that she could navigate the Briarbranch without one. "Thank you for your time," she sighed. She pushed herself up from the chair, careful to avoid the bubbling lava with her toes, and headed toward the door. "I have to go. It's a long way to Briarbranch Woods."

Just then, a great, rumbling roar exploded through the statehouse. It came from somewhere outside Abernathy's office, and it was so loud and so low that it reversed Mabel's heartbeat and made her blood pump backward. "What is that?" she asked, clutching her chest.

But the Viceroy waved it off. "That's just the Fullroy, bellyaching in the lobby. He's got a bad toothache, and he's being a horrible nuisance about it."

Mabel looked uncertainly out toward the statehouse lobby. Then she looked back at Abernathy. "Is there a back way out?" she asked.

"I wouldn't worry about him," the Viceroy said, waving his hand dismissively. "He's not a bad sort. You'll be fine."

Then the roar came again, and Mabel was certain that if she heard it one more time, her heart would seize up and shrivel into ashes. She was about to say so when a massive monster, the biggest she'd ever seen, burst through the door, clutching its mouth with both hands. Mabel dove into the corner of the room and took cover between a bright pink skeleton and a lime green one.

The monster was as tall and as wide as some houses. It had red fur, yellow eyes, and a huge, round, yellow nose. Every time it took a step, the floor shook and the lava in the pit sloshed up over the edge.

"Abernathy!" the big monster cried, his voice muffled by his huge, furry paws. "I can't bear it any longer! This toothache is killing me! It's killing me from the roots outward! My tooth will die, then my gums, then my jaw, then my head, then my neck, and the rest of me will surely follow!" He plopped down on the floor, and the whole room shook. The lime green skeleton rattled loose from its hooks and clattered down on top of Mabel. The skeleton bumped its forehead against Mabel's and gave her a knowing little grin.

"I'm sorry, Fullroy Trampleton. It does seem to be giving you awful trouble," the Viceroy said.

"It's the greatest pain I've ever experienced," the Fullroy agreed. "Worse even than the time I got that broadsword stuck in my toe for a week. Where's the confounded dentist?"

Abernathy clapped his hands to his head, crumpling down his bowler. "I already told you, Fullroy: the dentist won't come. Your head is far too big for him to reach the tooth, he'd have to crawl right up into your mouth, and he absolutely refuses. He says he's lost too many colleagues that way."

"But what am I to do?" the Fullroy wailed.

"I honestly don't know," Abernathy admitted.

"The pain is too great!" the monster sobbed. "I desperately require relief! This is all too much—it's too much, I say! Abernathy, consider this my resignation!"

"Your resignation!" the Viceroy exclaimed, nearly jumping out of his suit. "But sir! You can't resign!"

"I don't see any other choice," Fullroy Trampleton groaned. "This tooth requires my full attention. I cannot properly govern the district when I am so distracted by pain." He rolled onto his back and thrashed around a bit. Viceroy Abernathy hid behind his desk to avoid the much bigger monster's flailing limbs. "Starting tomorrow, *you* will be Fullroy."

"Me?!" Abernathy cried.

"Of course! When the Fullroy retires, the Viceroy assumes his position."

Abernathy dragged his hands down his face. A few dozen yellow scales flaked off and floated to the floor. "I'm molting from the stress of it!" he gasped. "I can't be Fullroy...I don't *want* to be Fullroy!"

"You *must* be—the pain is simply too great!" the Fullroy insisted.

"But—but—but—" Abernathy stammered. He turned and looked at Mabel as if he'd completely forgotten that she was present. "You!" he cried, leveling a finger at her through an opening in the green skeleton's ribs. "You're going to Briarbranch Woods!"

"Who on earth are you talking to?" Fullroy Trampleton asked. He rolled over to see where Abernathy was pointing, accidentally leaning on the side of his face with the sore tooth. He howled in pain. The force of his breath threw the skeleton clean off of Mabel, and thus was she revealed to the monster. "A human girl!" he cried.

Mabel clamored awkwardly to her feet. "Hello," she said.

"Hello," the Fullroy replied, quite surprised.

The Viceroy ran out from behind his desk and took Mabel's hands in his own. "You did say that, didn't you? That you're going to the Briarbranch?"

"Yes," Mabel said, hoping the Viceroy didn't notice how sweaty her hands were as she rubbed them on her pants. "It's...rather far. I should be on my way."

"Yes, of course! You have a long way to go, so go you shall! And you shall take the reflectoken with you."

Mabel started. "I shall?" she asked.

"Yes, of course! We must do all we can to keep you safe so you can find the Fullroy his moffat mushroom, mustn't we?"

Mabel took a deep breath and considered holding it until her lungs exploded and she expired on the spot. This entire experience was just so infuriatingly confusing. "I'm not going in after a moffat mushroom, I'm going in after a—" She caught herself just at the last moment. *Better to keep that part secret,* she thought. "After something else."

"Yes, yes, of course, but you shall *also* fetch back a moffat mushroom!" the Viceroy said excitedly. "It grows only in the Briarbranch Woods, you know, which is a place where we monsters are forbidden to trek. Oh, yes; the witches have seen to that. If we step inside, we'll burst into flames! But *you*, dear girl, you're going to the woods, and you could uproot one or two moffats for the Fullroy!"

"Is that right?" the Fullroy asked hopefully, tears of gratitude welling up in his eyes. "Are you braving the Briarbranch to bring me moffat mushrooms?"

Mabel looked from one monster to the other, then back. "I... well, I *am* going to the Briarbranch," she said slowly. "But...what is a moffat mushroom?"

"A *very* powerful healing agent and anesthetic," Abernathy explained. "Powerful enough to numb the Fullroy's tooth for years— perhaps longer!"

"Oh, please say you'll do it," the Fullroy pleaded. "I'm in such incredible pain!"

"And when he's in that pain, he's unable to assume his duties as Fullroy," Abernathy said pointedly. "Do you understand? He needs to be his regular, pain-free self. *I* need him to be his regular pain-free self. I shall lend you—not *give* you, you understand, but *lend* you—the reflectoken to help you along your way. What do you say?"

As I believe we have already discussed at some length, Mabel was not a dimwitted child. In fact, quite the opposite was true. She did not fully comprehend the words or actions of these monsters, but she did know that agreeing to this new chore was the quickest way to get the reflectoken and, perhaps more importantly, the quickest way to leave Devilden behind and be on her way. Besides, she was headed to the Briarbranch anyway...surely she could pick a few mushrooms on her way to the Grandfather Tree. Despite her distrust of the monsters, the wisdom of accepting the proposal was rather apparent.

"I'll do it."

The Fullroy cheered, and Abernathy exhaled with relief. He unfastened the pin from his necktie and placed it in Mabel's hands. "Do take great pains to keep this safe," he said. "There's not another one like it in the world."

"I will," Mabel promised. "And I'll bring it back...I swear on the moon."

"Tonight," Abernathy said, his eyes hard. "Bring it *and* the mushrooms before the morning moon rises."

"I can't bear the pain longer than that!" Fullroy Trampleton wailed.

"Before the morning moon rises," Mabel replied. *If I'm still alive then,* she thought. She fixed the pin to her shirtsleeve, just above her wrist. This placement seemed to offer some amount of utility; she could hold it up like a shield, if need be. "How will I know a moffat mushroom when I see one?"

"Oh, they're quite hard to miss," the Fullroy said, rolling upward to a seat. He seemed to have forgotten the pain of his tooth in his excitement, at least temporarily. "They're shaped like round pillows, bright orange with purple stems, and they're always quite wet."

"Yes, you shall know them when you see them," the Viceroy agreed. "Oh! And one other thing: you said you were in a hurry, did you not?"

"Yes," Mabel said, despairing at the distance she had to cover to reach the forest. It would be well past midnight before she entered the woods, and that was if she ran half the way.

"I believe your haste will serve us both," the Viceroy said, "and I can be of assistance in that regard." Abernathy scurried over to a tall, bright blue skeleton fixed to the wall on the far end of the room and waved for Mabel to follow. "Herbal," he said, addressing the skeleton, "jump down off the wall for a moment, will you?" Herbal acquiesced, lifting himself from the rack and stepping gingerly off his platform. Abernathy leapt up in his place and ran his hands over the wall, looking for a particular stone. When he found it, he gave the stone three sharp taps, and an entire piece of the wall broke away and swung open.

"A secret passageway!" Mabel cried. She clapped her hands over her mouth. She hadn't meant to get so excited, but she was something of a secret passage enthusiast, if you'll recall her various escape routes from St. Crippleback's. It was always very exciting to learn of a new, unexpected passage.

"Not a secret passageway," Abernathy corrected her, "a secret *portal*way. There's one behind every skeleton, and they all lead somewhere different." He pointed excitedly through the opening. "Look here! Tell me what you see!"

Mabel squinted through the darkness on the other side of the portal. She saw a line of trees, tall, dark, and scraggly, with branches like fingers and leaves the color of blood. "It's Briarbranch Woods!" she cried.

Abernathy folded his arms in a particularly self-satisfied manner. "I'd wager that'll save you a good few hours of a journey, will it not?"

Mabel's heart swelled with so much joy that it rippled and skipped and began to pump blood in the correct direction once again. She hadn't lost much time by coming to Devilden after all, and she had a weapon against the Shimmers to boot! "Oh, thank you!" she said. She threw her arms around the little yellow monster, squeezing him so tightly that his shoulders popped.

"Think nothing of it," he gasped. Mabel released her grip, and he smiled up at her. "The quicker you arrive, the quicker you return, with my pin and with my mushrooms." He leaned in closer and whispered, "Do hurry. No one wants to be Fullroy, least of all me."

"I thought you said Fullroy Trampleton wanted to be Fullroy

least of all," Mabel said.

"That was before I was awarded the promotion," Abernathy frowned. "Now I am quite sure there is no one who wants it less than I do." He turned Mabel around and pushed her through the portal. "Goodspeed, child."

Chapter 8
Witches and Stone

Mabel shivered as she stared into the Briarbranch Woods. The air was cool—quite colder, in fact, than it had any right to be—but that wasn't what made her shiver. There was a strange energy pulsing out from the forest, an aura of dread not too unlike the feeling you get when you are called into the principal's office for a bit of horrid behavior.

She looked over her shoulder and saw Abernathy standing in a rectangle of glowing lava light in the center of an otherwise empty field. He gave her a sharp little wave, then he closed the door to the portalway on his end. Suddenly the rectangle was gone, and there was nothing behind her but the nighttime horizon.

The evening moon was beginning its slow ascent, and it shone brightly on the field, coating the grass in a silvery gloss. But within the woods, the trees nudged each other for position and blocked out the light with their reaching, searching fingers. It was very dark in the woods, and for the second time, Mabel cursed herself for not spiriting away the elder's Luna Lamp.

A hand-painted sign posted in front of the woods read "Devilden Monsters Extremely Welcome." Strewn just inside the tree line lay several charred skeletons that had once belonged to monsters who had fallen for the trick. Mabel knew human children weren't prohibited from entering the woods—in fact, conventional wisdom held that the witches preferred if human children *did* enter the woods. Even so, the roasted skeletons gave her pause.

She approached the forest path, but stopped at the threshold of the woods. She closed her eyes, clenched her teeth, and inched one toe into the forest.

She did not burst into flames.

Thus encouraged, Mabel entered the Briarbranch Woods.

It was even darker within than it had seemed from without. The trees wove their branches together, covering the forest in a spindly web. They seemed to close behind her as she went, for after a few minutes of walking, she turned to assure herself of the path, and she could no longer see the open field for the limbs and leaves that clouded the view. What's more, the path behind her had been ravaged, and what had only moments ago been a smooth dirt clearing was now choked with thistle and stones. There was no discernible track to be seen.

I suppose there's no way to go but forward, Mabel thought. She raised the arm with the reflectoken pinned to the cuff and pushed on into the woods.

Before long, the path split into three new trails. The one on the right seemed to be made of glass. It was smooth and polished, and it glistened as if it were paved with shooting stars. The path on the left was consumed by fire; tall orange and yellow flames crackled up from the dirt as the path wound deeper into the forest. And the path in the center was constructed of deep sand.

She had not been expecting three trails. The map in Elder Alder's book had shown only one—the correct one, she supposed. But she didn't know which of the three that was.

She'd have to make a choice.

Mabel couldn't abide sand in her shoes, so that particular path was really no kind of choice at all. She considered the trail on the right, the path that glistened. "It really is rather beautiful," she said, weighing her options aloud, "but then, things which seem beautiful are often really quite horrid." She thought of Penelope Bluewhistle, a girl who had aged out of St. Crippleback's two years earlier. Penelope was a beautiful waif, the most beautiful child to inhabit the orphanage since the last stone was laid. But oh, she was a wicked girl. She used to tie spiders together by their legs and weave great, living chains with them, then use the chains to tie other little girls to their bunks. The more time she spent at St. Crippleback's, the meaner she became, and the meaner she became, the more radiantly her beauty shone. It was what one might call an *optical illusion*. Mabel wondered if the glistening trail was just such an illusion. And she didn't care for spiders, or for treachery, or for Penelope Bluewhistle, so she opted not to take the trail of glass.

That left the trail of fire. The path that looked most difficult was often the path most worth taking, Mabel knew, though the flames were certainly a detriment. At first blush, such a path was impossible, impassable, and a highway to certain death. "But if it were *real* fire," Mabel said, "then surely the whole forest would be aflame." Many fingers and tendrils of dry brush hung over the path, and though the fire flickered up and over them, they did not burn. Mabel approached the trail of fire and held her hand over the flames. The air was cool. She floated her palm down into it, and her hand passed easily through. "This is an illusion, too!" she said, delighted. The fire was just smoke and mirrors, heavy on the smoke. Someone had gone to great lengths to completely and complexly camouflage the path, and Mabel knew precisely what that meant; there was something worth hiding at the other end of it.

"The fire it is, then," she decided.

Another benefit of taking the fiery road, she found after just a few steps, was that while the flames were only falsely warm, they were authentically bright, and they bathed the woods in a warm orange glow. She was able to see her way easily. "How wonderful this light is!" she declared. The light and the wisdom of her decision had given her a much-improved outlook on her journey through the Briarbranch Woods. "I'm sure that without it, I would stumble over a root and break my head upon a rock. With all this light, I shall have no trouble finding the Grandfather Tree at all!"

But hubris is a blight to good fortune, and with her very next step, Mabel plunged into an enchanted well that had been hidden by a crust of burning leaves bobbing atop the surface. Mabel fell down, down, down into the pool and hit the bottom with a soft, muted *plunk*.

This was all quite a shock to Mabel. She had not expected to come across a hidden well, and she thought that if she did have to fall into one, she should float rather than sink, being a light, buoyant girl. Therefore, it was surprising on multiple levels to find herself at the bottom of the pool. She pushed off the bottom of the well, but her body did not move a bit. She tried again, but to no avail. She made a third attempt, giving it her all, and although her knees did not bend—although they literally *refused* to bend—she really put her back into it, and she did move, just one half of one bit, with a short, soft scrape. But nothing more.

This is odd, Mabel said to herself. *Why can't I move?* She tried to flap her arms, but like her knees, they were frozen in place. She cried out in surprise, but no breath escaped her lungs. *And what of that?* she asked herself, somewhat frantically. *Why am I not running out of air?*

We must forgive Mabel her confusion, for how could she know the horrors of an enchanted well? But oh, dear reader! The word "horror" cannot adequately capture it! A piece of me wishes to avoid a true description of what awaits poor little Mabel so that I might save you the heartache that you will surely feel for her. But even though my motives would be pure, I could no longer expect to be taken seriously as a narrator if I brushed it under the rug, for it is my sacred duty to relay the adventure in an accurate manner. I fear I must expose the truth of the enchanted well, no matter how much pain it might cause me, and no matter how much fear it might cause in you. But if you wish to close the book right this moment and never open it again, I will not blame you. Mabel's fate is not for the faint of heart, and you may be more comfortable in another, safer story.

If you do choose to go on, I applaud your bravery. I hope you do not regret it.

This particular enchanted well, you see, was one of the most horrid traps the Briarbranch Woods had to offer. It lurked beneath the leaves, blending in with the forest floor, and though we may chide Mabel for letting down her guard, the truth is, many more experienced adventurers had fallen into the trap under similarly well-lit conditions. The enchanted well was a very old type of witchcraft, and it had many long centuries to perfect its concealment technique. The well was seemingly little more than a deep cistern dug into the earth and filled with brackish water—and indeed, that is how it started out. But when a witch whispered a devilish spell upon the water, it became silvery and dense. When a person stepped into the pool, she instantly transformed into a limestone statue and sank straight to the bottom, where she sat for the rest of eternity, cracking and wearing and collecting moss.

Unfortunately, dear reader, Mabel was not immune to the magicks of the water, and her reflectoken, which was designed primarily for Shimmers, was no match for the power of the well. And so, when she plunged into the pool, she turned instantly to stone and sank right to the bottom.

This wasn't readily apparent to Mabel, though. Limestone statues have very poor eyesight, especially when under water. In fact, she might have spent her entire underwater career not even guessing that she'd turned into stone, except for the fact that the silvery water of the well reflected the light from the flames above, and she could see three other statues at the bottom of the pool; she had come to a rest quite near one of them. All three statues were men, and they all three had big stone axes, and Mabel had landed in such a position that the axe of the statue nearest her was poised to strike right in front of her nose. *These men are stone,* Mabel thought, amazed. *Stone does not breathe, and stone is heavy and difficult to move, and stone makes a scraping sound when it is thrust across the bottom of a pool. Is there a chance that I have turned to stone?*

She became acutely aware that she was not likely to find the second key now.

She did her best to stay positive as she bided her time at the bottom of the well. *Someone will come for me,* she thought. *Just as in Briny Field, and just as on Gallows Hill, someone will come, and I will be saved.* But it is a foolish thing to pin one's hopes on the pluck and fortune of another, and as the clock ticked on, and as little barnacles began to attach themselves to Mabel's shoulders and make little *pop-pop-pop* sucking sounds with their little mouths, Mabel began to think that perhaps no one would come for her after all.

"You don't look like much of an adventurer," she heard a voice say. It was a bubbly sort of voice, the way a fish might sound, if it was bewitched and therefore able to speak. Mabel looked about as best she could, given the fixed state of her eyes, but she could see no fish, or any living creature at all, for that matter. Only the three statues.

"She's just a child!" said a second voice, which was just as bubbly, but deeper.

"A child? Poking about in the Briarbranch Woods?" said a third voice. "Hmpf. Serves her right, falling down here. The forest is no place for children."

"Don't be a brute," the second voice chided. "She's probably frightened."

"How about it, girl?" the first voice asked. "Are you frightened?"

Mabel hesitated. She knew that a person wasn't supposed to try to talk while submersed in a well, because her lungs might become filled with water, and that was a very reliable way to expire. But since she didn't seem to be breathing, she wondered if it might not hurt her to speak up after all. She tried to move her lips, but they remained steadfastly closed. She wanted to say, "I'm sorry, who's speaking?" but what came out sounded more like, "Errmfferriking?"

"You've got to use your throat, girl," the second voice said.

"Yes, speak from your chest," the third voice added.

I shouldn't have to tell you that speaking from your throat, without the use of lips or a tongue, is really quite difficult. If you don't believe me, I invite you to try it, right now. Try saying, "Hello, my name is Mabel, and I'm a brave little waif" without working your mouth. You'll see how trying it was for our poor heroine. But with a little practice, Mabel was able to grunt out, in a throaty sort of croak, "Who's speaking?"

"Who's speaking?" the first voice asked, incredulous. "Why, *we* are!" Just then, one of the statues scooted itself just a tiny bit on the floor of the well, and Mabel realized that, of course, the three men were just as alive as she was, and they were the ones speaking.

"Can *all* statues speak underwater?" Mabel wondered.

"Only statues that are really humans under a curse," the first man said. "Now, I ask again; are you frightened?"

Mabel searched her feelings are discovered that she was a little frightened, but she was mostly annoyed at having her progress hindered by this enchanted well. "Only a little," she finally said.

"That is exactly the wrong attitude to have," said the second statue. "You should be *very* frightened. You'll never get out of this well, you know. None of us will. We're stuck down here for all eternity."

"That's true enough," the third statue added. "But I, for one, am glad you've joined us. I'm happy to have a new bit of company. These two blunderheads are awful conversationalists."

"Speak for yourself! I was known as quite the wit in my day!" the first statue blustered.

"Some trick, being conceived of us a wit by a bunch of swamp loggers," the second statue soured.

"And what, pray tell, is wrong with swamp loggers?"

"It'd be shorter to ask what *isn't*?"

"See what I mean?" the third statue sighed.

"Are you all woodsmen?" Mabel asked, trying to change the subject. "Were you all here logging in Briarbranch when you fell into the well?"

"I was," said the first statue. "My name is Hiram of the Highlands, and I came in search of the stoneoak trees that only grow in the western groves of the Briarbranch Woods."

"I was a woodsman as well," offered the second. "I was the

best woodsman Brightsbane has ever seen. Are you familiar with Starved Root Field?" he asked.

"I am," Mabel said.

"Well, it used to be Starved Root Forest, before I got ahold of it," he said smugly. "My name was Lameron Supperbun, of the Salt-wind Supperbuns. I'd wager that name's more than a bit familiar to you." It was not, but Mabel thought it impolite to point this out. Thankfully, the third statue piped up before she had a chance to reply.

"I was not a logger," he said, and Mabel thought she heard Hyram and Lameron scoff a bit at this. If the third statue heard them, he paid them no heed. "My name was Phineas Growinkle, and I was a great hunter."

"I've never known a hunter who hunts with an axe," Mabel said. She could just make out the shape of his blade through the silvery water.

"Then you've never known a hunter who hunts witches," Phineas said. "An axe is the best way to do away with them."

"Fire also works in a pinch," Hiram added.

"Fire will do," Phineas agreed. "But an axe is better."

"You came to the woods to kill a witch?" Mabel said, unable to keep the awe out of her throaty grunt.

"I was sent in after the Bad Witch by a private employer…but I'm afraid I was bested by this well's enchantment," Phineas said sadly.

"So were we all," Hiram sighed.

"Yes. So were we all," Lameron agreed.

"And what about you?" Phineas asked. "I take it you are neither logger nor hunter."

"No. I'm…well, I'm a waif. But I'm also on an adventure."

"An adventuring waif!" Hiram declared. "That's a new one on me."

"You're not out here alone, are you? Surely there is a guide and protector of some sort, an *adult*, standing at the top of the well, contemplating some ingenious method by which to get you, and by extension, us out of here?" Lameron said hopefully.

"I'm afraid not," said Mabel. "I'm on my own."

Lameron grunted. "Parents these days."

"Parents," Hiram agreed.

"My parents are dead," Mabel said matter-of-factly.

"Oh, my dear child! How terrible for you!" Phineas cried. "I am so sorry! Please excuse these two blunderheads. They really have no matters whatsoever."

"It's all right," Mabel said. "I'm only *mostly* sure they're dead anyway."

The three statues fell silent, and the water grew thick with an awkward tension. It seemed that nobody quite knew what to say next. Finally, Phineas cleared his throat and said, "Might we get to know your name?"

"Oh! Yes, of course. My name is Mabel. Mabel Gray." She exchanged pleasant and proper how-do-you-dos with the other statues. "You all keep saying that your names *were* such and such. Aren't they your names still?" she asked.

"Names are for the living," Lameron grunted. "We gave up on that particular chore long ago."

"But surely we're not dead!" Mabel said, a little startled.

"No," Hiram admitted, "but neither are we particularly alive, are we? We are no longer Phineas Growinkle and Lameron Supperbun and Hiram of the Highlands. We are now just statues of men who used to go by those names."

"I don't think you should give up hope," Mabel said. "After all, statues cannot die, can they? We could survive down here for a long time, I should think. Maybe for all eternity. Who knows who might come along and save us before eternity is done?" She knew, of course, that without her interference, the wizard Croup would soon destroy the entire world, but it seemed cruel to bring that up just now. *One must always have hope when one can,* she thought.

"It's not much of a life," Lameron said, and even Mabel couldn't argue with that. There wasn't anything about spending eternity as a limestone statue at the bottom of a well that seemed particularly appealing.

"Well," Mabel said glumly, "how do we pass the time?"

But just then, there was a disturbance in the water. Something plunged down into the well from above, and Mabel's heart sank at the thought of yet another wayward adventurer falling into the enchanted well (both because she didn't wish her limestone predicament on anyone and because it was already a little cramped down there). But it wasn't another statue that drifted down into her peripheral vision; it was a large, three-pronged claw fixed to a steel cable. Someone had dropped it down from above. She heard the soft *chink-chink-chink* of three claw points sinking into her limestone head, and presently, the water began rushing past her as she was hauled up, up, up through the water. "I'm being saved!" Mabel cried. The other three statues grunted various impolite phrases as she ascended, but the specific nuances of the syllables were lost in the rushing bubbles of the silvery water, and their rather choice words did not quite reach Mabel's ears. It shall suffice to say they were not terribly pleased that Mabel was being rescued while they were being left behind.

But, oh! The statues did not know how lucky they were. And poor, dear Mabel! If only she knew who her rescuer was, she might have begged the claw to let her go so she could sink straight back down to the bottom of the well.

But she did not know, and so she did not make the request, and even if she had, the claw would have likely ignored her plea. It lifted the Mabel statue above the water line and hauled her over onto a much sturdier part of the flaming path. In the newly glaring light of the fire, her eyes had a difficult time adjusting, and she could not see the person who had dragged her up. Not at first, anyway.

The metal claw released its grip and raised itself into the air. It became soft, then it became cloudy, and then the claw and the cable disappeared altogether in a puff of smoke.

"Well!" cried an old woman's voice, obviously quite pleased. "What an unexpected catch!"

As Mabel stared on, the woman walked into her periphery and circled around to face her head-on. She was pretty, if plain, with brown hair pulled up into a bun, a thin nose, and pale cheeks. She wore a black crepe dress in an older style, with a high collar buttoned at the throat and a dark red bustle pluming out the back. She was neither fat nor thin and had just the right amount of wrinkles for a woman of her age and appearance—and they were just the right amount of wrinkled, too, as if she had creased and folded her skin with care and exactitude before leaving the house. There was, in fact, much about the woman's appearance that looked so perfectly normal as to cause one to be suspicious. It was almost as if she wanted to look exactly plain, and not one bit more exotic nor one bit frumpier.

"There are generally three types of people who come tiptoeing through my woods," the woman said, clasping her hands behind her back and lecturing like a schoolteacher. "Men with axes who wish to cut down my trees, men with axes who wish to cut off my head, and horrid little children who have lost their way." She narrowed her eyes and inspected the Mabel statue carefully. "You are clearly no man with an axe, so I am inclined to think you have little interest in cutting down my trees or cutting off my head. But if I'm not mistaken, you are also not a child who has lost her way. You're a child, certainly. But your eyes belie a certain…focus. Am I wrong? Are you a wandering waif?"

Mabel tried to respond, but without the water to carry her words and give them a fluid sort of shape, her words came out as indiscernible grunts.

"Where are my manners?" the woman said with a smile. "How can one be expected to speak under the circumstances? Allow me to intrude." She produced a long, thin wand of iron oak from somewhere within the folds of her dress and tapped it once against Mabel's stone lips. Though they remained stony, she found that she could move them if she put some effort into it. Her tongue worked too, after a little coaxing. But when she spoke, her voice was gravelly and full.

"I *am* a waif," she said, testing out the words on her new tongue of rock, "but I'm not lost that I know of, and I'm not simply out for a wander."

The woman pressed her lips together in a tight little line. "Mmhmm," she said primly. "I thought as much."

Now, I must tell you, dear reader, Mabel did not know who this woman was at first. She didn't know what sort of person trucked with clouds of smoke that could form themselves into claws and drag statues out of wells. But between the dress, and the way she spoke, and the wand that she so blithely produced (and really, it was this that sealed it), Mabel came to understand that she was addressing one of the Witches of Brightsbane.

For those of you who have not studied the history of the village, there are precisely three Witches of Brightsbane. There always have been, and I suspect there always will be, in one manner or another, though I do not pretend to be a witchologist. The Brightsbane witches were all distantly-related sisters, but they didn't care much for each other, and even though they all lived in the Briarbranch Woods, they did not see each other except on holidays, when they would gather at one or the other's hovel and work at making pleasantries while enjoying a ham or a goose or some such festive culinary lynchpin. These family gatherings routinely devolved into a chaos of dredged-up memories and wildly flung accusations, as family gatherings tend to do, but they continued to get together for them anyway, for tradition is important, don't you think?

The three witches were as different as three flavors of pudding, and each had a very distinct purpose in life. There was the Good Witch, who mixed good potions and wove good spells that helped good people in need. There was the Bad Witch, who mixed bad potions and wove bad spells that helped bad people with evil agendas. And then there was the Witch of Neutral Position, who mixed both good and bad potions, and who wove both good and bad spells, and who engaged in good magic for good people, bad magic for bad people, bad magic for good people, and good magic for bad people. The Witch of Neutral Position had no ethical constraints; she worked as a witch-for-hire who would do any bit of magic requested, if one could pay a decent price.

Mabel knew that her fate depended on which witch had caught her in the enchanted well. The Good Witch would be good to her, the Bad Witch would be bad, and, since she had no money, the Witch of Neutral Position was likely to lock her in a dungeon with rats and bones and leave her there until someone came along and offered a good price for a potion that required the blood of an innocent little girl. "Are you the Good Witch?" she asked hopefully.

The witch looked at her, astonished. "Do you think the Good Witch goes in for turning people to stone?" she asked.

"No, I suppose not," Mabel sighed. It was difficult to sigh, now that her lungs were made of stone, but she managed anyhow. One will always find a way to sigh with disappointment if one feels the need. And oh, how Mabel felt the need! Being trapped in stone by a witch who was not the Good Witch was a terrible fate. If her heart hadn't been cemented in place, it surely would have sunk a bit in her chest.

"Of course not! An enchanted well that turns people into stone is a Bad Witch's tool, make no mistake."

There it was, then: Mabel was a prisoner of the Bad Witch. She had to think, and think fast. She summoned up all the courage she had. It was no small amount on its own, but it may have been that the weight of the stone made her spirit sturdier, for she must have had quite a bit of courage to say what she said next. "I was wondering, Miss Witch—may I call you Miss Witch?"

"You may," the witch said with a graceful nod. "Or you may refer to me as The Witch Belinda."

Belinda seemed a far too innocuous name for a Bad Witch, and Mabel thought that it fit her captor like an ill-stitched, oversized coat. She did not think it prudent to call that to attention, however. "I was wondering, Miss Witch—Witch Belinda—since I'm not a woodsman with an axe looking to cut down your trees, and since I'm not an adventurer looking to cut off your head, and since I'm not a girl who's lost herself in the woods, perhaps I might be allowed to go along my way? I could even scour the trail for woodsmen and adventurers and lost little girls as I walk and send them your way," she said, quite pleased with her own cleverness.

"Hmm," said the witch, scratching her chin. "It may be helpful to have a lookout of sorts on the trail. And it is certainly true that you are not a man with an axe. And it may be that you are not a girl who is lost in the woods. But just because you are not either of those things, that does not necessarily mean it is in my best interest to let you go free. I could not be sure that you would send other woodsmen and children my way. Would you agree?"

Mabel tried to shrug. "I suppose that's true," she said. "You would have to take my word for it."

"Indeed I would. And in my experience, children are often apt to lie. Therefore, I believe I shall take you home and have you for dinner. How would you like that?"

Mabel could feel salty drops of perspiration squeeze themselves out of her insides and drip down the stone of her brow. "Do you mean have me as a *guest* for dinner?" she said hopefully. "Or have *me* for dinner?"

The witch cackled again. "Why, that's the excitement of it, isn't it?" she cried, quite delighted. "We'll go to my hut, and you'll tell me your story about why you're skulking about in my woods, and then I shall determine if you will *share* my meal or if you will *be* my meal! Does the offer please you?" She waved her hands dismissively. "Bah, no matter," she said, "It's the only one you'll get!" Her face grew suddenly solemn, then, and all mirth evaporated from her lips. "You did say you were in a hurry, didn't you?"

"Yes, Miss Witch. Er, Witch Belinda."

The witch *tsk-tsk*ed. "We can't have that. If you stress about the time, the strain of it will make you less than tender if I decide to boil you up in my broth. Therefore, I shall remedy the issue." She plucked a pocket watch from the folds of her skirt and held it triumphantly above her head. "Do you see this?" she asked, shaking it close to Mabel's eyes. "What do you think it is?"

"It's a watch," Mabel said.

"Not just *any* watch—it is the *Eternity Watch*! This is the watch that lets life in Brightsbane keep on ticking! It was entrusted to me, you see, because time is a great enemy, especially to us witches… we are greatly concerned with chronological matters, and I would not wish to run afoul of time. Who better to guard something than a person who is terrified of losing it? Now, hold this, will you?" She draped the chain of the watch over Mabel's stone arm so the clock dangled freely. "Thank you!" The witch pulled out her wand and gave it a little shake. A wooden mallet grew out of the tip. She swung the wand with both hands, and it smashed the clock into a thousand tiny pieces that went skittering through the flames and out into the forest floor. "There! Now we have all the time in the world!"

Mabel looked down at the flames. They had ceased their mesmerizing dance. They no longer flickered and flared, but were frozen in place. Time, it seemed, had actually stopped.

"You broke time?" she asked, her gravelly voice horrified. "Surely there's no worse way to run afoul of time than to stop it forever."

"Tosh!" the witch declared. "Breaking a watch does exceedingly little harm to time; you can always repair it and get it ticking and tocking again. If you want to insult time, you need to speed it up or slow it down—*that's* what does it in. Stopping it altogether is perfectly allowed, so long as you remember to get it going again." The witch tapped the wand with her palm, and the mallet melted off the end. "Let's be off! Step lively, child, I've got a wicked hunger. Oh, dear me, you *can't* step, can you? Lively or otherwise?" The witch cackled gleefully and tapped her wand against Mabel's stone feet. Then the Mabel statue lifted into the air, levitating with astonishing ease.

The witch bounced through the woods, back toward her house, and the Mabel statue floated close behind. Her hut wasn't terribly far away, and it wasn't much of a hut, either. It was more like a castle built from trees. Four great oaks served as turrets at each of the four corners, and the walls between them were great, felled trunks stacked one atop the other. The door was little more than a pine bough curtain, and circular husks of tree bark served as roof tiles. Even the windows were set with panes of pressed and dried sap.

"This is your home?" asked the Mabel statue as it floated toward the house. It was much less drab and spidery than she expected it to be. Even frozen firelight of the trail served to give the witch's hut a merry glow.

"You were expecting a shell of intertwined corpses, perhaps?" the witch asked, raising an eyebrow.

In truth, that was exactly what Mabel had expected.

"It's very nice," said the girl.

"Even Bad Witches enjoy the comforts of a good home," said the witch.

They entered through the pine boughs, and Mabel was immediately stricken by the fact that the house was bigger on the inside than it was on the outside. *Much* bigger. Even though the exterior was quite large by typical residential standards, the interior stretched on and on and on, for miles, for *more* than miles. The main hall was so large that Mabel could not see the other end of it; it stretched even beyond the horizon.

"This way," the witch said cheerily. She beckoned to a side room with her wand, and the Mabel statue danced through the air behind her. This second room was a kitchen, and in the center stood a big copper cauldron that practically could have held the entire contents of Boiling Lake. The logs beneath it were already lit, and apparently immune to the whims of time, for the flames flickered hungrily, and the stock in the pot was beginning to smoke. "Soup's almost ready," the witch said shrewdly. "You had better talk quickly.

If you're not lost, tell me, where are you bound? And why are you bounding there in such a hurry?"

The Mabel statue came to a rest close enough to the cauldron to feel the heat from the fire. She could just barely peek over the rim of the pot and see the brownish-red mixture bubbling about. "I'm in a race against a wizard," she said. She was getting used to her limestone tongue, and her words formed themselves a little more easily now.

"A wizard?" asked the witch. "Which wizard? The wizard who drank the Eastern River? The wizard who set fire to the petrified lands? The wizard who tumbled down Wishy-Washy Falls?"

"No, Miss Witch. Er, Witch Belinda. The wizard who swallowed the sun."

"Oh," said the Bad Witch, her cheeks draining a bit. "You mean *the* wizard."

"Yes, Miss Witch."

The witch burst into another bout of cackling laughter. "I'm afraid you're adorned in the wrong footwear for that sort of race, my girl! You'd not beat the wizard if time stopped forever and *he* were the one made of stone!"

Just then, a large bird swooped into the kitchen and helped itself to a perch on the Mabel statue's shoulder. Its feathers were glistening orange with fiery red tips, and its beak and eyes were as black as obsidian. The creature was so large that only one talon could fit comfortably on Mabel's shoulder; the other found purchase nearer her elbow. "Meow," said the bird.

"Did your bird just meow?" Mabel asked.

"In the first place, Gertrude is not just a *bird,* she's a *familiar.* Be sure to treat her with plenty of respect, or she'll chisel away at your nose with her break and cast a dozen different, exquisite, and horrible spells on you. In the second place, yes, she did just meow," said the witch.

Had Mabel not been made of limestone, she surely would have frowned. "But oughtn't birds *caw*?"

The Bad Witch scoffed. "Ordinary birds might. But as a familiar, she is not bound to the normal rules of things. Sweet Gertrude chooses to meow in honor of my last familiar, Magritte, who was a very talented and very dear cat. She was squashed flat by the wooden wheel of a wayward apple cart." Belinda frowned a bit at this memory. "The merchant who owned the cart now wears his stomach on the outside of his body." This little recollection returned a bit of brightness to her eyes. "At any rate, Gertrude meows because she and Magritte were companionable friends, and she knows I miss her so."

"Meow," Gertrude agreed.

"Now," said the witch, plucking a wooden spoon from the wall, "what is it you're racing the wizard *to*?" She gave the soup a good stir. Some vegetables, some roots, and a number of odds and ends that rightly belonged to woodland animals bobbed up to the surface.

Mabel weighed her words carefully. She did not want to give too much away, but she wasn't sure if she should lie. Even though she was not yet a Lady of High Station, and was therefore not necessarily expected to always be forthright, she had an inkling that Bad Witches were liable to become cross when they were lied to. She certainly did not want to anger the witch further. "I'm in search of a certain tree," she finally said.

"Ah! The Grandfather Tree, is it?"

"How did you know?" Mabel blurted in surprise. She immediately cursed herself, for now she had given far too much away.

"It's practically the only tree worth finding." At these words, the witch's entire log house bristled. "Oh, apart from *you* trees, obviously. Compose yourselves."

Now that the witch knew the truth of her mission, Mabel didn't see much reason to hold back. "Do you know where to find it?" she asked.

The witch dropped the wooden spoon in surprise. It sank in the murky soup. "Do I know where to find it? Child, I helped plant the seed!" She suddenly became quite suspicious, and she rushed over to the statue, sticking her nose within a hair's breadth of Mabel's. Gertrude meowed in surprise and took to the air, flying out of the kitchen in search of a more peaceful perch. "What would a girl like you want with the Grandfather Tree?" the witch demanded. But she didn't wait for an answer. Instead, she gasped. "You're after the Skeleton Key!" she said, pointing an accusatory finger at the Mabel statue's chin. "Isn't that right?"

"I need to find it before the wizard does," Mabel said, her gravelly voice tinged with desperation.

The witch narrowed her eyes. "Answer this next question honestly, child. Your culinary fate depends on it. Does the wizard possess *The Boneyard Compendium*?"

"Yes, Miss Witch."

Belinda's face fell. She tapped the Mabel statue on the forehead with her wand, and the limestone cracked and fell from her skin in a great heap, leaving her a human girl once again. Mabel brushed the rock dust from her arms and her hair. "Thank you," she said. Her tongue felt strange again. She had just gotten used to speaking with a stone in her mouth.

"Don't thank me, child," the witch muttered. She began flitting around the room, opening up cabinets of bark and pulling down books and roots and jars filled with awful, horrid things, the descriptions of which belong only in the pages of a much more sinister book than this one. "Don't ever thank a Bad Witch. She's never done anyone a favor."

"I much prefer not to be made of stone," Mabel said. She stepped over the pile of rubble at her feet and backed away from the cauldron, just to be safe. "Changing me back into a girl seems like a favor to me."

"I changed you back because the path you're headed down is far more treacherous than any evil spell I could possibly weave for you. You have no idea what the wizard Croup is capable of, child. No *idea*. The horrors he has wrought on Brightsbane—and on us witches—they could fill a book of their own, and then some. Seeking out the keys to the Boneyard's book and matching wits with the sorcerer? Child, before the morning moon rises, you'll wish I'd popped you into my stew."

"You know the wizard, too?" Mabel asked. She had always perceived the man as a figure of legend, a great, evil hermit who was only seen in the storybooks she read in the orphanage…but it seemed he wasn't quite so reclusive after all.

"Know him? Ha! I should say so. I wish to the moon that I didn't." The witch put two fingers to her mouth and whistled. A large, empty bag came traipsing into the room and plopped itself down at her feet. She dumped her armful of goods into it, and the bag swallowed them up. Mabel thought she even heard it gulp.

"What are you doing?" Mabel asked. "Are you going on a trip?"

"Oh, you bet your young life I am," said the witch. She gripped one end of the cauldron and heaved with all her might, but she wasn't strong enough for the huge pot. "Give me a hand, will you?" Mabel cautiously approached the other handle. She grabbed it and helped the witch push. The cauldron tipped over, and the soup went spilling into the bag. "I won't be around when the wizard snuffs us out once and for all…oh, no. I leave that to the rest of you." She turned back to the bag. "Go get the rest of it. All the important things." The bag leapt up and trotted out the door and down the hall.

Mabel suddenly felt very much in the way. Against the witch's flurry of activity, she decided that she did not know what to do with her own arms. She folded them, and unfolded them, and stretched them, and circled them, and crossed them, but nothing seemed quite natural. "Do you need help?"

"Ha! Help from a child? I think not. You best be on your way." The witch fished the broken watch from her pocket and set it on the floor. She whispered a low incantation, and a green light began to glow from within the broken sprockets. The watch rattled as the witch's lips moved. Then the pieces straightened themselves out and knitted themselves together, and with a little *pop*, the watch was whole once again. It ticked along as if it had never been broken at all.

The witch picked it up and plunked it back into the folds of her dress. "You'll find the Grandfather Tree at the end of the path, where the three trails meet." The witch gave her wand a good spin, and everything in the room floated up into the air a few inches and hung there, suspended in space. "Good luck to you, girl," the witch said. "I doubt you'll survive the night." Then she snapped the wand through the air, and everything, the cauldron, the hut, the books, the bird, the bag, the jars, the fire, and the witch herself disappeared, leaving Mabel alone in a very empty clearing in the woods.

And that is how, quite by accident—and quite singlehanded-ly—young Mabel Gray dispatched the Bad Witch of Brightsbane.

CHAPTER 9
RIDDLED TO DEATH

The rest of Mabel's journey down the trail of flames was rather uneventful. Or perhaps I should say that it *seemed* uneventful to Mabel. You see, as helpful as the fire was for illuminating the woods in the close vicinity of the path, it was also helpful in another respect. Like all light shone into a great darkness, it made the outer darkness look *very* dark by comparison, and it made it very difficult for the person standing within the light to see much of anything beyond the light's glow. Do you see? Perhaps you do not, for the preceding sentence has a somewhat slippery syntax. But surely you must know what I mean. If you do not, then try this little experiment: next time you are able, pick up a flashlight at the very darkest part of night and wander out into the middle of a dark wood. If you can find a fairy tale wood that is filled with grubblets, grimlets, goblins, and ghosts, that would be best, for then you would *really* get to understand Mabel's situation. And if a fairy tale wood cannot be found? Well, more's the pity for you, but any old wood will make a decent stand-in. Wander as far into the forest as you dare without turning on the light. Walk until you hear branches snapping and hungry animals panting all around you. When the snapping branches and the panting animals grow very near, switch on the flashlight and shine it into the woods. Notice, then, how the path of the beam of light is extraordinarily illuminated, and you can see everything in its glow. But also notice that if you look *away* from the light, the rest of the woods seem much darker, and as well as you are able to see with the help of the flashlight, that is how much worse you are able to see *outside* of the flashlight's light. It is practically impossible to see creatures lurking out in the darkness beyond the glow. Who knows what might be waiting out there to gobble you up? *You* don't, that's for sure, because you can't see a thing.

But because you are standing with a light in your hands, the monsters can see *you*. Oh, my, yes…they certainly can. They can see you, and they can salivate over you, and they can lick their lips at you, and they can creep up on you in the quietest manner, and you will never be able to see them coming, because that is the nature of a light in the darkness.

Now, quickly—shut off your light and run as fast as you can back to the safety of your house, for you are in grave danger.

That is exactly the sort of danger Mabel came into as she crept down the fiery trail toward the Grandfather Tree. She saw nothing within the fire's glow that could harm her, and so even though she knew the legends of the woods and the devlish beings that lived there, she considered herself to be quite safe because of the light. But if I were to tell you of the sort of creatures that watched Mabel pass through the Briarbranch, you would have nightmares for a month at least. Let us leave that information tucked away, then, at least for now, and let us all be glad that Mabel did not have the sight that your narrator has. Elsewise, she should have died of fright on the spot.

But before too terribly long, she saw a shimmering light through the trees, and she recognized the shooting star pattern of the first path. The glimmering lights twisted and turned but eventually merged closer to the path of fire. And the path of sand returned as well, though more quietly. It snaked its way beneath the fallen leaves of the spindly trees, and suddenly, there it was, spilling its sandy edges onto the path of fire and making the false flames sputter. The shimmering path met up with them soon after, and the three trails became one new trail of sandstone alight with shimmering blue star flames.

A stone outcropping jutted up from the ground where the paths became one, a huge sledge of rock blocking the view deeper in. Mabel followed the new path around the edge of the rock, and there, fairly glowing in the darkness, stood the Grandfather Tree.

It was big, but not as big as Mabel had pictured in her mind. It really was no larger than most of the other trees in the woods. But oh, it was a special tree, there was no doubt about that. The trunk was as green as a meadow's soul, and bright against the darkness of the woods, so that it appeared to be a tree-shaped hole in the air (assuming, of course, that the air has dark green felt beneath it, and who's to say that it does not?). A thick patch of white fungus draped along the branches, waving bashfully in the breeze. It crept along the sides of the trunk, too, and came together near the roots, forming the tree's snowy white beard.

But the most astonishing thing about the Grandfather Tree was the sheer number of keys that dangled from its branches. There were thousands of them, keys of all shapes and sizes, hanging from the limbs of the trees by long white ribbons. The light from the shimmering blue flames of the trail reflected off polished and tarnished metal alike, and the keys hung so thickly in the air that it seemed as if the tree were awash in a sea of sparks. They jangled in the breeze, clinking and clanging like an entire of orchestra of wind chimes. There were keys made of iron, keys made of brass, keys made of stone, keys made of tin, keys carved from roots, keys made of paper, keys formed from sand, and keys made of glass. Mabel was dismayed to see there were also quite a few keys carved from bone. How was she supposed to know which key was the Skeleton Key? Or if it was even still hanging from the tree at all?

She closed her eyes and recited the Warden's poem:

To find the next key, you'll need a stout heart;
Witches and owls and Shimmers play a part.
You'll find many keys in the Grandfather Tree.
Speak the right answer, set the real one free.

Mabel approached the tree. "Speak the right answer to what, though?" she wondered.

The trunk of the tree began to creak to life. It sounded like logs popping slowly in a hearth. As Mabel looked on, a knot twisted into existence on the front of the trunk, and then two others grew above it, until the tree had squeaked and popped itself a knobby face. The tree blinked its eyes open and sniffled through its new nose as it regarded the young girl. "What sort of woodsman might you be?" the old tree asked, his voice slow and cautious.

"I'm not a woodsman at all," Mabel said.

"I should say not. Why, you haven't even an axe. How would you even begin to chop down my trunk?"

"I wouldn't!" Mabel cried, somewhat alarmed. Did woodsmen really come through the Briarbranch Woods to cut down a tree as old and large and magical as the Grandfather Tree? "Why would someone want to chop you down?"

The tree gave a scornful little snort. "There is an idea in the world that if my trunk were hollowed out, it would make a fine, magical ship; one that could take an army of men clear across the Saltwind Sea without fear of tipping or wrecking, even in the most treacherous waters."

"Is that true?" Mabel asked.

"No one has yet managed to put it to the test," the old tree said. He spread four of his limbs wide and slammed them into the ground so that the whole forest shook. When he lifted his limbs once again, they left deep depressions in the earth.

"You seem very capable of protecting yourself," Mabel admitted.

"I am that," the tree agreed. "Now, young lady, if you are not a woodsman, you must be an adventurer. I assume, then, that you are after a key. I shall assume the formal manner of speech." He cleared his throat. A cloud of white moss puffed out from his mouth and settled on the forest floor. With its vocal chords thus properly cleared, the tree began: "Speak ye the truth, and the key shall fall away. What is the greatest desire of the young Mabel Gray?"

Mabel was astonished—and a little honored—that the Grandfather Tree knew her name. And she was elated to hear that the question was so simple; she knew the answer practically before the Grandfather Tree even finished speaking the question. "My greatest desire is a Letter of High Station," she said. She held out her hands and waited for the key to fall into it.

But the tree shivered and shuddered, and with the loud clang of a hammer striking forged metal, one hundred new keys blossomed forth from the branches, adding to the tangle of keys already there. Mabel recoiled in surprise. "What happened? Where is my key?"

"You spoke a lie, so the key was not revealed. Much like the truth, the key you seek grew more concealed. Speak ye with care, for opportunities are few. You have two more chances to answer me true."

Mabel remembered what the Warden of the Boneyard said about rhyming, and she knew the Grandfather Tree must be a very wise and very powerful bit of topiary, since he liked to speak in verse. Therefore, if the tree told her she was not being truthful, then surely the tree was well informed. After all, he knew her name and everything. But the Letter of High Station *was* what Mabel desired more than anything in the world...

Wasn't it?

She closed her eyes and thought as hard as she could. What could she possibly want more than the letter? There was so much that came with it; an education, a social circle, a chance to explore the world.

The letter was everything.

Wasn't it?

"No," Mabel realized aloud. "It's not." For a Letter of High Station was like one of the paper keys that hung from the Grandfather Tree. It could open many doors for her, but it could not open *all* of them. There was only one thing that could open *all* doors.

"A wand," she said. "A wand filled with magic that will do anything I wish." How had she never even considered the possibility of having a sorcerer's wand before? Probably because it was so out of reach. A wand was beyond impractical, it was impossible. But that didn't mean she couldn't want one. "A wand would give me complete power over anything, over *everything*! Why, with a powerful enough wand, I could move the moon and the stars! With the right bit of magic, I might even be able to grow a new sun! I could do away with our eternal nighttime, and I would no longer be Mabel Gray the Waif, but Mabel Gray the Girl Who Dispelled the Night!" Once that idea took root in her mind, it refused to be shaken loose. "More than anything else, more than a Letter of High Station, I want a sorcerer's wand."

The Grandfather Tree buckled and groaned. The sound of hammering metal rang through the air, and *two* hundred new keys popped out from the branches, suspended by white ribbons.

Mabel gasped. Then she gaped. Then she gasped again. "But—but—" she said, for she was very near to being speechless. "But" seemed to be the only word she could dredge from the depths of her vocabulary.

The Grandfather Tree was very wise, and very intuitive, and he did not need to hear more than that one word. He understood Mabel's consternation perfectly. The knobby lips creaked again, and the tree said, "The truth within ourselves is quite the paradigm. If you want the key, take care, and answer one last time."

Mabel was flabbergasted. What could she possibly want more than a magic wand full of sorcerer's magic? There was nothing—*nothing*—that would not be available to her with the right bit of magic! A wand was all-encompassing. A wand represented every good and wonderful thing she could ever desire; a wand made the future limitless. With a magic wand, she could have everything she ever wanted from here on out.

All of that is well and good, whispered a voice in Mabel's head, *but what about things that have passed?*

A wand, she knew, couldn't change the course of history; it might conjure up any number of magicks to change the future, but it couldn't change what had always been. And as Mabel thought about her own past, she realized that there *was* something her past was missing, a thing that no magic could ever grant her. Not anymore. She had never truly considered it a want or a desire, because it was almost certainly an impossibility, but once her mind found it, picked it up, shook it out, and hung it on the line, there was no denying the way it tugged at her heart. She yearned for this thing more than anything else in the world, more than a Letter of High Station, and more than a sorcerer's wand. In an instant, she knew she had the true answer. It was the thing that drove her from the orphanage on quiet nights, and it was the thing that she could never quite let go of.

"What I desire more than anything else in the world," she said quietly, holding back a tear, "is a family. *My* family."

The Grandfather Tree closed his eyes, and the knobby features drew back into the bark. The entire tree shuddered, and the keys drew up into the branches, curling and rolling themselves into little key-sized pods. One by one, the keys drew up and disappeared into the fluffy leaves until they were all gone. Then the tree sighed and said, "You have spoken well." One of the branches dipped low, reached out, and presented itself to Mabel, as though inviting her to take the Skeleton Key that dangled from its tip.

But there was no Skeleton Key. There was only an empty white ribbon, swaying in the breeze.

"I'm too late," Mabel said. "I'm too late!"

The Grandfather Tree typically didn't go in for emotion. But he couldn't help sharing the poor girl's disappointment, and he drooped sadly. "I am sorry, young adventurer," he said, his white leaves fluttering against the forest floor, his limbs dragging downward with despair. "Perhaps you would have better luck as a woodsman after all." But Mabel didn't hear; she had already started walking away, her head low. "Are you all right, child?"

Mabel couldn't keep a tear or two from leaking out of the corners of her eyes. "I—I had hoped the key would still be here," she said.

"Is it the key?" the tree asked, raising an eyebrow of bark. "Or is it the family you spoke of?"

"Maybe...maybe a little of both," she whispered. "Goodbye, Grandfather Tree."

"Goodbye, little adventurer," the tree said. It spun its knobs back into its trunk, and with a creak and a twist, it was just a regular tree once more.

Lost in thought, Mabel wandered slowly back down the path of blue-fire sandstone, not paying much attention to anything in particular, least of all to the devious owl hovering above the outcropping of rock with a small wooden cage caught in its beak. The owl rubbed its wings together greedily, and as soon as Mabel stepped into the right spot on the path, it flew into the air and let loose its cargo.

The whole ordeal caught Mabel by surprise, and she cried out as the cage came to a crashing down on her from above, trapping her on the forest floor. "What is this?" she shouted, which may seem like a strange thing to say, but I should wonder what *you* might say if an owl tossed a wooden crate over *your* head, especially after all that Mabel had gone through that day. She gripped the wooden slats and shook them roughly. They rattled but didn't give. She tried to lift the contraption, but it wouldn't budge. "Help!"

"No sense in that! You're as trapped as trapped can be!" giggled the owl. It fluttered down onto the top of the crate and leaned forward, poking its beak into the cage upside-down and gazing gleefully at Mabel. "No fits or flashes of furtive fearlessness can free you. There is only one way out of a Riddle Raven's cage." The owl hopped down to the forest floor and stood before the crate, looking very smug indeed.

"A Riddle Raven?" Mabel asked. "I don't see any ravens..."

"*I* am a Riddle Raven," the owl said, somewhat testily.

"But you are not a raven at all," Mabel observed. She was not yet of an age where she knew that when a creature puts you in a prison cell, you should behave very politely toward it and refrain from pointing out its flaws. "You're an owl."

"Obviously, I am an owl," the bird said crossly, shaking its feathers. "But Riddle Raven is alliterative." He pronounced the word with sharp pauses between the syllables: *al-lit-er-a-tive.* "It is important to be as alliterative as availability allows." He thought for a moment, and then he added, "Assonance is also acceptable."

"You seem very advanced with language," said Mabel, who was a little bit impressed in spite of herself.

"I am," the bird said smugly. "I have dictated dozens of dictionaries and doted on dense dissertations for days."

"Still, I don't think Riddle Raven is the right title for you. Perhaps you could be called an Ornery Owl?"

"I am not ornery!" the owl declared, in a decidedly ornery manner. "Besides, the word 'riddle' is really rather a requirement, my churlish child, for it explains quite a lot. I must be the Riddle *something*. I bandied about as the Riddle Rook for a spell, but something about the sound seems somehow subtly surreptitious, don't you agree?"

Mabel did not know whether she agreed or not; she did not know the definition of the word surreptitious. She said as much, and the bird shook out its wings in consternation. "Your lack of vocabulary is appalling. Where do you go to school?" Mabel wondered what the matrons of St. Crippleback's would think of the popular opinion all these creatures seemed to have of their educational abilities. Before she could answer, the owl pushed on. "Wouldn't you like to learn how to loosen the lock of your cage?"

"Oh, I should like that very much," said Mabel, nodding vigorously. She had just one more key to search for, and if there was any hope at all of getting there before the wizard, she couldn't very well spend all of her time locked away.

"To free yourself from your fetters, you must give accurate answers to all three of my riddles. If you cannot answer appropriately, I will leave you here for an entire eternity. You shall wallow and waste away within these wooden walls. Do you understand?"

"Answers to three riddles? You're not serious!"

"I am incessantly serious," the owl said.

"Riddles from the Warden of the Boneyard! Physical attacks from razor-footed crows! An enchantment spell from the Bad Witch! Three questions from the Grandfather Tree! And now answers to three new riddles? This is getting out of hand."

"And yet, here we are," the owl beamed.

Mabel sighed. She gripped the bars and planted her forehead against the wood. "Give me the first riddle, then, Riddle Raven. I am in a great hurry."

The owl puffed up a bit at being recognized as a raven and grandly bestowed upon Mabel the first of three riddles. "I howl in your ear, but you have never seen me. I have many trades, but I have no occupation. I can carry many things, and though I sometimes whistle, I cannot carry a tune. What am I?"

"Hmm," said Mabel. "There aren't many things that whistle *and* howl." She thought very carefully for a moment or two. Then she said, "Is it the wind?"

"It is, it is!" the owl chirped, delighted. It clapped its wings together happily. "Clever girl…how did you know?"

"A monster taught me about the geography of the lands to the north and to the east, and he showed maps of the trade winds on the Saltwind Sea."

"I see! Perhaps you've had an encompassing education after all. What a singularly spectacular set of circumstances! But that was an easy one," the owl added, tempering Mabel's excitement. "Let us see how you fare with the second riddle."

"Yes, please," Mabel said, nodding. She had lit upon the first answer quite quickly, and she was greatly encouraged.

The owl took a deep breath and delivered the next riddle. "My insides are bare and my soul is black. I like to be uplifting, but I can't control my own tongue. I'm often tied up, and usually underfoot. What am I?"

Mabel pulled at strand of her wild black hair and twisted it thoughtfully around her finger. "I should think that a horrid prisoner would fit the bill, if not for the last part. I can't imagine that a murderer or thief would be underfoot. They usually toss them into prison cells, or else they hang them on Gallows Hill and bury their bodies in paupers' graves, and no one ever walks over those, because it's bad luck. Hmm…May I ask a question?" she asked.

"You may ask only purposely particular ponderings," the Riddle Raven said. "You may not ask if an answer is correct, for example, but you may call for clarification of lexiconical confusion."

"What is lexiconical confusion?" Mabel asked.

"Yes—it's that exactly! Now, what is your question?"

"I'd like to ask if you could spell a word that you used."

"Ah! A shrewd girl, a shrewd girl, indeed! Which word would you have me spell?"

"Did you say s-o-u-l…or s-o-l-e?"

The bird hopped about from one foot to the other and hooted excitedly. "Brilliant girl, clever girl! I shan't tell you the answer to that question, but I'm extremely excited that you emitted such an extraordinary examination and were mindful of my masterful manipulation!"

"Manipulation?" Mabel said. "Then you must have been trying to trick me, and the spelling you *really* meant was s-o-l-e. The answer is a shoe."

"I see you struggled with that one," the owl said happily, clacking his beak together with devious excitement. "The riddles get harder, you know. Did I mention that?"

"You did not, but I suppose it only makes sense."

"It does! It does! Now, properly prepare your person," said the owl, "for the third and final riddle is positively perplexing! Are you ready?"

"I am," Mabel said. She gripped the wooden bars of the crate tighter, anxious to be free of the little prison and be on her way.

"I am sometimes celebrated, but always reviled. The longer I live, the more rotten I become. Once I go, I almost never return.

Individuals are silent when I am near, but masses sing for me. What am I?"

Mabel gaped at the owl like a fish. "I'm sorry…can you repeat the riddle?" she asked. She suddenly felt a nervous puddle forming in the pit of her stomach.

"I cannot," said the owl. "The rules are as old as time and relentless as rhyme. Do you find yourself struggling?" The bird had a wicked smile upon its beak.

"It is harder than the first two," Mabel admitted. "I—I—I'm not sure I understand it."

"Ah, but that is the nature of riddles! We have the urge to understand, and once we know the answer, we can never *un*-understand. Wouldn't you agree?"

"Yes, I suppose so," Mabel said. "Once the answer is known, it always seems very obvious."

"Yes, indeed. But, ah, you are stalling! Clever girl, clever girl, but not clever enough, I fear. Answer the riddle…what am I?"

Mabel turned her brain over and over and over again, but the answer did not tumble forth. She did not know what sort of thing could be both celebrated and reviled, or could became more rotten the longer it lived, or could almost never return once it left, and she certainly did not know what thing masses of people would sing for when individuals found the need to be silent around it.

"I need a moment to think, please," she said, trying to keep the panic out of her voice. What would happen to her if she were left in the cage to wither away to dust? The wizard would open the elder's book, of course, and use its spells to destroy all of Brightsbane. And she, Mabel, would be forced to watch from the confines of her cage. She would have to know that the death of her village was all her fault, for not being clever enough. And when all the villagers were dead, no one would be left to come seek her out in the woods. She would die from hunger and thirst on the forest floor, and her body would be lost in the blue star flames that burned without burning, until the woodland creatures pulled her apart and gnawed her bones to splinters.

It was a somewhat discouraging thought.

The Riddle Raven hopped closer to the cage and stuck its beak through the bars. "For the third and final time, I ask you... *what am I?*" he demanded.

Mabel bit back a tear. *This is the end*, she thought.

"You are the dead," came a cheery voice from up the fiery path. Mabel and the Riddle Raven both started in surprise.

"Who speaks?" the owl demanded, his voice high and irritated. "Who dare interrupts a riddling?"

"I do." A lanky, affable-looking man stepped forward into the blue light, his hands tucked into the pockets of his shabby trousers. He wore a once-white long-sleeved shirt, with the sleeves pushed up to his elbows, revealing patches of dried mud splotched across his forearms. It was crossed with a pair of suspenders that held his pants just a bit too high, so that his ankles peeked out below his cuffs before disappearing down into his shoes. His face was thin and sharp, but it was a gentle sort of sharpness, so that he looked as if a very nice but very simple-minded carpenter had carved him from a block of wood. His hair was tidy enough, the same midnight black as Mabel's. It flopped freely over his forehead, and it contained a small sampling of the Briarbranch Woods' leaves and twigs.

"And *who* are *you?*" the owl snipped.

"A concerned citizen," smiled the man. "Well? Do I have it, or do I not?"

"The accurate answer is not yours to ascertain," the Riddle Raven huffed, crossing its wings angrily. "This is a private riddling, and it is not directed toward you."

Mabel looked wide-eyed at the stranger. The stranger winked back. She didn't know if it was the right answer, but it was certainly *an* answer, and *an* answer was much better than *no* answer. "The dead," she said as confidently as she could manage. "The answer is the dead."

The owl turned on her and scowled. "You're not to have help

from him!" he complained.

"What's done is done, and I have the right to answer," Mabel pointed out.

"She's right; she does," the stranger agreed.

The owl hooted loudly and unfolded its wings, shaking them wide and ruffling his feathers. "This is an aberration!" he squealed. "An absolute and abominable aberration!"

"But is it correct?" Mabel asked.

The Riddle Raven glowered. "Yes," he said through a gritted beak. "It is."

There was a loud *crack*, and the cage fell apart from the top down. The little wooden slats collapsed to the forest floor and lie there, innocent and harmless. Mabel leapt up and stretched her arms and her legs, and even though she hadn't been contained for very long, she thought that the ability to reach herself high had never felt so good. "I'm sorry to have spoiled your game, owl," she said, though she was not really sorry at all. She said it in order to gloat a bit, you see. Sometimes people do that; they say they are sorry for something when they are *not* sorry for it in order to make sure the person knows that they are actually even less sorry for it than that person thinks.

Humans are sometimes very complicated.

"Carry yourself away from here at once!" the Riddle Raven screamed, stomping around on its little clawed feet. It bustled over to the broken cage and began to set the slats up against themselves again. "If you are still here by the time I finish rebuilding the cage, I shall drop it on you a second time, and the riddles will not be so kind!"

"Yes," agreed the stranger, whose hands still remained casually in his pockets. "Let's remove ourselves, shall we?"

Now, Mabel knew that you should never go wandering off into the woods with strangers. But this particular stranger had saved her life, which made her less afraid of him than she might be of a different stranger, and something about him seemed somehow familiar.

"I suppose we'd better," Mabel said, skirting away from the frantic owl. "I'd like to stay free of cages if I can."

"So would we all," the stranger agreed. And so together, they left the Riddle Raven behind, cursing and spitting and gathering together its little crate.

"I don't mean to be rude," Mabel said after they'd taken a few steps together, "but what are you doing walking through the woods alone at night?"

The stranger laughed at that, a loud, pleasing sound that showed no sign of fear or malice. "Why, looking for you, of course!"

Mabel stopped in her tracks. "Looking for me?" she said. "Why were you looking for me?"

"I thought you might need my help," the stranger grinned, moseying on down the path.

Mabel gasped. "It was you!" she cried. "You were the one who threw mudroot at the crows! And you were the one who shone the green light on Gallows Hill!" *That* was why he seemed so familiar. She had already seen his shadow and heard his voice. And the stranger was favoring his left hand, where Mabel knew that, if she looked, she'd find a burn from where he had touched the bright green light.

"I was," the stranger said, "and I'm something more than that, I think. Perhaps I should properly introduce myself." He stuck out his hand, which was splotched with dried muck, and his skin appeared to be covered in lichen…or was it naturally that pale greenish color? "My name," he said happily, "is Zoumbrus Gray."

"Gray?" Mabel asked, surprised. She had never met anyone else with that surname before. It wasn't nearly as common as Brickletooth or Spindlespear. "Gray is my last name, too."

"I know it is," Zoumbrus said. His smile had become somehow nervous. "I know quite a bit about you, Mabel. You see, I am your great-great-granduncle."

Mabel was so astonished, she laughed out loud. Zoumbrus looked a little taken aback. "That's impossible," she said. "I don't have any living relatives. The village has checked and double-checked."

"And they're quite right," Zoumbrus said. "You don't have any *living* relatives. But you have me, and I've been dead for a rather long time."

And then, without warning, a Shimmer of Time and Place decided to appear and swallow Mabel up.

CHAPTER 10
SHIMMERING TO AND FRO

The Shimmer of Time and Place appeared as Shimmers often do, which is to say, without any warning at all. It had been lurking a little ways down the path, where it had set itself up and stood very still so that the oncoming travelers would not see it shimmer. You see, Shimmers are bred in the Briarbranch Woods, and most of them spend their entire existences lurking behind trees and preying on unsuspecting travelers. They are very adept at camouflaging themselves in the forest.

Simply put, Shimmers are like very clear doors, so they are almost perfectly hidden from sight no matter where they loom, except for the small detail that they gleam a little. Some people wonder *why* they gleam a little, but what they *should* wonder is why they don't gleam a *lot*. There is quite a ferocious amount of space-time continuum compression happening within each paper-thin sliver of Shimmer. Frankly, it's astonishing they don't constantly combust in the most violent manner.

Shimmers work on a rather simple principle; if you step into one, you will be removed to another time or to another place, or sometimes to both another time *and* another place, depending on the type of Shimmer.

This particular Shimmer— a Shimmer of Place more than of Time (several dozen leagues of space, to be specific, and only a few hours of time)—had been waiting for Mabel and Zoumbrus to wander helplessly into its clutches, but when they stopped in the middle of the trail to have their discussion of lineage, the Shimmer grew anxious, for it had been months and months since anyone had stepped through its portal. It hadn't sent a single person to the far reaches of the world that entire calendar year, and it practically salivated glimmering drool in its excitement. Just as you might feed on a bit of cheese or on a roast duck, you understand, a Shimmer feeds on humans that it sends through to various Other Times and Other Places.

And this Shimmer was hungry.

It crept up behind young Mabel and old Zoumbrus as quietly as a dormouse. Just as Zoumbrus confessed to Mabel that he had been dead for a rather long time, the Shimmer leapt into action and made to swallow both parties whole.

Zoumbrus had never been through a Shimmer, but he had spoken to plenty who had, and he knew what a Shimmer looked like when he saw one. He didn't recognize the glimmer in the air until it was too late and the Shimmer was descending upon them. He threw his hands up over his face and cried, "Aieeee!" in a decidedly uncivilized manner. Mabel saw the glimmer, too, and she threw up her arm on instinct. As it turns out, she threw up the *wrong* arm, the one that did not have Abernathy's reflectoken pinned to the cuff (a small blunder for which we can surely forgive her, given the immediacy of the event), but it didn't matter. The reflectoken was old, and old objects can be very powerful. It cast its reflective spell on the hungry Shimmer from down at Mabel's side, and rather than the glimmering portal sending Mabel and Zoumbrus to the far side of the Black Flint Mountains, Mabel sent the Shimmer there instead. It doubled up on itself and sucked itself inside out with a loud *POP!*

And that was it for the Shimmer.

"Good gracious!" Zoumbrus cried, peeking through his fingers. "How did you do that?"

Mabel showed him the little yellow-stoned pin on her cuff. "I borrowed this from a monster."

"And a blessing that it works!" Zoumbrus exhaled with relief. "Is that why you went to Devilden? To fetch that wonderful little pin?"

Mabel nodded. "I was cross with Elder Alder for making me

retrieve it before coming into the woods, but I suppose I owe him an apology now." Mabel squinted one eye and peered up at her great-great-granduncle. "Did you follow me to Devilden, too?" she asked.

"I did indeed. I didn't make it very far, though. I was accosted by a horde of street merchants who insisted that I taste their inhuman wares. Awful stuff, monster food. By the time I managed to slip away and find a statehouse window to peek through, you were being shooed out the secret portalway in that Abernathy creature's office. I had to cover the distance between there and here the old fashioned way. I ran with all haste, which is why I'm a bit late. I see you were able to manage yourself quite well in my absence."

"I dispelled the Bad Witch," she said, lifting her chin proudly. "All by myself."

Zoumbrus' eyes grew large. "Well. That is certainly some feat." He sounded as if he did not quite believe her.

"If you ran all this way, why are you not out of breath?" Mabel asked, suddenly a bit suspicious. It is a strange and surprising thing to meet an ancestor who has been dead for many years, and she wasn't convinced his story held much water.

Zoumbrus tilted his head and frowned at her. "I don't *have* breath. As I said, I've been dead a rather long time."

"Oh. That makes sense," said Mabel, feeling a little foolish. She resumed walking down the blue-flame path.

"Since we are walking away from the Grandfather Tree, I assume you have already made its acquaintance," Zoumbrus said, falling into step with her. "Did you find a Skeleton Key there?"

"No," Mabel frowned. "It's already gone."

"Then we must not dilly-dally," he said seriously, quickening his step.

"We?" Mabel asked. She wasn't even quite convinced that this Zoumbrus was the relation he claimed to be, and despite the grand realization she'd recently had about her desire for family, a great-great-granduncle risen from the grave wasn't at all what she expected. Besides, family or no, she didn't know how she felt about letting someone else in on her adventure. Adventures, she knew from reading books, tend to get a bit overcrowded.

Zoumbrus frowned down at her, looking a little hurt. "Haven't I been helpful?" he asked.

"You have been *extremely* helpful," she admitted. "But why would you want to help me? Why show yourself now, when I'm on a grand adventure, and not when I was locked away in St. Crippleback's? If you were really family, I don't think you would have let me stay in that horrible orphanage. But now, here you are, desperate to help? I hope you'll excuse me, but it's suspicious."

They reached the point where the path broke into three trails again, and Zoumbrus stepped onto the shining path with no hesitation. "Come," he said, noting Mabel's pause. "This is the fastest route back."

"I think maybe we should take the path of fire," Mabel said. "I know that one is free and clear of witches."

Zoumbrus smiled. "Not to worry. The path that glistens is the path of the Good Witch. If we make her acquaintance, we'll be all the better off for it. Come, now. Walk with me, and I'll answer all of your questions, and then some. I promise."

Mabel was uncertain. She knew the fiery path was the safest path, having already tested it, but the glistening path was a trail of great curiosity, and curiosity will always win out in a child, for children have not made enough good decisions yet to know a bad decision when they see one.

Mabel decided to follow the man who claimed to be her great-great-granduncle.

"We'll go together as far as the edge of Briarbranch Woods," she said. "If you're still of a suspicious nature by then, I'll go on alone from there."

"You have a deal. And, here, as a show of good faith, I'll give you my beaconstone." He fished into his left pocket and withdrew a lime green gem. He placed it in Mabel's palm. "Hold it between two fingers and say, 'Beacon bright!' It'll glow the same green that you saw on Gallows Hill. If I give you a single answer that displeases you, you can blind me with it and run away while I stumble about with my eyes burning."

Mabel nodded her agreement. It seemed like a fair deal. "Maybe I can use it to shine light into the forest, too. I'm supposed to find some mushrooms for the monsters, and it's too awfully dark to see anything on this path."

Zoumbrus smiled as he reached into his right pocket and pulled out a handful of small, round, pillow-shaped mushrooms. They were bright orange and had purple stems. They were also quite wet. "I made a slight detour on my way here and fought off some hungry forest grimlets to pick a handful of these. Will they do?"

"Moffat mushrooms!" Mabel squealed. "Oh, thank you!" She took the mushrooms and examined them closely. They fit Abernathy's description perfectly. "This will save me loads of time. What a wonderful surprise!"

"I like to think I'm full of surprises," Zoumbrus said with a satisfied smile. He offered Mabel his arm, and with only a little bit of hesitation, she took it.

Together, they started down the glistening path.

Chapter 11
The Abbreviated Tale of Zoumbrus Gray

Zoumbrus Gray was as good as his word. As they walked briskly along the glimmering path, he gave Mabel all the answers she requested, and then some. And this is what he said:

"In my youth, I was something of a rascal. I'm not proud of it, Mabel, and I certainly don't condone it. But I don't deny it, either. I made my living on the roads, purloining purses and burglaring billfolds. I was a highwayman, a scoundrel, a footpad, and a cutthroat. I fancied myself a gentleman thief, though there was nothing so awfully gentlemanly about any of it. My partner Fogg and I, we were low men who thought ourselves quite high.

"But my decisions caught up with me, as decisions are wont to do, and in the end, I was hanged, right atop Gallows Hill. Fogg and I, we swung until dead, and then we were left for the night, as was the custom back then. 'The Crows' Tithe,' we used to call that practice.

"We chatted to pass the time until the rope man came to cut us loose. And I realized as I hung there that I'd wasted the absolute entirety of my life. I'd always wanted to see the world, but I'd never made it beyond Brightsbane. I'd made a wreck of my relationships, including the one with my brother, Bartlebous, your great-great-grandfather. I'd learned a thing or two, and I had a taste for further education—I took quite well to geography and the basic sciences, I found—but I'd squandered any chance of formal learning by turning to a life as a cutpurse. And as I swung above Gallows Hill, I realized that I had a chance to go forth and retrieve for myself an *in*formal education. The dead aren't supposed to walk about, of course. It's highly unorthodox. We're supposed to have stiff upper lips and shuffle off into our graves. But I thought, why not? Why should I give myself to the ground? I felt fit enough, and I was hungry for experience. I finally had the nerve to leave crime and villainy behind and embrace a larger worldview. Do you see? Death was my chance to live.

"Fortunately, the snap of the rope had broken my neck, and I was able to wriggle out of the noose quite easily. Fogg wasn't so lucky. I offered to cut him down, but he was scared." Zoumbrus sighed and gazed wistfully up through the canopy of tree limbs. "Ah, Fogg. I hope you're comfortable enough, in your pile beneath the ground.

"At any rate, I ambled down Gallows Hill, ventured across the Slurptongue Swamp, shook the dust of Brightsbane from my feet, and, for the first time, I crossed over into Parts Unknown. I spent the better part of two centuries exploring the Lands Far Beyond. What sights I saw! The Floating Rocks of Tarmandine! The Great Cloudy Canyon! The Desert of a Thousand Steps! The Wishy-Washy Falls! The Saltwind Sea! There are great wonders beyond our borders, and oh! They are beautiful in the moonlight. The world is wide, much wider than you'd think.

"I did come back to Brightsbane now and again, to check in on the family line. Blood is thicker than brine, as they say. The family had disowned me for my deplorable actions, and I didn't blame them, but they were still dear to me. I watched helplessly through a garden window as my brother died of consumption in his bed one night. I used to watch his children, and then his grandchildren, play in the sands near Boiling Lake. One of my brother's grandchildren, his name was Baldrous, he got too close to the lake and was lost in the boiling waters. Did you ever hear about your great-uncle Baldrous? No? Just seven years old when he perished. Your grandfather wasn't born yet." Zoumbrus sighed. "I've witnessed a great many tragedy in our family line." He glanced nervously at Mabel from the corner of his eye. "I—I heard of your parents and their awful pumpkin accident, as well. We seem to be a family destined for sadness. I *did* want to help you, Mabel; I wanted to help quite desperately. I even had an audience with Mayor Poppet and pleaded with him to let me raise you. But he made it quite clear that only *living* relatives can be granted custody of orphans—apparently there are now several of us undead wanderers requesting rights to the town's orphans—but not being alive, well, we do not fit the bill. I began to stay closer to Brightsbane, and I checked in on you twice each year, though the matrons of St. Crippleback's would not allow me to enter the home. They have heard awful rumors of the traveling dead devouring other human beings, and other such nonsense. Every rational person knows that the traveling dead only hunger for human flesh on Pere Suppleup's Day."

This bit of information was new to Mabel. "You eat human flesh?" she blenched.

"Hungering for it and partaking of it are not the same thing. And it's only for one day of the year."

"Why only on Pere Suppleup's Day?" she asked cautiously, widening the slight distance between herself and her walking partner.

"The same reason any odd thing happens at all," Zoumbrus said with a shrug. "Someone cast a spell that made it so. Oh, but do not be worried. We're still several weeks away from Pere Suppleup's Day, and we traveling dead take great care to lock ourselves in pantries from first moonrise to second moonset."

"Alone and without other humans to feed on?" Mabel asked, because clarification is important.

"Yes, exactly," Zoumbrus confirmed. "Just with salted lamb and the like. Sometimes there's barley. Usually, there's flour. At any rate, I'm consistently turned away from St. Crippleback's, no matter which day the calendar shows. I hope you'll forgive me for not visiting you. I did try. Many times."

Mabel felt a lump rise up in her throat. "So I *did* have family looking for me," she said, her voice quavering.

"Looking for you and after you," Zoumbrus said. "I know you

must have felt horrendously alone, and I apologize for that. I—I did not know how best to reach you…or how you might react to having a traveling dead relative, especially since I—well, you see, I—I'm rather greenish about the skin." He held one arm up and pushed back his sleeve so Mabel could see his green-tinted flesh. "It's from a lack of oxygen, I think, and from being so curiously nourished. There's not much to eat on the roads between Brightsbane and the Lands Far Beyond aside from lichen and some various green leafery. I was afraid that—well, you see…I thought that you'd be afraid of me."

"Greenish skin doesn't bother me," Mabel said. "I wasn't afraid of the Devilden monsters, and they come in all *sorts* of strange colors."

"Yes, that's exactly true! After I saw how you handled yourself with the monsters, I knew you were a good and kind girl who wouldn't be put off by a greenish tint. It made me feel much better about my own state, and I thought perhaps you *wouldn't* be too put off by having a traveling dead uncle."

A tear spilled out of Mabel's eye, and she scrubbed it away. "I think I quite like it," was all she said.

Zoumbrus smiled, looking relieved. "Well. At any rate, I stop in the village to look in on you from time to time, and I happened to return to Brightsbane just last week. I was reading a book near the square this morning when I spied a great exodus of children from the orphanage. Children are rarely quite as sneaky as they fancy themselves. They kept to the shadows, but there's nothing natural about three dozen children creeping through shadow. I thought something must be wrong at the orphanage, and I hurried up the hill, which is when I saw you peek out from an alleyway. There was no mistaking you, my dear! You look so much like your father, who looked so much like *his* father, who looked so much like *his* father, who looked so much like my brother. I followed you, then, and offered what help I could along the way."

"I'm glad you decided to reveal yourself," Mabel decided. "I wouldn't have guessed the answer to the owl's final riddle."

Zoumbrus smiled. It was a tender, fatherly sort of smile. "You asked why I would want to help you and why I should show up now, desperate to help, when you're on a grand adventure. I want to help you because you are family. In fact, you are my *only* family. There are lots of smaller reasons that get wrapped up into that one big reason, but that's the gist of it. Blood calls to blood, as they say. And as for your second question, it is not suspicious that I should show up now, but lucky, I think. I haven't just shown up now, I have shown up to look in on our family twice or thrice a year ever since my untimely expiration, long before you were born, and I am fortunate that one of my visits has coincided with a time of great need. You are on an extraordinary quest, and if you fail in it, then Brightsbane shall be lost, and I do not wish that on the villagers who inhabit it. The dirt of Brightsbane covers the bones of my family, and I shouldn't like to see it all destroyed.

"That is my general story, Mabel. There is much more to it than that, of course, and while I shouldn't wish to ever horrify you with the details of my sordid life, someday I hope to share with you the marvels of my travels, and maybe take you on a journey of your own. But for now, let it suffice to say that I have had a long and interesting life, but the thing I am most interested in is my last remaining bit of family, my great-great-grandniece, Mabel Gray." They reached the end of the glimmering path just as Zoumbrus finished his story. The trees suddenly parted, and the empty field spread before them once more. "And here we are," he said, stopping at the edge of Briarbranch Woods. "As promised, I've answered your questions, and now you shall decide whether or not to continue on alone."

Mabel turned and crossed her arms, eyeing her long-lost relation carefully. "You did answer all my questions, and it seems that you really must be my relative. There is much about you that's familiar, including your need to wander and explore. I think that would explain why I escape from St. Crippleback's so often, even though I know I shouldn't."

"We Grays have always been well-regarded wanderers," Zoumbrus admitted.

"And I've recently discovered that family is very important to me. I think I would very much like you to accompany me on my mission. But if all this turns out to be a lie, and you end up being a spy sent by the wizard, I'll tell the elder, and you'll be clapped in the stocks."

Zoumbrus smiled with relief, for if the truth is to be told, then I should tell you, dear reader, that he was quite nervous that Mabel would reject his offer and banish him from her life forever. "That is a fair deal, and true," he said. He extended one slightly greenish hand, and Mabel shook it.

"Where to now?" Zoumbrus asked as they stepped out into the field. "The Elderary?"

Mabel clicked her teeth together and thought for a moment. "I'm supposed to deliver the moffat mushrooms to Viceroy Abernathy before moonrise. I don't know how long the next bit of adventure will take, and it would probably be best to bring them to him now."

"I can tell you from experience, Devilden is a long run from this point," Zoumbrus said with a frown.

Mabel nodded. "And I don't see the portalway open anywhere—do you?"

"No," Zoumbrus agreed. "I don't see anything but grass and stars."

"Well, we don't have time to waste," she decided. "The wizard is a greater evil than some silly monster's toothache. We'll just have to hope we can return to Devilden before morning."

"That, my dear child, seems like sound advice."

And sound advice, it may have been, but I shall let you in on a secret now, if you promise not to tell Mabel, for that might spoil the course of her grand adventure. Do you promise? If you do, place one pinky on the page, and I shall do the same on my end, and then we will have a pinky agreement, which, as I'm sure you know, cannot be broken without a permanent hex being cast on the breaking party.

Are you ready? Is your pinky in place? If you do not promise to keep this secret, and if you are not proffering your pinky, please do not read these next two sentences:

Mabel is going to regret her decision to put off Abernathy's mushrooms. Not for some time…but eventually she will regret it very much.

With their path thus decided, Mabel and Zoumbrus began the trek back to the Elderary, where Elder Alder was fidgeting nervously about the answer to the problem of Boiling Lake.

Chapter 12
The Most Dangerous Bell
in the World

Elder Alder was surprised to meet Zoumbrus Gray, and, as I am sure you can imagine, a somewhat prolonged session of introductions and explanations was necessary in order to ease his mind as to the dead man's presence. He, too, had heard the tales that the traveling dead hungered for flesh on all days and not just on Pere Suppleup's Day, and he required quite a bit of convincing to the contrary.

"Have you found a way across Boiling Lake?" Mabel asked, getting down to iron tacks once proper introduction etiquette had been met. She didn't like the fact that they had lost almost an entire day seeking out keys that had already been swiped.

"As it happens, I have," said the elder, though judging by the look on his face, he might have just said, "As it happens, I've found a small, slimy squid lodged in the bottom of my throat."

"Is it a troublesome way?" Zoumbrus asked, noticing the sour look.

"Troublesome would be a very mild way to put it."

The elder pressed the spine of a particularly nondescript book on one of his many shelves, and the entire bookcase swung out from the wall. "A secret passageway!" Mabel cried. This time, she could see stone steps descending into the wall behind the case, and she knew without a doubt that it was a passageway and not a portalway.

"Each elder's chamber has several secret passageways, I'm told." Elder Alder said. "I have only just begun to find the ones in my room. Apparently much that is done in this building is done in secret." He lit a torch, and the trio stepped into the wall and wound their way down the steps. The elder spoke as they made their descent. "Do you know why Boiling Lake boils?" he asked.

Mabel admitted that she did not. Her exploits beyond the walls of the orphanage, which had once seemed so large and exciting but now paled in comparison to her current adventure, had never taken her near the boiling waters. "Maybe the lake is really a gigantic cauldron?" she guessed, remembering the witch's soup and the way the surface of it bubbled and roiled.

"I've heard a tale or two," Zoumbrus chimed in. "I don't like to think of the stories as true, though. If they are…" He let his voice trail away.

"I'll tell you why it boils: There are three irascible fire daemons living at the bottom of the lake, and by their very presence, they heat the water to unfathomable temperatures."

Zoumbrus groaned. "Those *are* the tales I've been told," he said sadly.

"It's…unfortunate," the elder said. "Irasible fire daemons are wearisome things, to put the matter lightly."

"Doesn't the water douse their flames?" Mabel asked.

"Fire daemons don't burn from the outside *in*; they burn from the inside *out*. And their insides are tethered to the Place of Brimstone, which is where the fires are stoked. I'm afraid you'd need more than the water of one lake to put out those flames."

"Do they ever cool?" she asked. "Even a little?"

"To my knowledge, they only burn hotter, and they never burn cooler."

"That means no crossing in a metal boat," said Zoumbrus.

"Quite right," Elder Alder replied, "unless you want to be fried alive. Boats of any kind are out while the lake is a-boil. Some people have had limited success in wooden rafts, but they are unreliable, and the water tends to seep up through the cracks and the knots."

"Is there a way *over* the water?" Mabel asked.

The elder shook his head. "Not a reliable one. Even if we had a flight craft or a hover spell, the convection would throw you into a tizzy. You'd likely tip right into the lake, or careen off course and smash into a tree."

"Then how do we get to Steamsoak Island to retrieve the key?"

The elder hesitated as he reached the bottom of the stairs. "Well," he said uneasily. "The only way I've been able to determine is for us to get the daemons out of the lake."

Zoumbrus missed a step and tumbled the rest of the way down the spiral staircase. "Did you say get the daemons *out* of the lake?" he asked, his body lying in a twisted heap.

"I did." Elder Alder stuck the torch into a brass holder set into the wall, and the flame grew three times brighter. As if on some secret cue, other torches along the wall caught fire, and the chamber in which they found themselves became awash in flickering orange light. It was a storeroom, but unlike the storeroom at St. Crippleback's, where the matrons kept extra sacks of sugar and mysterious liquids in dusty bottles, this storeroom had cages filled with old, dusty, and dangerous trinkets, and everything in it was under lock and key.

Mabel had an idea about something that seemed very obvious, so obvious that she felt foolish asking it. "This might be a poor question," she said, "but won't it be bad for Brightsbane to have three irascible fire daemons roaming around the land?"

"Yes, of course it will," Elder Alder said, as if she'd just asked if one plus one were two.

"Then…is it right to do it?"

"The fire daemons are bad, and awfully destructive. But they'll do less damage than the wizard will do with his spell book. Mark my words on that." The elder fished a ring of keys from his pocket and hurried down one of the rows of locked cages.

Mabel helped Zoumbrus to his feet, and they followed quickly after the elder. "But is it worth the trouble?" the girl asked. "I'm so far behind the wizard, it's been almost a full day now since he came to you, and the other keys were already gone. He's surely made his way to the third key as well."

"Actually, I think there's a good chance he hasn't," murmured the elder, searching the cages. "I did some research while you were in the Briarbranch. Steamsoak Island is actually a very small volcano, thanks to the daemons firing up the temperature of things below, and judging by the Warden's rhyme, that's where you'll find the key. According to *A Study in Magmas, Lavas, and Other Orange-Colored Viscous Things*, which is the most reliable text on the subject, the Steamsoak Island volcano is permeated with daemon magic. It's especially designed to keep out *other* magicks."

"Like the Elderary's blue magic!" Mabel said.

But Elder Alder shook his head. "Not so very much like that. Quite a bit stronger, I should think. And more fearsome. At Steamsoak Island, the more magical powers one has, the less likely one will be able to cross into the volcano."

"The wizard is the most powerful magician Brightsbane has ever known," said Zoumbrus, his voice taking on a tinge of excitement. "If what you say of daemon magic is true, he won't be able to set foot there!"

"And I'm not magical at all," Mabel pointed out. "I should have no trouble."

"Yes, quite right," said the elder, "though let's bear in mind that you are not invulnerable to fiery lava or extreme temperatures. There are still plenty of dangers awaiting you in Boiling Lake. Ah!" He crouched down and examined a cage that sat against the stone floor. "Here we are!" He fiddled with his keys until he found the right one, then he opened the padlock on the cage and swung open the door. He reached in and carefully pulled out the object inside. It was wrapped in rags, but the shape was unmistakable.

"Is that a bell?" Mabel asked.

"It is," the elder confirmed. "A very special bell."

"You don't mean—" Zoumbrus started with a gasp. "Is that— the Blacktower Bell?" The elder nodded. Zoumbrus' knees turned watery, and he plopped awkwardly down onto the floor. "I never guessed it would really exist," he whispered.

"It does." Elder Alder pulled back the rags and revealed a shining copper bell underneath. The clapper was wrapped in many layers of dense cotton so that it could not ring against the casting. The elder's face became grave as he beheld the instrument.

"What's the Blacktower Bell?" Mabel asked.

"Do you know the white bell tower in the town square?" the elder asked. Mabel nodded. Everyone knew the bell tower. It was the tallest structure in Brightsbane, apart from the Elderary. "That tower is not original to the village; there was another tower that once stood in its place, a tower built to the same specifications. It housed a great, silver bell once, the largest bell in any of the lands. But one day, a mysterious rider appeared with a new bell—*this* bell." He held up the shining copper thing. It was as bright as if it were brand new and freshly smithed. "No one knew where the bell came from, or who the man was who delivered it. Some stories say it was The Great Evil. Others say it was the wizard Croup. But wherever the bell came from, its effects are well-documented.

"The man lied and told the mayor of the day that the elders had ordered it especially for the white tower and that it was to be installed posthaste. The mayor, eager to please the elders, had the instrument in place within the hour. That night happened to be a town meeting. When time came to sound the gathering chime, the pullman rang the bell. And then..." The elder's voice drifted into silence.

"Then what?" said Mabel.

The elder lifted his eyes to hers. "Then the villagers found out exactly what the bell could do."

"It called forth the fire daemons," Zoumbrus said. "The sound of the bell drew them out of Boiling Lake."

"Really?" Mabel said, gaping at the bell. It was a fairly small thing, and it seemed very innocent. It didn't seem possible for such a thing to cause so much danger.

"The truth of that day has been wiped from the official history so that we may be spared anguish over the foolishness of our ancestors. But the rumors persist, and there are still books that hold the truth…and the truth is that at that time, the people didn't know what made the lake boil. They believed it was just the nature of the water. But when the bell sounded, something stirred deep beneath the waves. The fire daemons rose from the depths and stormed the town square, dripping fire." The elder paused, as if considering how to tell the rest of the story. "There are differing accounts of what passed then," he finally said. "What is known for sure is that when the daemons were done, the square was in ruins, and the white bell tower, like so many of the other buildings, was charred black. But the bell inside remained clean and shining, bright as the day it was made."

Mabel's eyes were wider than saucers. "And you want to *use* that bell?" she asked, incredulous.

"I don't see any other option," the elder frowned.

"You're going to call three irascible fire daemons out into Brightsbane?" she said, her voice taking on a high squeak.

"Shh!" the elder urged. "There are ears everywhere." He threw the rags back over the bell and tucked the bundle under his arm. "But yes. Drawing forth the daemons is the only way to stop the water from boiling."

"But they'll destroy the village!" Zoumbrus cried.

"*Please* keep your voices down," Elder Alder begged. "They won't destroy the village. Listen well: you two will go to the edge of Boiling Lake—the *western* edge, do you hear me? Be sure to hide yourself in the brambles on the western side, and stay out of sight. I'll take the bell into Slurptongue Swamp and ring it there. There's nothing in the swamp for the daemons to destroy."

"Except trees," Mabel pointed out. "And you."

The elder waved her off. "I'm more than capable of giving this assistance. I may be a coward, but there is some small courage in me yet. You wait until the daemons leave the lake. The temperature of the water will fall almost instantly, and you can take a boat to the island."

"What boat?" Zoumbrus asked. "I don't suppose you have one waiting for us in the brambles?"

"I'm sure you'll figure something out," the elder muttered.

"This is a dangerous plan," Mabel observed.

"It is that," said the elder. "If you've got a better one, I'm all ears."

"I didn't say it was a *bad* plan." She crossed her arms defiantly. "I think I might like to see some fire daemons up close."

"Not *too* close," Zoumbrus frowned.

Elder Alder raised an eyebrow. "Then we're agreed?"

"I'm agreed," said Mabel.

Zoumbrus sighed. "Agreed, I suppose. Just promise not to burn Brightsbane to the ground."

Elder Alder nodded, though none of them was entirely certain that he could keep that promise.

CHAPTER 13
THE KEY OF THE FIRE DAEMONS

"Do you think this is a bad plan?" Mabel asked, now that they were far out of Elder Alder's earshot.

"I definitely wouldn't call it a *good* plan," Zoumbrus admitted. "Though to tell the truth, I've heard worse."

They had scouted out a patch of brambles on the western side of the lake, just as the elder had directed, and they were currently perched precariously against the sharp thorns. "A bramble patch doesn't seem like a very good place to sit and wait," Mabel said.

"No," Zoumbrus agreed, pulling his shirt free from the barbed clutches of a bramble twig, "it does not."

They were not alone on the banks of Boiling Lake. Far from it, in fact. Despite the great heat that rolled off the water, Boiling Lake was considered one of the more romantic spots in Brightsbane. The bubbling water of the lake reflected the moonlight in remarkable shifting patterns, and it was a pleasing sight. Dozens of couples reclined on the shores around the lake, smiling and laughing and generally having no idea that any second three ill-tempered fire daemons would come slithering out of the water and squish them to death under their burning, blazing feet.

"Do you think we should do something to get them away from here?" Mabel asked, eyeing the villagers on the banks.

"Yes," Zoumbrus nodded. "We probably should."

They picked their way out of the brambles and hurried to the southern shore, where the daemons would emerge from the water on their way to Slurptongue Swamp. If, of course, everything went according to plan.

"Excuse me," Zoumbrus said as he approached the nearest pair of lovebirds, pulling down his sleeves to hide his greenish arms. "Have you seen the view from the north side of the lake? It's absolutely exquisite this time of night!" The man and woman leapt up from the beach and screamed.

"You're hideously green!" the woman shrieked, picking up their beach blanket and tossing it over her head to hide her vision.

"What extraordinarily good eyesight," Zoumbrus muttered.

"Sir! How dare you approach us thusly!" cried the man, a knobby thing of knees and elbows with a bushy moustache. He wore a red and orange striped bathing shirt, though of course no one ever even considered taking a dip in Boiling Lake. "And the lady is correct: you have a distinctly greenish hue! Therefore, I must challenge you to a contest of fisticuffs." The man raised his fists and held them awkwardly in front of his face.

"Fisticuffs?" Zoumbrus said. "I'm not trying to fight you, young man—I'm trying to *warn* you!"

"Someone should have warned *you* not to threaten young, innocent ladies with your horrid verdigris!" the man in the bathing suit said. "If she'd fainted, I should have called the constabulary! Comfort yourself that your slight only comes down to pugilism." He threw one jaunty fist forward, missing Zoumbrus' cheekbone by several wide inches. "Stop moving!"

"Give him his comeuppance, Galthwaite!" the young lady cheered.

"I'm trying, dear, but he moves like a snake." The young man threw a second punch, this one missing by an even wider margin. "Are you made of water, sir?" he cried.

"Look, we're just trying to warn you that any moment now, a bell will ring in the swamp, and three irascible fire daemons will come stomping out of the lake, and if you don't move your blanket to one of the other beaches, you'll be right in their path!"

The man in the bathing suit guffawed so hugely that his mustache bounced. "Fire daemons? A bell in a swamp? A different beach? You are mad, sir, and for your own good, and since you cannot hold still, I shall call forth the constabulary. Clementine! Fetch my shoes! I'm walking back into town!"

"No, Galthwaite! We're having such a lovely time!" the woman called with her head still buried beneath the blanket. She put her hands out and groped blindly for her lover, but she had gotten herself turned around, and she planted her hands down on Mabel instead. "Galthwaite? Oh, Galthwaite! He's rendered you legless and brought you low!" she wailed. Mabel looked quizzically up at Zoumbrus. The dead man shrugged.

"I am over here, Clementine!" Galthwaite said. He stomped over to his shoes and picked them up himself, not even bothering to slip back into his breeches before jamming them onto his feet. "Come, darling. We're going for the police." He grabbed Clementine's hand and pulled her along the beach, tucking the bundle of his clothes under his arm and leaving a lit candelabra and a full picnic basket behind.

"Are all romantic people as odd as that?" Mabel asked, stunned.

"Most of them, yes."

They looked out over the beach at the dozens of other young couples canoodling under the glistening moonlight. Not a single one of them had even lifted an eyebrow at the scene that had just unfolded on the beach, so enthralled were they all in their own individual affairs. Passionate feelings do make you something of a dunce, after all. "Maybe we should let them get trampled by the daemons," Mabel suggested.

But Zoumbrus gave her a wink. "I have a better idea," he said. "Wait here."

He pushed up his sleeves and rolled up his pants so that a goodly amount of his skin was exposed. He picked up some wet sand and smeared it on his cheeks, just below the bones, making him look especially gaunt. Then he staggered about the beach, snarling and slurping and clamoring on about a hunger for human flesh.

"An ambling dead!" the young lovers squealed. "Help! Help! Oh, help—he's hungry for our flesh!" They leapt from their blankets

143

and scattered off into the trees beyond the beach, running blindly through the darkness, most of them leaving their other halves to fend for themselves. There were muted crashing sounds and groans as a handful of the moonbathers knocked into tree limbs and bashed their toes against rocks.

Zoumbrus watched them flee, then pushed down his sleeves and his cuffs and sauntered back down the beach to where Mabel stood. "That," he said, his voice chipper, "is rather the good side of those hopeless rumors."

Mabel could not argue that the method was effective. "But you're not doing much to change their minds on the matter," she pointed out.

"True, true. But all for the common good, I think." And just then, as if to exacerbate his point, the peal of the Blacktower Bell rang through the air, the clanging as clear as a shot.

The sound was nothing like Mabel had ever heard before. It was so clear and so crisp, she felt as if she could reach up and snap a piece of the sound from the air. But it was also somehow hollow. The tone rose and fell on the wind, seemingly meant not to peal, but to *sing*. It was the sound of an angel's choir sealed inside an ocean of bubbles. That was the best way Mabel could describe it.

"Oh, dear," Zoumbrus fretted. "Run!"

They slugged across the beach, pulling hard against the sand that sucked at their feet as they ran. "He made it," Mabel said as she struggled back toward the brambles.

"Did you think he would not?"

She shrugged mid-run. It was not an easy thing to do, but Mabel thought the question called for a good shrug. "He's a bit of a coward. I thought he might go yellow about it."

"Maybe he tripped and fell and rang it by accident."

Mabel nodded. That was entirely possible.

They reached the brambles and dove into the sharp branches, wincing at the pain. They peeked their heads up just high enough to see over the scraggly scrub. They sat like that for some time, watching the boiling water anxiously.

"Do you think it worked?" Mabel asked.

"I didn't see any daemons leave the lake. Unless they are very tiny daemons, almost too small for the eye to see, in which case I question the reliability of the old stories of their destruction."

"Maybe it takes them a while to wake up."

They continued to wait in the brambles, but nothing unusual stirred in the lake.

"The bell may be in disrepair," Zoumbrus said, rubbing his chin thoughtfully. Little flakes of sand and mossy dirt flaked away. "Or perhaps the story of the Blacktower Bell really is just a legend after all." He stood up from the bramble patch and brushed the briars from his shirt. "I'm sorry to say, I don't think this is going to—"

But he didn't get a chance to finish his statement, because just then, Boiling Lake began to gurgle and churn far out toward the center. The water seemed to rise up into a low hillock, and it glowed a watery orange from below the surface. Steam sizzled throughout, and the hill of water rose higher and higher, until an orange dome burst through.

The water sluiced down the sides and crashed back onto the bubbling lake as the first fire daemon rose. It was a massive, hideous thing, with the appearance of a hulking, short-necked dragon, covered in burning scales that gave it a charred-yet-still-on-fire look. Viscous lava dripped through the fiery cracks between the scales and sizzled as it hit the lake. It clawed its way through the water with huge, curving talons of brimstone that smoked in the air. Its tail was long and ended in a three-pronged fork, each prong as long and as thick as a fencepost that had been whittled to a fine point. Fire blazed from the creature's nostrils as it breathed, and its large, orange eyes were set into dark pools of inky blackness. The irises themselves seemed to flare with heat.

As the daemon approached the shore, it reared back onto its hind legs and stomped slowly up the sandbar. It was incredibly tall—more than twice the height of the Elderary. It straightened itself and unfurled huge, ragged black wings that were ripped through in several places, giving them a dead, half-eaten appearance.

Two other daemons followed, rising from the lake in much the same manner and lumbering in tandem behind the first monster. They looked quite similar to the first, except the second one had great, twisting horns, and the third had a gaping hole in his chest through which Mabel could see a swirling, churning pit of lava that fueled the beast and kept its fires burning.

I hope you'll believe me when I tell you it was a rather horrific sight.

When the daemons had gathered on the shore, they lifted their heads in unison and belched forth a terrific series of roars that shook the branches from the trees and sent shockwaves spilling across the lake. Mabel covered her ears with her hands, and still she feared her eardrums might explode. Then the daemons lumbered off toward the trees, in the direction of Slurptongue Swamp. Their burning feet left footprints of smooth glass in the Boiling Lake sands.

The air around the lake was still as the daemons crashed into the woods. As the crashes began to die away, Zoumbrus whispered, "I think it worked."

"Look!" Mabel pointed to the water. It was already beginning to cool. The rolling boil was slowing, and the edges of the lake were already growing smooth.

"Excellent," the dead man declared. "Now let us find a boat."

This proved to be a task of great difficulty. There were many boats littering the shore, but they were decorative boats, not built to sail. This made sense, of course; no one ever actually sailed them on Boiling Lake. The wealthier Brightsbanians liked to have huge, garish ships built and wheeled to the shoreline so that they could impress the other wealthy Brightsbanians who wheeled *their* huge, garish ships to the shoreline. But since no one planned on actually setting sail, seaworthiness took a backseat to aesthetics. Here was a glass craft shaped like a diamond and polished to a high sheen; over there was a ship of heavy onyx chiseled to look like a raven. One of the boats was shaped and painted to be a facsimile of a quarter moon, and another was a velvet-covered, ruby red shoe for four people. There was even a boat designed to be a floating carousel with 12 life-sized stallions, each carved from a different precious gem. All these ships and more dotted the shores of Boiling Lake, but, of course, not a single one of them would float.

"Oh dear. This is a predicament," Zoumbrus frowned.

"Perhaps not," said Mabel. She pointed to a little crate set up near the northwestern corner of the lake. "Look there!"

The crate was actually a booth, which sat before a makeshift dock that tethered three small boats of questionable sturdiness. They bobbed and struggled in the water, but they floated, and they did not steam from heat, despite the recently high temperature of the water. Nailed to the crate was a sign that read "Boat Rides – 2 Bits." From the look of things, it wasn't an offer anyone much liked to take the owner up on, because the crate was rickety, the dock was in disrepair, the sign was hanging by one nail, and the dock worker sitting behind the crate was long dead, and only his skeleton remained.

"Business must have been bad," Zoumbrus decided as they approached the booth.

"Why would he have sat there until he died?" Mabel asked, amazed. She poked the skeleton's skull with her finger. It tumbled off the spine and fell into the lake.

Zoumbrus shrugged. "Some people are stubborn to a fault."

Mabel tested the water with her fingers and found it hot, but not overly so. She reached in, retrieved the skull, and balanced it atop the spinal column. It stood upright, but very shakily. "Shouldn't the Warden of the Boneyard have collected his remains?"

"The bone warden has his limits like the rest of us, I suppose. He probably didn't want such a stubborn boar trolling about the yard." The skeleton raised its hand and made an obscene gesture directed at Zoumbrus, but remained silent on the matter. Mabel ignored it.

"Do you have two bits for a boat ride?" she asked.

Zoumbrus started. "Two bits? For him?" The girl nodded. "Why would we pay him two bits? He's dead!"

"You're dead too, and I bet you could still use two bits."

"That's different," Zoumbrus said, crossing his arms. "I still have my faculties. I haven't given myself to rot, unlike some." He coughed and gestured very obviously at the skeleton behind the booth.

"Yes, I've been wondering about that," Mabel said. "How do you keep from going all soft and full of worms? And if your neck broke at your hanging, why does it stand up straight on your shoulders?"

"That, my child, is a long story for another time. Remind me to tell you the tale one day. It involves much determination, extreme amounts of danger, and a little poddlewoddle juice." He moved toward the dock, but Mabel leapt into his path.

"Uncle Zoumbrus," she warned, her voice tinged with steel. "We're meant to respect the dead. Do you have two bits to pay?"

"But Mabel! What on earth will he do with two bits?"

"That's his business," the girl said. The skeleton rattled his jaw in agreement. It tapped the top of the counter with a disjointed finger that cracked and broke off upon impact.

Zoumbrus grunted. "Fine." He reached into his vest pocket and fished out two bronze coins. He slapped them down on the counter. "May we please rent a boat for the evening?" he asked the skeleton. The skeleton gestured happily toward the dock. Then it scooped up the two coins and dropped them into a coin purse near its feet.

Mabel was pleased. "Now we may go."

They chose the shaky boat at the farthest end of the dock. The water had all but ceased its bubbling now, and the surface was fairly calm. They stepped cautiously into the boat and found that if Mabel sat in the bow and Zoumbrus distributed his weight a bit unevenly to the starboard side of the stern, they could both inhabit the craft without it capsizing.

"What's this made of?" Mabel asked. The curved planks looked like wood, but the felt much smoother, and much lighter.

"It's polywood!" Zoumbrus exclaimed, rather surprised. "It only grows in one forest I know of, way out behind the desert. I wonder where a stubborn skeleton like that found enough polywood for three boats…" He reached for an oar and began to paddle for what he felt sure was the little craft's maiden voyage. "That explains why the boat hasn't boiled up and warped beyond floatability. Polywood is impervious to heat."

"It feels impervious to water, too," Mabel said, grasping the sides of the boat for support. But with their careful balancing act, and with Zoumbrus' steady rowing, they managed to stay afloat. Before long, the boat bumped against the rocky shore of the little volcanic island in the center. They leapt out of the boat and pulled it up the sloping sides, securing it in place with a few well-placed stones near the stern.

"Well," Zoumbrus said, dusting off his hands. "That part was surprisingly easy."

"Easy enough to be worth two bits, I think."

They scaled the little volcano, careful to navigate around the looser bits of rock. Before they had gone ten feet, Mabel noticed white etchings in the stone underfoot. "Look," she said.

Zoumbrus nodded. "Ancient runes," he said, squinting down at the esoteric lines and squiggles on the ground. "Daemon language, I'd wager. Meant to keep out the magical types, just like Elder Alder said."

"So that magical folk can't cross?" Mabel asked. She'd never heard of markings that exerted so much power.

"That's my guess. You'd be amazed what a few good runes can do."

Even though she was in no way magical, Mabel held her breath as she stepped over the chalky markings. She passed over them without incident, however, and she breathed easily as she left them behind and continued her climb up the slope. Zoumbrus passed over them, too, for although we may think a walking dead person exceedingly odd and dependent on some sort of black magic or other, there was no spell required to animate the dead—not back then. That rule didn't come into effect until much later.

At the top of the slope were three small holes. The one in the center opened up into the island below and showed the rolling, spitting lava within. This was the volcano's crater. The hole to the left was filled with a thick, bubbling, milky white substance, and the one on the right was an empty bowl of rock. A loping channel carved into the stone around the crater connected the two outer holes.

"What a strange volcanic formation," Mabel mused.

"Where are we meant to find the key?" Zoumbrus asked nervously, peering carefully down into the crater. "Are we too late once more?"

Mabel recited the last poem from memory. "The next key, I fear, is harder to take. You'll find it in the middle of a fiery lake. The heat of the place may have caused it to melt, spill common blood to operate the smelt." She gazed down into the bubbling white liquid inside the hole on the left. "Does that look like melted bone to you?"

"I have no earthly idea what melted bone looks like," Zoumbrus said, a hint of disgust in his voice. "It's certainly not lava, though…"

"It must be! It *has* to be! What Elder Alder said must be true," Mabel said, barely able to contain her excitement. "The wizard can't pass the runes onto the island! He's not powerful enough to cross them!"

"You mean he's *too* powerful to cross them," Zoumbrus corrected her.

Mabel got down on her hands and knees and examined the black rock around the craters. "Where do you think you spill the blood?" she asked.

"The more important question is, whose blood are we meant to spill? I find it curiously alarming that that's not your first question."

"We'll shoot hands for it," Mabel said. "If I win, we'll spill yours first, and if that doesn't work, we'll spill mine…and if *you* win, we'll spill mine first, and if *that* doesn't work, we'll spill yours."

"Good grief!" Zoumbrus cried, slapping his hand to his forehead. "Mabel! You macabre thing! Listen to me! In the first place, I do not have blood—not blood that flows, at any rate. It congealed long ago. It's probably the consistency of wood by now. In the second place, I am not allowing my young niece to open her veins into some crater on a lark! In the third place, we have no idea what 'common blood' is, or if you have it, or if even I had it when still my blood flowed! You are being quite cavalier about this whole thing, and, as your elder and the standard-bearer of your lineage, I do not approve."

"Whose blood did you *think* we were going to spill when it came to it?" Mabel asked.

Zoumbrus closed his eyes. "To tell the truth, I didn't expect we would get this far," he said. "Certainly not before the wizard did."

"But here we are. And if your blood is stiff in your veins, then there's only one option." Zoumbrus opened his mouth to protest, but Mabel silenced him with a wave of her hand. "Relax, old uncle. I'm not going to spill *all* of it. I couldn't do much with the key if I were dead, could I?"

"Hrmph," said Zoumbrus. "I still don't like it."

Mabel resumed her inspection of the craters and the curving channel, poking and prodding the stone. "Do you think the blood goes in this empty hole?" She leaned closer and saw that there was a little piece of flint standing at the edge of the channel, closing it off from the empty chamber. "Well, regardless, this bit of stone will have to come out before anything can be done." She reached down and grabbed the flint. It changed shape all of a sudden and twisted itself into a sharp point that drove into her fingertip. "Ouch!" she cried, falling backward and shaking the pain from her finger.

"What? What happened?" Zoumbrus demanded. He hurried over and inspected her hand.

"It stuck me!" Mabel stared down at the pad of her finger and saw a bead of blood ooze up from it. What she did *not* see was the blood that coated the little point of the shape-shifting piece of flint. She didn't see the blood spread down the base of the point, either, and she certainly did not see the little piece of flint morph back into a flat, solid barrier, now covered in a thin veneer of Mabel's blood. Nor did she see the flint melt into the crater, evaporating the barrier between the channel and the empty bowl. But she distinctly heard the *click-click-click-whirrr* as some age-old mechanism spun to life near the volcano's surface. She instantly forgot about the pain in her finger and lowered herself back down to the three craters. "Look!" she cried, pointing down at the crater on the left. The bubbling white liquid was rising in its bowl.

"And look here!" shouted Zoumbrus, suddenly taken with excitement. The rock wall of the empty crater on the right was rearranging itself. Pieces of it broke away and swapped places with other pieces, stacking and adjusting and situating themselves just so. When they were finished, the crater was no longer a smooth, empty bowl. There was a mold of stone, built up on the sides with rocks. The shape of the mold was a key. "Your blood must have set it off!"

"I'm perfectly common!" Mabel squealed, delighted.

The white liquid continued to rise, pushed to the crust of the volcano by some unseen platform lifting from below. When it reached the lip of the crater, it spilled down the channel, arcing its way over to the depression with the key mold inside. It poured down into the stone mold until the left crater was empty and the key shape in the other leveled off. The subterranean whirring stopped and was replaced with another series of clicks, this time emanating from beneath the key mold stones. The rocks crusted over grey with hoarfrost, and the white liquid hissed and steamed against the quickly cooling rocks. The key solidified; it was no longer a mass of key-shaped liquid, but an actual key made of solid bone. The bow of the key was a solid vertebra, circular and knobby; the shaft was a short, gently curving clavicle; the teeth were actual teeth, pearly greyish things, with roots that wrapped around the far end of the shaft.

One of the teeth had a gold filling.

"It's a Skeleton Key!" Mabel squealed. She bounced to her feet and leapt excitedly around the crater. "We beat the wizard! We found the third key!"

"Careful, child—careful!" Zoumbrus cried, snagging her elbow and yanking her back before she could plant a foot into the lava crater. "Fall into the volcano, and it won't matter who got here first."

"But *we* did," she said triumphantly. She reached down into the little crater and peeled the bone key from the mold. It was a little big for her hand, and it was heavier than she'd expected. "The wizard won't be able to open the book without this! Uncle Zoumbrus, we've just saved Brightsbane!"

The dead man rubbed his jaw with one hand. More bits of green skin flaked away. "This is undoubtedly an extraordinary moment. You've done an incredible thing, Mabel, outwitting a wizard, and I don't wish to take away from that…but now that we have the key, what, exactly, do we *do* with it?"

Mabel frowned. "I don't know," she admitted. "I guess we should bring it back to the Elderary?"

"Or perhaps we should bury it deep within the ground and not tell a single soul where it's hidden."

Suddenly, there was an explosion from the base of the volcano, and a puff of blue smoke billowed into the sky. "I have a suggestion," offered a voice within the cloud.

Mabel and Zoumbrus both jumped in surprise. The voice in the smoke was soft, yet strong. It was the voice of much experience. It was a voice under perfect control. It was a voice that could crack stone or cradle a broken heart. It was a voice that could command legions and make mountains fall. It was a voice that could whisper a secret that could carry on the wind for centuries at a time. It was a voice that ebbed and flowed like time itself. It was a voice of steel cloaked in honey.

It was a voice that could only belong to one man.

"The wizard," Mabel breathed.

The old man leaned on his staff and gazed up at them through his clear blue eyes. The points of light on his dark blue robe spun lazily about the folds of fabric, constellations drifting against a night sky. His grizzled white beard was bunched and tied by a loose blue bow far below his waist, and his dark blue cap slouched languidly on his snowy white head. "Mabel Gray, is it? And you must be great-great-granduncle Zoumbrus." The wizard shifted his eyes to the walking dead man. "It has been many, many years since I last saw your face. I did not think to find you looking so...well. How remarkable."

Zoumbrus moved between his grandniece and the wizard. "Leave us be, sorcerer. You cannot cross the runes!"

"Oh, quite right...quite right." The wizard removed his hat and placed it atop the staff. He ran his fingers through his mop of fluffy white hair and crouched to a seat atop a boulder on his side of the white markings. "This spell is quite ancient. It's daemon-made, you know." Then he muttered to himself, "Fascinating creatures, daemons..."

"We're not coming out," Mabel said, crossing her arms. She held the Skeleton Key tightly in her fist. She knew the wizard's magic couldn't pass the runes, but she wasn't taking any chances. That key wasn't leaving her hand without a fight.

"Oh, I doubt that," the wizard said with a smile. He crossed his right ankle over his knee and pulled off his clog. He set about rubbing the sole of his foot. "Walking is a rough business," he frowned. "I should look into one of those flying carpets they have in the desert." He looked up and blinked, as if he suddenly realized he was getting off track. "Where was I? Oh! You said you're not coming out, and I said that I doubt that. That was a clever thing the elder did, drawing the daemons out with the Blacktower Bell. Clever... and foolish. Though I find that many very clever things *are* rather foolish, don't you? At any rate, once the fire daemons have had their fill of destruction, they'll lumber back to the lake. And believe you me, my dear, you'll want to be off this island before that happens...

oh my, yes. Otherwise, you'll never get out. You'll either die of starvation or boil until your tender meat slides right off your bones. None of us wants that." He made a little clucking sound with his tongue.

Mabel scowled. The wizard was right. They couldn't stay on the island forever. But then she had another thought, and she was sure this idea was both clever and not at all foolish. "I'll throw the key into the crater," she decided. "I'll drop it into the volcano, and it'll melt down to goo, and it'll mix with the lava, and no one will ever be able to mold it back into a key."

"How very short-sighted of you." The wizard put his shoe back on his foot and then switched his legs and set to work on his other foot. "If you destroy the key, *The Boneyard Compendium* will remain forever closed. No one will ever be able to open it again... not even the Warden of the Boneyard. Think of the knowledge that would be lost."

"It would be worth it," Mabel said. She moved closer to the crater and held her fist over the opening. "Leave us alone, or I'll drop it in."

The wizard shrugged. He slipped his foot back into his shoe and heaved himself up from his stone. "Well, if that's what you truly want," he said. He plucked his cap off the staff and plopped it back on his head. Then he turned and walked down the island to the water's edge, where his own rickety boat was moored.

"What's he doing?" Zoumbrus asked. "Where's he going?"

"It worked!" Mabel whispered. "We've out-leveraged the wizard!"

But Zoumbrus shook his head. "I don't think we'll have such an easy time of it." And indeed, when the wizard reached the water's edge, he did not climb into his boat and push off. Instead, he turned his staff upside-down and dipped its blue jewel into the water. He closed his eyes and murmured some sort of spell, and the water around the staff began to bubble and boil.

"What are you doing?" Mabel asked, suddenly very alarmed.

Something dropped away from the pit of her stomach, and though she didn't understand how, she had a suspicion that she perhaps didn't have any leverage over the wizard at all.

"If you wish to melt the key, I shan't stop you. But time is short. The daemons might return at any moment, so I'm speeding up the process." The rippling circle of bubbles spread across the water as the wizard's staff heated it to extraordinary temperatures. The amount of steam that rose from the lake suggested that the sorcerer was turning the water even hotter than the daemons did. Soon the little island was surrounded by roiling, popping, hissing water, and the steam was so thick Mabel could only just make out the wizard's blue robe by the pinpoints of light that shone through the fog. She looked down into the crater and saw the lava becoming fussy. It bubbled and popped and began to rise.

"Stop it!" Mabel shouted. "Wait!"

"Feel free to drop it in, if you like," said the wizard.

The lake grew hotter still, and scalding water splashed up the slopes of the island. The lava became tumultuous, rising in sputtering waves and splashing over the edge of the crater. Mabel jumped back and narrowly avoided a glob of hot lava on her toes. "What do I do?"

"I don't know!" Zoumbrus cried. He was presently very distracted by keeping his own feet lava-free. He danced out of reach of the spreading liquid, which crested the crater and spilled over the edge, sliding slowly down the volcano on all sides. Mabel backed away from the slow, viscous slide.

The lava was forcing them down to the runes.

Mabel began to panic. If she threw the key into the lava, all would be done: The book would forever remain closed, and the wizard wouldn't be able to destroy Brightsbane…at least not right now. But the lava was coming whether she threw in the key or not, and if she destroyed it, the wizard had no reason to keep her alive when the red-hot flow forced her back across the runes. If she held fast to the key, maybe—just maybe—the wizard would let her live.

I would like to take this opportunity to address a concern that you might have at this point. Surely you have read stories where the heroine has encountered a similar predicament and has been forced to choose between her own survival and the survival of the many. In the majority of these tales, we see the heroine make a selfless choice, sacrificing herself for the common good. And perhaps we are inspired by this brave choice, and perhaps we think to ourselves, *Gosh, what an incredibly brave young woman, to give her life so that others may remain unscathed.* And sometimes, we may even decide that if we are ever faced with such a decision in our own lives, we, too, shall make the selfless decision to throw ourselves upon the pyre, as it were, and take one for the proverbial team.

But most of those stories are full of bunk. Because, historically, while there have been a number of extremely courageous men and women who have made such a brave and selfless choice, most of us, if given the opportunity to choose, would quiver and shake and bargain and ultimately decide that the rest of humanity can sod right off, because death is a terribly frightening thing.

Therefore, I hope you will not judge Mabel too harshly when you learn that when she stared down the barrel of this very important and very harrowing decision, her brain went into desperate survival mode, and she decided not to toss the key into the lava after all, but to hop across the runes and throw herself on the mercy of the wizard.

I can tell you without shame that I believe I would have done the same thing, with the important difference that, given the position between an evil wizard and an advancing wall of lava, I would likely have reduced myself to a bawling, blubbering mess.

Now, let us return to our story.

The lava pushed Mabel back to the white runes, and she held her breath as she stepped over them, into the wizard's territory. When Zoumbrus saw her cross the threshold, his heart broke a bit. Of course, he was very worried for the fate of Brightsbane, but he was very happy that Mabel had not thrown the key into the lava, for he, too, believed the wizard would strike her down if she did, and the safety of his great-great-grandniece was far more important to him than the future of the village.

The wizard withdrew his staff from the lake with a little exclamation of delight. The water immediately stopped boiling, and the lava cooled on the slope until it became black and hard and immobile. It seeped down to the line of runes but did not advance. Zoumbrus danced away from the cooling lava and leapt across the white markings. The three of them stood in a triangle—the dead man, the wizard, and the waif.

"That was a wise decision," the wizard said. He reached out a hand to take the key, and in that moment, Zoumbrus made a rash decision. He decided his best bet to save Mabel was to take the wizard unaware and wrestle him down to the ground. Maybe, just maybe, this would give Mabel enough time to hop into the boat and start back across the lake. The head start might not do a lot of good, but it might do *some* good, and some was better than none.

And so Zoumbrus Gray launched himself at the wizard. "Mabel, run!" he cried as he sprang through the air. He flew at the wizard with hands outstretched, ready to tear at whatever pieces of the sorcerer he could. There was a snarl on his lips and an undeniable purpose in his eyes. But the wizard did not flinch. In fact, he looked rather bored as he waved his magic staff in the dead man's general direction. A pale force field appeared in the air, and Zoumbrus slammed into it at full speed. His dead, slightly greenish, somewhat-rotted body popped apart at the seams, and his arms, legs, and head plopped to the ground completely separate from his torso and rolled down the slope toward the water. "Oh dear," the head fretted as it skipped down the stones.

"Uncle Zoumbrus!" Mabel cried. "You've killed him!"

"That's quite impossible," the wizard said. "He was killed long ago, and I had nothing to do with it." He waved his staff again, and the force field evaporated. "He may need a few stitches, though." Zoumbrus tried to say something, but his head had rolled to a stop facedown on the rocks, and his voice was too muffled for anyone listening to make out the words. "Come now, child," the wizard said, "may I have the key, please?"

Now that Mabel saw the truth of things, she sorely regretted her decision to cross the runes. The wizard was pure, limb-ripping evil—there was no denying it. And no matter what happened, she would die at his hands on the Steamsoak Island volcano.

She had one last chance to make it right.

"No," she said. "You may not have it." Then she turned and hurled the Skeleton Key through the air and into the crater, where it splashed down into the lava and melted down to white goo, never to be molded into a key of bone again.

At least, that was how she saw the whole thing playing out in her mind.

In reality, as soon as the key left her hand, the wizard winked, and the bone key froze in midair, just before it broke the plane over the runes. Mabel froze, too, fully against her will, and the wizard stepped easily up the hill and snatched the Skeleton Key out of the air. "I thank you for your help, Miss Gray," the sorcerer said, pocketing the bone. "I hate to grab and run, but I've got quite a bit of reading to catch up on tonight. I do hope you'll excuse me." He doffed his cap, held it to his heart, and gave Mabel a low bow. Then he stamped the staff on the rocky ground, and in a puff of smoke, he was gone.

Mabel found herself once again able to move. She felt a deep despair unlike any she'd thought possible. The keys were gone; the spells inside the compendium belonged to the wizard. Her Letter of High Station would never come, and even worse, Brightsbane, along with all its citizens, was doomed.

All because she hadn't had the courage to destroy the key.

"I've doomed us all," she said in utter disbelief as she sank to her knees. "Uncle Zoumbrus...I've doomed all of Brightsbane. The wizard will destroy us all, and it's all my fault." The Zoumbrus head responded by mumbling nonsense into the rock. "I had the key in my hand! I had it *in my hand*! And I just—I just—*gave* it to him!" Tears sprang to Mabel's eyes, and she didn't even bother wiping them away. They spilled over and streamed down her face. "Brightsbane will be reduced to rubble, and it's all because I was too afraid to melt the key." She reached out and picked up the Zoumbrus head. "Why didn't I just melt the key?" she wailed, driving her forehead into her great-great-granduncle's. Zoumbrus opened his mouth to answer, but Mabel shook her head to silence him. "There's nothing left to be said," she whispered. She gathered up the pieces of her uncle, dumped them into the boat, and paddled back to the shore. She laid Zoumbrus' limbs on a blanket left behind by one of the beach couples, then, with her head low and her heart heavy, she dragged him back to the Elderary to prepare for the end of the world.

CHAPTER 14

DIRE DESPAIR, DEPRESSION, AND DEATH

Elder Alder pushed back his smoldering hood, and his entire robe crumbled away in a heap of ash, leaving him standing in his long, white linen shirt. Pieces of the singed robe still flashed orange with the fire that had torn through it. The elder stamped them out. His face and arms were covered in soot, his left hand was pink with a bad burn, and his smoking hair stood up on end.

Overall, he didn't look so great.

But that's what one gets when one mucks about with daemons.

"So…how did it go?" the head of Zoumbrus asked from the floor.

The elder huffed. "I fared better than you did, I'd wager."

Zoumbrus' arms flopped about as they tried to shrug their shoulders. "Fair point."

"Oh, Elder Alder…I'm so sorry." Poor Mabel rushed forward and hugged him, tears streaming down her cheeks. The elder flinched in pain as the girl embraced him, but he did not push her away.

"Sorry for what, child? For a few burns? I've had worse, I'm afraid."

"We had the final key," she whispered, burying her face into his belly so he couldn't see her crying. "I had it in my hands, and I should have destroyed it, but I couldn't, and now the wizard has it, and we're all going to die."

"Oh." Elder Alder stared blankly forward as he patted her on the head. "I see." He paused for a moment, letting the finality of the failure sink in. Then he looked down at the discombobulated

Zoumbrus. "Is that what happened to you, then? The wizard?"

Zoumbrus' head tried to nod. "Popped me apart at the seams," he said sadly.

"Well." The elder peeled himself away from Mabel's grip and pulled the bell rope near the door. "If nothing else, we can fix *that*."

Before long, the Elderary's seamstress bustled into the room, a lopsided, poorly woven sewing basket in tow. She was an elderly woman with thinning white hair and grumpy old gums. She knelt on the floor next to Zoumbrus without a word and set to work stitching his limbs back to his torso. It seemed rather odd to Mabel that she didn't flinch at the unwelcome sight of a disjointed dead man, and that she didn't take a moment to ask how such a thing had happened. Perhaps this sort of thing was commonplace outside the walls of St. Crippleback's.

"So *The Boneyard Compendium* is lost," the elder said softly. Mabel's eyes grew wide with alarm, and she silently indicated the seamstress with her head, but the elder waved her off. "Not much point keeping it secret now, is there? Besides, Mrs. Pucklebuck shan't be telling anyone. She doesn't have a tongue. She's mute."

"She doesn't have a tongue?" Mabel started. She immediately flushed with embarrassment, for it was impolite to call out some-one's handicaps with that someone kneeling five feet away. But the woman kept on sewing and did not seem bothered in the least.

"She may also be deaf," Elder Alder surmised.

"How did it happen? Was it natural causes?" Mabel asked.

"Natural causes? You mean, did her tongue just rot off and fall away with age?" the elder asked, knitting his eyebrows together. Mabel just stared at him and shrugged. Stranger things had happened. "No," the elder continued, "I don't suppose it was natural causes. But I don't know how it happened. Mrs. Pucklebuck can't write, nor can she read, so she hasn't been very forthcoming with information."

"She can't speak or hear or write or read?" Mabel asked, amazed. "How does she get on?"

"She sews remarkably well." And, indeed, she was already finishing up Zoumbrus' left side, and the stitches were so tight, one could scarcely see the seam between shoulder and socket.

"I wonder if she can sew all of Brightsbane back together," Mabel said glumly, plopping down into a chair before the fire.

The elder frowned. "Yes, things do appear to be rather bad just now, don't they?" He joined Mabel by the hearth, taking the chair opposite her own. "I don't suppose we can place hope in the other orphans to accidentally stumble across the wizard's cave in their picking and scraping of Gallows Hill?"

Zoumbrus cleared his throat. "Ah...that's probably unlikely, since I sent them scampering into the desert with my beaconstone."

Elder Alder buried his face in his hands. "That is...unhelpful," he said.

"As somewhat of an expert on Gallows Hill, I'd say it's highly unlikely they would have discovered the wizard's cave anyway," said Zoumbrus. "I died there, you know. On the hill, I mean, not in the cave."

"I don't suppose—"

"No, Elder Alder, I haven't the slightest idea where to find the entrance to his lair."

The elder sighed. He raised his head and brushed at the soot that stained his shirt. "Then I suppose we are lost," he said quietly. "Nothing left to do but wait for the end." He looked toward the ceiling, as if imploring some mystical deity up there. "I'm sorry, grandfather. And father, wherever you are. I've shamed the Alder family and destroyed the village." Then he began to weep quietly.

Mabel squirmed in her chair. It made her feel uncomfortable, watching a grown-up cry. Grown-ups were supposed to be strong, solid, full of confidence. Even grown-ups who were somewhat cowardly were expected to be stoic in the face of imminent demise, and Elder Alder was less of a coward than he let on, for he had successfully lured the fire daemons out from Boiling Lake at great personal risk. But here he was, crying, and it made Mabel feel awkward. She reached out and patted him on the shoulder. "Perhaps we'll be all right," she suggested, though she knew that wasn't possible.

"I don't see how," chimed in Zoumbrus, rather unhelpfully. "There's only one someone in the world who can tell us how to find the wizard now, and that's the wizard himself. I don't exactly expect him to babble on about how he can be stopped."

Mabel gasped. She suddenly became so excited that she leapt from her chair, knocking it over. "Good heavens, child!" the elder said, wiping tears from his eyes. "Are you all right?"

"Uncle Zoumbrus!" Mabel said, ignoring the elder for a moment. "You're a magnificent genius!"

Zoumbrus frowned. "I'm touched, and I prefer to agree, but I'm afraid I don't follow your reasoning," he said. Mrs. Pucklebuck clapped his jaw shut so she could focus on sewing his neck to his shoulders without missing a stitch.

"Why didn't we think of it from the beginning?" Mabel was pacing up and down the elder's chambers now, her hands beating an excited tattoo against her hips. "It would have saved us an awful lot of trouble."

"Would you please relieve us of the suspense, child, and tell us what exactly you're talking about?" Elder Alder asked.

Mabel stopped pacing and stared at the elder as if his head had just sprouted mudroot. "Don't you see? Isn't it obvious? The wizard won't babble on about the entrance to his cave…but there *is* something that *will*!"

Elder Alder opened and closed his mouth many times in rapid succession, looking quite like a lost fish. Finally, he said, "But surely, you don't mean—"

"The Babbling Brook!" Mabel declared, quite pleased with herself. "It's not far north of the village proper. I learned all about it in my geography lesson," she added.

"Surely you don't believe that old wives' tale," Zoumbrus frowned. "The Babbling Brook is the oldest fable in the book."

"Have you been there for yourself?" the elder asked, clearly intrigued, though if he had been asked, he would have been forced to admit that he quite agreed with Zoumbrus Gray on the matter of the brook's probably non-existent powers.

"I have," Zoumbrus nodded. "I asked a question of no small importance, and the brook did nothing but bubble along. Believe me when I say that it absolutely does not work. In other words, the tales of the brook's babblings are a lot of bunk."

"I don't think it's bunk," Mabel insisted. "I believe the stories are true."

"You're a child, you're *supposed* to believe the stories. That's why stories were invented: to convince children of things that aren't true. But I've just told you, the stories of the brook are false."

"Maybe you asked wrong," Mabel said, crossing her arms.

"Asked wrong?" Zoumbrus said, his voice rising in pitch. "Asked *wrong?* And how, pray tell, might someone ask a question *wrong?*"

"There are plenty of ways to ask a question wrong," Mabel insisted. "Maybe you asked rudely."

"Well, what cause would I have to be polite to a creek?" Zoumbrus demanded.

Mabel looked at the elder. The elder looked back at Mabel. "He asked rudely," they said in unison.

"I asked as politely as the circumstances allowed," Zoumbrus grunted.

"But isn't it worth trying?" the elder cut in. "Even if the tales are false, I don't see that we have any other hope."

"It's a waste of a trip," Zoumbrus sighed. "But one last walk under the stars would do us all good, I suppose. If we're going to be imploded or exploded or whatever it is the wizard plans on doing to us, I'd just as soon do it outdoors. But I don't want anyone to get any hopes up about the brook," he said, looking directly at Mabel.

"But hope is exactly what we are supposed to have, I think," she said. "Without hope, we're all just old men crying in front of children by a fire." She glanced nervously at Elder Alder. "No offense, Elder," she said.

"None taken. And you're quite right. If there is hope to be had, then we should have it, and in as great abundance as we can." He reached out and took Mabel's hands in his own. "Let's go, then. The three of us. Let's go seek out the Babbling Brook."

Zoumbrus, now fully restored, clamored unsteadily to his feet with a little help from the old, mute seamstress. He gave the elder a good once-over. "Perhaps you should stay behind and...mend yourself," he said pointedly.

Elder Alder looked at his badly burnt arm. Then he looked down at his soiled underclothes, and he caught Zoumbrus' meaning a little more clearly. "Ah. Yes. Perhaps you are right. My absence might arouse suspicion anyway, and if we are truly going to deal in hope, perhaps we should throw in a hope that none of the other elders begin to suspect that anything's amiss. Will the two of you go, then?"

"Might as well," Zoumbrus said. "Mabel, dear, let's hope you're right."

"I am, I think. At least, I *feel* right. So that's something. Now," she said, pushing up her sleeves, "which way is North?"

CHAPTER 15
BURBLES AND BUBBLES

Once again, our characters' travels give me ample time to fill you in on a bit of Brightsbane backlore without fear of missing an important plot point or two. While Mabel and Zoumbrus Gray make the trek from the Elderary to Parts Up North, I shall regale you with a brief synopsis of the Tale of the Babbling Brook. We should have just enough time, for the walk is not terribly long, but just long enough. Let us count ourselves fortunate that none of our characters owns a horse or some sort of bewitched cart, or else they would be too speedy to give us occasion to examine this auxiliary tale. I suppose it's unkind to express joy over the fact that Mabel and Zoumbrus are forced to walk, for as the wizard himself has already stated, "Walking is a rough business." But we may allow ourselves a small moment of merriment, for there is nothing in the world quite so wonderful as a full and satisfying story.

The Brightsbane Babbling Brook was a small offshoot of the larger Brightsbane River, and it was really not much of a babbler at all. In fact, it almost always declined to speak (ever so politely, you understand). When it *did* speak, though, its words were well heeded, because it spoke the absolute truth. If you stood at the edge of the little creek and whispered a question, the water would respond with the correct answer, no matter how difficult it was to come by. The brook's knowledge of the world was unlimited.

However, like so many wonderful things in fairy tale lands, the brook had a catch: each person could only receive the answer to one question in his or her lifetime, and never another.

This was a big predicament, as you can imagine. For example, you might ask, "Where will I find true love?" and the brook might respond, "In the marketplace." And that is all well and good as far as answers go, but *which* marketplace, and *where* in the marketplace? *When* at the marketplace, and *how* at the marketplace? *What will you be wearing* on that day in the marketplace? Will there be any false loves that take you by surprise in the marketplace *before* you end up finding your true love in the marketplace sometime later? Or you might ask, "What should I study at university?" and the brook might say, "You should study polyology," and you could rest assured that polyology was the field for you, but *where* should you attend university for polyology? Which school has the program best suited for you? Which branch of polyology should you focus on? Transformosis? Spectricism? Duobiologics? There are many follow-up questions that are necessary to really cement the truth of the thing, but you would not be able to ask them. Or, to be more specific, you could ask them all you wanted, but the brook would betray nothing more.

All of this, at least, is what the stories led one to believe. Mabel liked to think they were true. But, as we have seen, Zoumbrus was of quite a different opinion. He thought the brook was unlikely to babble at all…not even a little bit.

I suppose we shall have to wait and see.

Fortunately, we will not have to wait long, as Mabel and Zoumbrus have just reached the Parts Up North and are very, very close to the Babbling Brook.

The brook was very small by any reliable nautical standard, stretching just four feet wide at its very widest point, and often diminishing itself to a rivulet of no more than a few inches at certain points during the dry seasons. If you did not know it was the Babbling Brook, you would likely mistake it for some sort of runoff (though runoff from what, I do not know, since, as I have already said, Brightsbane was really very flat, and Gallows Hill loomed on the opposite end of the village). But there was one area of Babbling Brook that was really quite charming. Just beyond Lady Snickerton's stone farm (where the very best rocks in Brightsbane were harvested), the brook dipped into a little cove hidden in a thicket of leafy ash trees. It paused for a moment or two in a shallow pool before spilling under a rather charming footbridge that some nice person or other took the time to build long before our once upon a time. The brook then continued on through the edges of Brightsbane, trickling along in a decidedly mundane manner.

Perhaps it was the seemingly magical nature of the little cove next to the Snickerton farm, or perhaps there was some sort of enchantment in the grass. Whatever the reason, most people who sought out Babbling Brook for its truth-telling properties wound up approaching the banks within this little cove, even though it was hardly the most convenient way to arrive at the creek. Mabel and Zoumbrus were no exception to this strange rule of nature, and even though the walk was a bit longer than it had to be, they eventually found themselves pushing aside the leafy branches and easing themselves down the slippery grass hill to the water's edge.

"I'd forgotten how lovely it is here," Zoumbrus said, just before he lost his footing and slid the rest of the way down the slope on his back. "Though a staircase wouldn't go amiss," he groaned.

Mabel eased herself down to the water and peered into the gentle stream. "How is it supposed to work?" she asked. Then, very quickly, lest there be any confusion from the brook thinking it was being addressed, she added, "Uncle Zoumbrus! How do you think it works, Uncle Zoumbrus?"

"I just stepped up and asked it a question."

Mabel glanced doubtfully down at the water. "It doesn't look very magical," she said glumly.

"It's magical, all right," rumbled a low voice just behind Mabel. "What are you going to ask it?" The girl jumped with a little squeak and picked up a rock from the water. She held it up, ready to hurl it at the person who had snuck up behind her. But there was no one; only the grassy hillside, the trees, and a mossy stone outcropping set into the bank.

"Who's there?" she demanded, gripping the stone. It dripped

down on her head, and she shook off the drops, hoping that the accidental spilling of water on herself didn't make her look less menacing.

"It's just me." They heard the voice as clear as a bell, and it sounded as if it were coming from somewhere very close, but there was no one there, and not a single shadow stirred in the darkness.

"What sort of sorcery is this?" Zoumbrus demanded. "Voice trickery is considered low magic, you know," he added, hoping that insults would drive the creature in the shadows from its hiding place.

"There's no sorcery here," rumbled the voice. It sounded like two slabs of granite rubbing past each other. "I couldn't be in plainer sight." Then the outcropping of mossy stone blinked, and Zoumbrus wheeled backward in surprise, splashing down onto his backside in the brook. The stones shuddered and groaned to life. They were not stones at all, but a great, hulking monster, crusted over with hardened grime and spattered with lichen. "No one cares to see the monster," it grumbled. "Always looking away, always pretending he's not there."

"It's just that you blended in so wonderfully with the hillside," Mabel said. She strode forward and offered her hand to the monster by way of proper introduction. "I'm Mabel." One day ago, she might have run and hid from the great, heavy creature, but she had done much in the last few days, and she was much braver now than she had been before. After all, once you face an evil wizard, three fire daemons, a Riddle Raven, a Bad Witch, Devilden monsters, a murder of crows, and a Boneyard warden all in one day, you can handle just about anything.

The monster looked down at her hand suspiciously, but he took it in his own and gave it a good shake. His skin was rough and cold, and a little wet, too. It made Mabel's stomach turn a bit.

"Don't you have a name?" she asked.

"I've forgotten it," the monster grumbled.

Mabel crossed her arms and tapped her chin. "Maybe it was

Grommert?" The monster raised an eyebrow. Zoumbrus did the same. They both stared at Mabel. "What? He looks like a Grommert."

"I didn't always look like this," the monster muttered. A hungry gleam filled his eyes as he sized Mabel up. "Are you a good girl or a wicked girl?" he asked. His great, rough tongue licked his stony lips.

"She is an extraordinary girl," Zoumbrus said, floundering out of the creek and taking up his position by Mabel's side.

The monster eyed him slyly. "Are you her rightful guardian?" he asked.

Zoumbrus frowned. He looked down at Mabel. Mabel looked back up at him. "In a fashion, I suppose," the dead man decided.

"Would you like me to gobble her up?"

"Good gracious, no!" Zoumbrus cried. "Why would you ask such a thing?"

The monster shrugged his boulder-like shoulders. "Some guardians want their children gobbled up, they do." Somewhere deep inside of him, his stomach rumbled. "Tell me if you change your mind." The monster turned back toward Mabel. "What are you going to ask it, girl?"

"I don't believe that's any of your business," she said, folding her arms.

"Why so curious?" Zoumbrus asked suspiciously.

"I ask everyone," the monster said. "Do you know what you'll ask for? Or haven't you sorted it out yet?"

"I came all this way, didn't I? I think I know what to ask, thank you very much."

"No need for a tone," the monster said, sniffling. "Some people think they know what they want to ask, then they get here and have cold feet. I did that."

"You did what?" Mabel asked. "Got cold feet?"

The creature nodded. "Very cold, indeed. I've been sitting here for over five hundred years, trying to decide what to ask."

"Over five hundred years!" Zoumbrus cried. "That's preposterous!"

"Says you. *I* think it's preposterous that someone would know what to ask right away. You only get to ask one question per lifetime, you know."

"Well, I don't recognize you, and I was here not even a century ago," Zoumbrus said smugly.

"You didn't recognize me this time around either, did you? Not one for observation."

Mabel was astonished. She couldn't imagine spending five hundred years doing *anything*, except maybe decomposing down to dust and air. "What question did *you* come here to ask?"

"I was lost when I stumbled upon the brook," the monster said, "so I thought I'd ask directions."

"And why didn't you?"

"I almost did. But then I saw the sign that said you only get one answer per lifetime."

"What sign?" said Zoumbrus, looking around. "I don't see a sign."

The creature looked at him as if a more foolish statement had never crossed his ears. "Of course you don't. What sort of sign do you think would stand for five hundred years?" he asked. He shook his head and pointed to a spot next to a bend in the creek. "It was there. It rotted away some centuries ago."

"Was it written in rhyme?" Mabel asked on a whim.

The creature nodded. "It was."

Mabel smiled. "The brook's magic must be real, then. The Warden of the Boneyard said everything spoken in rhyme was great and important."

"It is," the creature said. "The brook answers, all right."

"Ridiculous. *My* question wasn't answered," Zoumbrus said.

The monster shrugged. "You must have asked wrong."

"Told you so," Mabel whispered.

"The brook *does* answer," the monster continued, "and only one question, as promised. So I began to think, what might I ask that's more important than directions? Should I ask about my lot in life? Should I ask who made me? Should I ask what I'm meant for? Should I ask when I'll die, or *how*? I was crippled with indecision. I have been sitting here thinking about the right question to ask for five hundred years." He sat back down on the hill. "I think I might be here for five hundred more. I haven't come close to settling on a question. So I ask you again: do you know what you're going to ask?"

"Yes," Mabel said. "We came all this way just to ask it." She decided there was no harm in telling the monster her question, as he was likely going to overhear her ask the brook anyway. "I'm going to ask how to find the cave of the wizard Croup."

The creature snorted. "If you ask how to find the wizard's cave, you'll be told how to find the wizard's cave. But what if it's locked? Won't you wish you'd asked how to open the door?"

Mabel opened her mouth to respond, but she stopped before sounds fell out. She closed it again and thought for a moment. "Hmm," she said. "I hadn't thought of that."

The creature nodded. "That's the way of it," he said.

"Come to think of it," added Zoumbrus, scratching at the new stitches on his shoulder, "shouldn't we ask what to do once we find the wizard in his cave? How do we expect to get the book back? With a pair of smiles and some passably good manners?"

"I wouldn't mind knowing if we'd survive the encounter," Mabel said grimly.

"Have a seat." The creature patted the grass next to him. "This thread takes much time to unravel."

"But we haven't *got* time," Mabel said. She glanced over her shoulder at the little brook. It burbled and bubbled innocently along. "We have to find the wizard *now*. I think the two most important things to know are how to find and enter the cave and how to defeat the wizard. Do you agree?"

"Now that I think on it, I'd like to know how to get back out of the cave as well," Zoumbrus frowned. "But, yes, I suppose those are the two most important questions."

"Then I'll ask how to find and enter the cave, and you ask how to defeat the wizard. But ask it the right way this time."

Zoumbrus frowned. "I'm not entirely sure I'll like the answer to my question one bit."

"Uncle!"

"And how do I know the right way to ask? You, monster, how does one properly ask the brook a question?"

The monster shrugged. "You just walk up to it and ask it."

"Preposterous!" Zoumbrus cried. "I *did* that!"

"Well, you must have done it wrong *somehow*," Mabel said. "Now, do you agree that those are the questions we should ask?"

"Yes, yes, I agree," he said, throwing up his hands. "Let the questions be those, and let us be done with it. The myriad questions I'll never get to ask are starting to flood my brain, and it's becoming quite irksome."

Mabel felt much the same way. If she let herself think about it even a little, she was sure she'd want to ask things like, Will I be an orphan forever? What exists beyond the Desert of a Thousand Steps? Are my parents really, truly dead? So before those questions could root themselves into her mind and blossom into bothersome flowers of regret, she turned to the stream and asked, "Babbling Brook, how will I enter the cave of the wizard who lives in Gallows Hill?" It was a very clever way to word the question.

The water began to roil faster. When the bubbles reached the surface, they popped and exhaled an answer. "You will find and pull the hidden lever beneath the gallows, revealing the entrance to the wizard's cave," said the air as it rose past Mabel's ears. "You will crawl through the hole on your belly and drop head-first into the cavern, knocking your skull on a piece of blackrock and causing yourself quite a bit of pain." The whisper evaporated into the night sky, and the bubbles in the brook thinned until the water resumed its normal easy flow.

"I don't like the bit about my head," Mabel said with a frown.

She splashed the water spitefully with her toes.

"But at least we know where to find the wizard!" Zoumbrus cried, overjoyed. "I can't believe the brook worked! What a wonder! And a hidden lever, set into the gallows? To think, I swung there for several hours and was positively none the wiser."

"You swung from the gallows?" asked the great, mossy creature from his seat in the grass.

"For a time," Zoumbrus said.

Mabel scrambled up the hill. "It's your turn, Uncle Zoumbrus. Hurry, and we'll be off."

Zoumbrus squatted close to the surface, lest he mishear the gentle murmur of the water. "Babbling Brook," he shouted, as if speaking to someone nearing total deafness. "How will we defeat the wizard?" He turned his head so that one ear was close to the surface, but the brook did not bubble up, and the water made no whisper. "What did it say?" Zoumbrus asked.

"I don't think it said anything," said Mabel. "Perhaps you should ask again."

"Not again," Zoumbrus grumbled. He turned back to the brook. "Hello! Babbling Brook! I said, how will we defeat the wizard?" But the little creek was silent. Zoumbrus turned and frowned up the hill at his niece. "What did I do wrong?" he demanded.

The creature on the hill snorted. "You died, is what."

"Pardon?"

"You get one answer in your lifetime," the monster said. "If you've swung from the gallows, your lifetime is over."

Zoumbrus gaped at the monster. "That hardly seems fair!" he cried. "I still have life…of a sort, anyway. Look at me! Can a man without life do this?" He lifted his knees in an awkward jig. The knot of thread at his left hip burst, and the sutures began to unravel. The edge of his leg peeled away from his side. "Drat," he cursed, and he set about to work retying his stitches.

The creature shrugged. "I don't make the rules," he said. He closed his eyes and returned to his deep contemplation.

"What a deplorable show of injustice," the dead man muttered as his fingers fumbled with a knot. "When we've finished with the wizard, I shall come back and dam this creek at the source. You see if I don't!"

"Assuming we survive," Mabel pointed out.

"If we don't, it's on *you*, brook." He kicked a stone into the water. "Choke on that," he instructed.

"Fighting with the water will get us nowhere," Mabel said. "It's already so late, surely the wizard is poring over the book while we stand here splashing around. Please, Uncle, we should go."

Zoumbrus sighed. "Yes, of course," he said. "Let's go. It's time to return to Gallows Hill."

Chapter 16

The Cave Beneath the Gallows

Gallows Hill was eerily still as they approached it from the north.

"I guess the other orphans really did scamper off into the desert after our little run-in," Zoumbrus said. He had been in a sour mood for the entire walk from Babbling Brook to the hill, but he brightened a bit with the memory of his extraordinary green light blinding the waifs and strays into a stumbling avalanche of confusion. "That was rather fun," he beamed.

"Or they've been rounded up by the matrons at last, or by the constabulary," Mabel said. "In which case, the matrons will undoubtedly see by now that I'm still at large."

"I wouldn't worry too much about that," said Zoumbrus, his good humor returning. "When we're done here, you'll either have your Letter of High Station, or you'll be dead. Either way, I don't think you need to worry about St. Crippleback's anymore."

Oddly, Mabel took a strange sort of comfort in that.

The trail to the top of Gallows Hill was steep, and it was arduous, but the difficulty of the climb gave Mabel something to think about other than her imminent duel with a centuries-old master of sorcery. She was grateful for every rock she tripped over and every bramble bush she stuck her finger on, for the obstacles cleared her head and gave her focus.

She was also glad, albeit somewhat less so, for Zoumbrus' chipper retelling of the last time he ascended the mountain. The story was a welcome distraction, though it did drag on a bit. "We'd been in the stocks for four days leading up to our trial," he said, tramping up the hillside, "so even when they handed down our sentence, hanging by the neck until dead, it was something of a relief to be out, trudging up the hill to the gallows. It was a clear night, but even so, my brother-in-thievery, Bartauk Fogg, tripped over so many stones on the way up that his knees were bruised worse than his neck when it was all over and done with! The best part, I think, was that the villagers wanted to see us hanged, because there's something of a macabre thrill in it, witnessing the mortal demise of someone who's wronged you. So they followed us up the hill, huffing and puffing and wheezing and falling, and, oh! I shouldn't laugh at the misfortunes of others, but when you're on your way to the hangman's noose, it's the oddest things that lift your spirits. One woman, I think it was Laurelei Bundt, she slipped and fell right over the side of the hill! She tumbled all the way down like a big, fat log, just when we were nearing the top, and since she was a major donor to Mayor Poppet's last three campaigns, he insisted that we wait for the hanging until she catch up. It took ages! It was practically a stay of execution! Oh, and the view from the top, Mabel! There is nothing that can compare. You can see the town square and Slurp-tongue Swamp and Briarbranch Woods and, if the moon is bright and if you squint your eyes, you can even spy the twinkling sands of the desert! Oh, it is beautiful from the top. I never saw such a sight before, and I haven't seen one since." He paused for a moment. "The hanging did dull the experience a bit," he decided.

"Did it hurt?" Mabel asked, hopping over a boulder that had fallen onto the mountain path and nearly falling into a bottomless crevice on the other side.

"What? The hanging?"

"Yes."

"Not at all! My neck broke instantly, it was over like that." He emphasized how quickly it was over with a snap of the fingers that Mabel thought probably sounded quite like the snap of her uncle's neck. "Poor Fogg wasn't so lucky, I fear. He had a very solid neck. Buffered about with plenty of padding. His held strong. He had to suffocate slowly. He said it was quite painful, though one never knew with Fogg. He was always going on about things in the most dramatic way."

They continued their ascent, and Zoumbrus began describing the exquisite craftsmanship of the gallows with smoothly planed and finely carved detail. His admiration for the woodwork was almost palpable, so thickly did his words drip with affection. Mabel, who did not particularly care for the finer details of carpentry, thought she might go mad when he began describing the mathematical perfection of the circular joint knobs inset with outwardly expanding nautilus shapes of sturdy blackwood. She began to wonder about the merits of a *second* hanging when suddenly, to her great relief, they reached the top of the mountain. The gallows themselves rose above at the apex of the curved mountaintop.

"Look!" she said quickly, silencing her uncle with a point of her finger. "We're here!"

"Isn't it exquisite?" Zoumbrus gushed. He actually wiped a tear from his eye. "It's just as beautiful as I remembered."

"It's a princely implement of death," Mabel agreed, for now that she saw the craftsmanship, she had to admit that it was rather fine. She scrambled across the level plane of the hill and began inspecting the ground below the gallows for the wizard's hidden lever.

"Now, don't be too discouraged if you're unable to find it, Mabel," Zoumbrus instructed. "Remember, the wizard is a master of shape-shifting and resizing. His lever might be small enough to be only seen by ants, grub worms, and stunted pixies. Or it might be large enough to comprise this entire mountaintop, and the only creatures who can pull it are giants, Cyclopes, or a mighty and magically enlarged sorcerer. Or it may be hidden in perfect camouflage, covered over by a spell woven with such intricacy and care that the wizard himself tends to forget where he set it into the stone. What I mean to say is, even though we know there's a lever, and even through the brook said you are bound to pull it, we might not find it for hours, perhaps days, and we must be prepared to—"

"Found it," Mabel said.

The lever was a smooth, flat rectangle of stone set into a channel carved into the mountaintop just beneath the gallows. It blended in perfectly, with its dappled black and grey texture, and the darkness made seeing it no easier. But when Mabel moved her head just so, the moonlight caught the flat surface of it just a little differently, enough to make it stand out. It lay more or less directly beneath where a hanging man's feet would swing."

"Good gracious!" Zoumbrus cried. "It was right beneath old Fogg the whole time! If he hadn't been whining so about his shoes being stolen by the villagers, he might have noticed it himself." Zoumbrus shook his head with rueful tenderness. "Oh, Fogg…"

"Do you think the wizard pushes bodies out of the way when he has to get to his cave after hangings?" Mabel asked with a bit of macabre delight.

"I suppose he must," Zoumbrus frowned.

"Well," the girl said, slipping her fingers under the free end of the lever, "here goes nothing."

"Wait." Zoumbrus rushed forward and stayed her hand. "Perhaps I should be the one to do it. I'm already dead, after all. I should go in alone and confront the wizard."

Mabel offered a little smile. "That is very gallant of you, Uncle, but it's my task. It's my fault the wizard was able to get his hands on the third Skeleton Key. It's my responsibility to see this through. And besides," she added, "you don't have a history of holding up well against him."

Zoumbrus covered his neck stitches self-consciously. "Well, you didn't have to make it personal," he said with a harrumph. "But, fine. We'll go in together."

Mabel grasped the lever and gave it a good pull.

A large boulder to her left immediately sprang to life. It hitched up and danced three steps to the right, then settled itself back down on the ground. A small hole revealed itself in the vacated space. Mabel and her uncle approached it cautiously.

"It's quite small," Zoumbrus frowned. His head would fit inside, but his shoulders never would. "The wizard truly must shrink himself down to fall through."

Mabel nodded. "It's small," she agreed, "but not too small for me." She swung her feet down into the hole and perched on the edge. "Wish me luck," she said.

"Absolutely not! Mabel Gray, you are not plunging into the depths of a wizard-infested cavern all on your own without any sort of protection whatsoever!"

"I've got my reflectoken," Mabel insisted.

"A reflectoken that works on *Shimmers*, not *sorcerers*!"

"We don't know that for sure," Mabel pointed out. "And I've still got your beaconstone. That's not nothing."

"It's not nearly enough!" Zoumbrus cried.

"It will have to be. Unless you want to untie yourself and come down in pieces."

Zoumbrus crossed his arms haughtily. "Certainly not."

"Then I'm afraid you'll just have to cross your fingers and hope for the best." Mabel hesitated. "If I die, I want you to know, I'm very glad we met." Then she dropped down into the hole, leaving Zoumbrus alone, and aghast, atop Gallows Hill.

"Mind your head!" he called down.

But Mabel had already cracked it on a stone far below.

CHAPTER 17

REGINALD

Mabel lay in a puddle of something cold and wet that she hoped upon hope was water. The world around her was filled with colorful lights, and they swam about her head in a slow, lazy dance. Her forehead throbbed, and for a few moments, she couldn't remember why. But she touched her fingers to her brow, and they felt something wet and warm, and the fall came rushing back to her. She couldn't see the rock she'd collided with, but she had sure felt it. She blinked hard, and the swimming lights pulled themselves together and firmed up a bit.

She sat up with a groan. Her head throbbed, and a small stream of blood trickled down her forehead and over her nose. She wiped her sleeve against her head and winced with pain.

Babbling Brook had been nothing if not accurate, she reflected.

She didn't know how far she had fallen, but it must have been very far, for she couldn't see the opening of the cave above. "Uncle Zoumbrus?" she called. Her head pounded with the effort of calling out, and her echoing voice bouncing through her ears didn't help matters much. She closed her eyes and waited for a response, but none came.

She was officially on her own once again.

She pushed herself up to her feet, and the ground pitched about beneath her. She threw out her hands and caught herself on a wall of stone. "This head wound is disagreeable," she decided aloud. She dabbed at her cut with her shift, and it came away soaked through with blood. She reached down with a mind to tear away a bit of her pants cuff to serve as a bandage, but in the darkness, her hands brushed against a small bulge in her front pocket. She reached in and pulled out the contents. "The moffat mushrooms!" she cried. She picked out a very small mushroom and sniffed it. It smelled like peppermint and copper. "Well," she decided, "if it works for Devilden monsters, surely it will work for a small person like me." She popped it into her mouth and cautiously began to chew.

The mushroom tasted like a tingle.

Ridiculous! you may be thinking. *"Tingle" is not a taste!* And I wish I could agree with you, for a narrator must be as agreeable as possible. But the simple fact is, you're wrong. You only do not *think* tingle is a taste because you have never tasted tingle. You might have tasted things that *do* tingle, but unless you've ever had a moffat mushroom, you've never actually *tasted* a tingle, for the moffat mushroom is the only food in history with that particular flavor. If you wish to experience this singular taste for yourself, you'll have to find your way to the Briarbranch Woods, which only existed very long ago. Do pack a sweater for your trip if you go, though; it tends to be quite chilly in Brightsbane.

Mabel chewed with caution; the tingle taste was a surprise. She also detected a hint of cranberry and just a touch of pine needle, but they were all but lost in the overpowering taste of tingle. As she chewed, something strange began to happen. It wasn't that the ache in her head began to subside, though it certainly did do that…and the dulling of the pain was very welcome. Something greater occurred, though: The gash in her head crackled to life, and the skin seemed to repair itself. Mabel reached up and touched the wound. Sure enough, the skin was knitting itself back together. The blood that flowed down her brow dried into a thin crust and flaked away, and the swelling quickly deflated. In just a few seconds, the entire cut was completely healed, and there was not a single trace that she'd ever had an injury at all.

Other aches and pains melted away, too. She'd banged her elbow on the way down, but that dull ache was suddenly no more. She'd scraped her knee at the orphanage last week, and she felt that scar mend itself, too. Though she was still wet, even the chill she felt from landing in the cold water evaporated. Her back now felt comfortable and warm.

"What an astounding bit of magic," she whispered. "I'm certainly glad I waited to deliver them to Mr. Abernathy." She placed the rest of the mushrooms safely back into her pocket and hoped that she would have a chance to bring them to Devilden before morning.

Thus restored, she eased herself off the wall and took stock of her surroundings. The bright lights around here were actually softly glowing gems of extraordinary color. There were emerald greens and rosy pinks and buttery yellows and fiery oranges and oceany blues. The stones glowed as if lit from somewhere deep inside, and they ranged in size from Mabel's Fist all the way up to Bloated Pumpkin. They were set into the cavern walls, filling it like stars in the night sky.

"They're so beautiful," Mabel murmured. She reached a hand out to touch one of the pink stones.

"And perfectly magical," intoned a stolid voice from the darkness.

Mabel gasped and drew her hand back, quick as an asp. "Who's there?" she demanded. She stepped back into a dimmer space between glowing stones where she might be a little better hidden and pressed herself flat against the wall.

"My name is Reginald," said the voice in the darkness. "What's yours?"

"You're not the wizard?" Mabel asked, equal parts disappointed and relieved.

The voice laughed gently, an uncomfortable chuckle that echoed through the cave. "Goodness, no. I'm something of a different sort." Two new gemstones sparked to life farther down in the cave, dazzling in their deep purpleness. Mabel tilted her head with curiosity, watching as the two stones moved in tandem down the long, dark tunnel, bobbing from side to side in perfect synchronization. Then the gemstones blinked, and Mabel gasped as she realized they were not gemstones at all, but eyes…glowing, violet eyes. "Won't you come closer?" the creature with the glowing eyes said. "You're so far away, it's difficult to see you, and I dare not venture farther and risk abandoning my post."

"No, thank you," Mabel said, backing away from the eyes.

"Such a polite thing, yes, yes. But there's no use *not* moving forward. Forward is the only way to go, you know, unless you are a creature with wings. Are you a creature with wings, polite thing? A fairy, or a billow beetle, perhaps?" The creature with glowing eyes sniffed in the air; Mabel could hear it draw a long inhale. "You do not smell like a fairy or a billow beetle, thank goodness…there is no scent as peculiarly distasteful as that of a ripe billow beetle."

"I'm not a fairy or a beetle," Mabel said. She took another step back, and her heart sank as the back of her foot struck stone. She had hit the wall, and there was no more room left to retreat. "Are you going to eat me?" she asked.

"I suppose that depends," said the glowing eyes. "Do you deserve to be eaten?"

"I don't think anyone deserves to be eaten."

"I have met *many* people who deserved to be eaten."

"Well, I don't think I'm one of them," Mabel said. "I'm a decent enough person."

"Then come forward; you might have nothing to fear."

Mabel bit her lip. She had bitten it so many times today, in both indecision and fear, that it was growing raw around the ridge. She crept forward slowly, keeping to the shadows as much as she could. The glowing gemstones lit a dim path down the tunnel, but they were not nearly bright enough to shine a revealing light on the creature. Mabel remembered the beaconstone in her pocket. Its light would be more than enough to reveal the creature at the other end of the tunnel, and surely enough to blind it so she could hurry past. But she couldn't remember the words that would bring it to life. Beacon on? Beacon beam? Beacon blaze? None of those seemed familiar. "What sort of thing are you?" she asked as she shuffled along in the darkness.

"I—well, I'd rather not say just now," the creature said, sounding embarrassed. "I'm afraid you'd judge me harshly, and without cause."

Mabel slipped on a loose bit of wet stone and threw one hand out for balance. It landed on a yellow gemstone, which was warm to the touch, but not overly so. The stone jiggled in its setting, loose as a tooth. *I wonder,* thought Mabel. The creature in the darkness had said that the stones were magical, after all...

"You must be something horrid indeed, if the very mention of it would make me think ill of you," she said in as normal and unremarkable a voice as she could muster. "Are you an ogre?" She pried her fingertips beneath the yellow stone as she talked, trying not to shake it too much.

"An ogre!" gasped the creature with glowing eyes. "Good grief! That I should be as simple and obnoxious as an ogre! No, no—certainly not that."

"Then a rotten ghoul, perhaps?" Mabel wedged her fingers under the gemstone far enough to be able to pull it out.

"A ghoul!" wailed the voice. "What business would a horrible ghoul have in a cave? Do you know nothing of ethereal phantoms? Where do you go to school? Oh, but a ghoul...the awful things you think of me already! I'm nothing as awful as all that, and I am better than what I am would have you think. Come forward, come closer, and I shall endeavor to explain, yes, yes."

"Okay," Mabel said. "I'll come closer." But instead of taking another step, she pried the gemstone out from its place in the wall and heaved it down the tunnel. The glowing eyes recoiled in surprise as the stone crashed to the floor and clattered down the tunnel. The eyes disappeared entirely into the darkness. As the light approached, Mabel saw why: the creature had covered them with huge, leathery wings, making them invisible in the darkness. Mabel also saw exactly why it didn't want Mabel to know what it was... because it was a huge, black-scaled dragon.

"Eeeeek!" the dragon squealed, shielding itself from the gem. "Eeeeek!" It stood like that for several long moments, hiding behind its great wings as the stone came to a stop at its feet. Then, slowly, it pulled its wings down and peeked over the edge. "Is it exploding?" the dragon asked.

Mabel's eyebrows twisted themselves suspiciously above her eyes. "It…doesn't seem to be," she said.

The dragon breathed with relief and wiped a bit of sweat from its scaly brow. "Thank goodness. You must not know the magic word to bring it to life." It poked the gemstone cautiously with one toe, and the stone clattered around on the stone floor, and it did not explode. "Phew."

"You seem rather scared, for a dragon," Mabel pointed out.

"You would be too, if you knew what these gems were capable of," the dragon said. Then it realized what Mabel had said and glanced sadly down at its large body. "So you can see what I am, then," he said.

"I don't mean any offense, but it's rather obvious, with the light and all." Mabel grabbed a few other stones out of the wall and rolled them down the tunnel, just to shine a little more light on the massive beast. It shied away from them as if they, too, might explode. But of course, none of them did, for as we have already noted, Mabel did not know the proper words.

"You might as well come closer now," the dragon said miserably. "Let's get this over with."

"So you *are* going to eat me," Mabel said glumly.

"Not necessarily," the dragon said, brightening a bit. "I only *sometimes* eat people who pass through!"

"How often do people pass through?" Mabel wondered aloud.

"Not very often," the dragon admitted. "In fact, you're the first in a long, long time. I hadn't encountered a visitor since the Time of Change, and that was ages and ages ago."

"What happened to that visitor?" Mabel asked.

"I ate him."

She clicked her teeth nervously. The only way out was in, and if the dragon didn't eat everyone who passed, there was still a chance. She began to walk cautiously forward. "How do you determine whether or not you should eat me?"

"Ah! I'm so glad you asked—yes, yes!" The dragon retrieved something from behind him and turned back with the thing in hand. Mabel saw a large board of slate, from which the dragon blew off a great cloud of dust. A little plume of fire belched out at the end of his exhale, and the slate began to smoke. The dragon waved it crazily through the air to cool it. "Sorry about that," he said, clearly embarrassed. "Now, this is a list of questions I've been instructed to ask anyone who would enter here to see the wizard. If you answer well, then you'll be free to pass into the sorcerer's chambers."

"And if I answer poorly?"

"Then it is my duty to dispose of you through esophageal means. Are you ready?"

"As ready as I'm likely to be," she said. *Dying alone in the throat of a dragon is no worse than dying with everyone else at the hands of a wizard's spell*, she told herself.

She wondered if it was true.

"Question one: what is your name?" The dragon placed a claw humbly over his heart and said, "As I have already mentioned, my name is Reginald."

"I'm Mabel. Mabel Gray." She gave the dragon a little curtsey, because a little bit of politeness is never a bad thing.

"It is a distinct honor to meet you, Mabel Gray. I hope I won't have to eat you. But you're doing remarkably well so far!" He made a little mark on the slate board with one of his claws. It squealed into the stone as he etched a small checkmark, and goose pimples popped up all over Mabel's skin. "Question two: what business have you with the wizard?"

"I'm here to reclaim something that the wizard stole from the Elderary," she said, surprised by her own bluntness. But you see, dear reader, when one's back is against the proverbial wall, one often realizes that one has nothing to lose by speaking the truth.

"Hmm." Reginald furrowed his brow in the most troubling manner. "There's no check box for that sort of answer, no." He turned the slate board over and read down the back. "Ah! Then it calls for question two, sub-question one. Do you mean harm on the wizard?"

Mabel had to think about that one. She didn't necessarily want to harm him, but she certainly *would* harm him, if it came right down to iron tacks, and if she were able. But she decided that willingness to harm someone and meaning to harm someone were two different things, and so she said, "No, I do not mean him harm."

"Oh, that's very good!" Reginald made another squealing checkmark on the slate board. "You're doing very well." He leaned forward conspiratorially and whispered, "I'm not supposed to tell the candidates about their progress, no." He said it with a self-satisfied little chuckle.

"Oh. Um…thank you," Mabel said.

"You're most welcome, yes! Now, question three: do you have an invitation from the wizard?"

"An invitation?" Mabel asked. "You mean, a formal letter of sorts?"

"Yes, yes—that, exactly! Do you have one?"

Mabel frowned. "No."

Reginald's face fell. His snout seemed to droop with disappointment. "You don't have an invitation?" he whispered gently. Mabel shook her head. "Oh." The dragon cleared his throat and reached down at the slate with a shaking claw. He drew a slow, small X in the last check box. "And you were doing so well," he sighed.

"Does every visitor need one?" Mabel asked.

"Every visitor who wishes not to be eaten." The dragon tossed the slate over his shoulder and settled down onto his belly. "I'm so very sorry, Mabel. You're a nice and brave little creature. I regret having to eat you." He opened his massive jaws and lay his chin flush against the floor. "Climb on in—yes, yes."

Mabel hesitated. "I'd rather not," she said. She suddenly decided that dying alone in a dragon's throat was *not* the same as dying in a group of townspeople from a wizard's spell, and she felt herself becoming desperate to find a way out of her current predicament. She grabbed glowing gems from the walls and hurled them in all directions, hoping against hope that they would illuminate a new escape route, but each glowing ball clattered against solid stone, and the light they threw revealed only solid walls of rock.

With the dragon blocking the tunnel, there was truly no way out.

Mabel tiptoed closer to the dragon's snout. "Reginald," she said, working hard to keep her voice even. "I forgot. I *do* have an invitation, it's just that I left it in my room."

Reginald squinted at the little girl. "Is that a truth, or is it a lie?" he asked. "Be honest, please, I can't bear to be lied to." Great, purple tears leaked from the corners of his eyes and splashed to the cave floor.

"I—I—I—" Mabel knew her life may well depend on the lie, but the dragon's sincerity touched her heart, and it sank like a stone in her chest. "It's a lie," she admitted.

The dragon began to weep. "I thought so," he said. "In you go, Mabel. Let's get it over with quickly."

Mabel was overcome with chills as she stared down into the creature's gaping maw. A fire burned somewhere deep in Reginald's throat, casting a shade of light into his mouth, but it was still awfully dark down there. "Might I bring a stone of light in with me?" she asked. "So I can see the way?"

"I should think you wouldn't want to," Reginald said miserably. "But I suppose if it gives you comfort, then please, yes, yes, by all means."

"Thank you." Mabel picked out a particularly bright green stone and carried it before her like a torch. The reflectoken at her wrist seemed to have no effect on the dragon, and that was too bad. She paused outside Reginald's mouth and reached in with the gemstone. "It's awfully slimy inside," she said.

"I'm sorry about that," Reginald said, sounding genuinely contrite. "I haven't eaten in so long, I'm afraid I've been salivating quite a lot."

Mabel glanced frantically around for something—*anything*—to offer salvation. With the help of the green gemstone, she could see an opening between the dragon's flank and the wall, an opening large enough for her to squeeze through. But running was futile; Reginald would fry her to a crisp before she'd gone four lengths. *Maybe it will all be over quickly*, she hoped.

She stepped onto the dragon's tongue.

"Your shoes taste dirty," Reginald said sourly as Mabel stepped inside his mouth.

"They've got dirt on them," Mabel said, rather churlishly. We may excuse her for a bit of unkind behavior, I think, for finding oneself in a dragon's mouth is a good a reason as any for taking a turn of temper, don't you agree?

Mabel was thinking of other churlish things to say, a set of uncivilized last words to utter so that she may leave some sort of mark on a world that would otherwise not miss her all that greatly, when she noticed something curious about Reginald's throat—or should I say, *throats,* plural. For you see, with the help of the green light, Mabel discovered that the dragon had two separate throats. The orange glow of the dragon's fire lit up the lower throat, but the upper, larger throat was dark. Mabel could just make out a bouncing uvula dangling there.

"You have two throats," Mabel called from inside the dragon's mouth.

"Yes, of course," Reginald replied, careful not to crush Mabel in his mouth as he spoke. "One for fire, one for food."

Mabel took another cautious step back on the dragon's tongue. She held up the gemstone and lined it up over the fire hole in the dragon's throat. It was just big enough to fit.

Mabel's heart fluttered with a chance at survival.

"Do you breathe out of either of these throats?" Mabel asked, taking one more step.

"Oh, no. We dragons have gills that feed into our lungs through other tubes and tunnels. Why do you ask?"

"Because you're such a pleasant dragon," Mabel said, "I'd hate to suffocate you." With that, she jammed the green gemstone into the dragon's fire throat and skidded back down its tongue and out of its mouth.

"Ulp!" Reginald cried. He lurched back, and Mabel cleared his teeth just in time. She leapt to the cavern floor just as the dragon reared up. Reginald clawed at his neck, trying to dislodge the stone. "What have you done to me?" he cried. He worked up a stream of fire and blasted it up from his chest. The flames pushed against the stone, but Mabel had jammed it in tightly. They had nowhere to go. The stream of fire backed up along Reginald's throat and pushed back down into his chest, where it exploded in a cloud of searing heat. Reginald squealed in pain and toppled over, howling and pawing at his chest, his great wings flapping frantically against the cave walls.

Mabel watched this spectacle with wide-eyed horror. *I've killed him*, she thought with a gasp. *I've murdered the dragon.* But she could not pause to weep for the poor, dying creature, for his thrashing was disrupting the cave, and great mounds of rubble were tumbling to the floor. Soon, the tunnel would be completely covered, and she would be sealed into the chamber with no escape. And so, with her heart heavy with sadness, she skirted past the squirming dragon. "I'm awfully sorry," she said as she leapt over Reginald's thrashing tail. "But you *were* going to swallow me whole." Remembering this made her feel a bit better.

She followed the path of the glimmering gemstones and pushed on deeper into the wizard's cave.

Chapter 18
Mabel Versus the Wizard, and Other Perilous Plans

The number of glowing stones grew as Mabel stepped carefully down the tunnel, descending deeper and deeper into the dark heart of Gallows Hill, and the world became somewhat brighter. The farther she went, the colder and damper the air became, until she was clutching her shoulders and shivering against the chill. She crept close to the glowing gems for warmth, but they had little to offer.

She wound her way down the sloping path, wondering if perhaps it would never end, but would continue on for all eternity, a deadly parlor trick set by the wizard to keep intruders at bay. But just as she began to feel the heavy fingers of claustrophobia close in on her shoulders, the tunnel widened, and Mabel stepped into the hall of the wizard.

It was a starkly beautiful chamber, as long as any Great Hall in the palaces Mabel had read about in her books. It seemed to be bigger than the mountain could bear, and Mabel wondered if she'd wound her way so deeply into the hill that she was below the surface of the earth. A seemingly infinite number of gems radiated with their soft glow, filling the walls, the ceiling, and the floor, too. The great dome above them was supported by a series of massive stalactites that stretched downward and came to a rest atop stalagmites that jutted up from the cave floor, creating row upon row of tall, hourglass-shaped stone columns. The rock formations glowed from the inside, like the gemstones, but their colors changed from green to pink to blue to yellow to purple to orange and back to green again. The slowly shifting colors were soothing, and Mabel wondered if this was what it would be like to live in the sea, where, she knew from her studies, bioluminescent creatures floated about, filling the waters with the most remarkable colors.

In the center of the hall, behind a huge, flat stone that served as a writing desk, sat the wizard himself. His robe hung from a stone hook on the glowing column to his left, and he looked somehow innocent in his white linen plainclothes. He had placed both his hat and his staff on the flat surface of his desk, one on either end. Two yellow gemstones illuminated the contents in the center of the desk, and Mabel could just make out the three Skeleton Keys, lain out in an orderly line. *The Boneyard Compendium* rested quietly in the center of the desk; the three locks had been cast aside, and the book sat open to two pages covered in small script writing.

The wizard was learning his new spells.

"Young Mabel Gray," the old man said without looking up from the book. "What a pleasant surprise! I was hoping it would be you. Please—come in." He waved her forward. "How ever did you manage to get past Reginald?"

Mabel took an awkward step into the hall, suddenly feeling very vulnerable and exposed. She walked with her reflectoken wrist in front of her, just in case. "I slayed him," she said, trying to sound fierce but not entirely able to keep the wobble out of her voice. She wasn't proud of having murdered such a dear dragon, even if his intentions had been somewhat malicious.

"Oh, I doubt that," the wizard said with a smile. "Let's see, shall we?" He looked up from the book and took hold of his staff. He tapped the gem twice against the desk, and a fine mist sprayed forth from the end of the blue jewel. The droplets hung in the air like a thick fog, and an image flickered to life, as if someone were projecting it with a lantern onto an unstable screen. Mabel found herself watching a moving picture of the black dragon writing about on the floor of the cave. He was currently in the process of whacking his chest with his small, clawed hands, and though the image came with no sound, Mabel could clearly hear his cries for help deep in her mind. She was sure that the wizard was showing her poor Reginald's death. But just as she was about to turn away from the awful image, Reginald heaved his hands hard against his sternum, and the green gemstone popped out of his throat and skittered off along the tunnel. The dragon took a deep breath and wiped a flood of perspiration from his brow. He sank happily back against the cave wall and belched out a good spray of fire that seemed to leap right off the canvas of fog.

"You see?" the wizard smiled. "He's right as rain. Quick thinking, blocking off his minor trachea like that."

Mabel was truly relieved that she hadn't killed Reginald after all, but she didn't want to show the weakness of mercy to the sorcerer. So she crossed her arms and said, "I'm sure I'll slay him properly next time."

"Nonsense," said the wizard, waving off her words. "Now come, come, have a seat, we have much to discuss." He winked at the ground in front of his desk, and a fat new stalagmite spun into existence. It had a flat top and was just Mabel's size.

In her head, Mabel made a list of things she needed to do in order to best the wizard and make it out of the cave, with the book, alive. The list went something like this:

Incapacitate the wizard.
Snatch the compendium.
Find a useable exit.
Do not die.

It was a somewhat disheartening list, and one she was rather uncertain how to successfully complete.

"Is this the only way in to your cave?" she asked, trying to sound casual. She walked slowly across the hall, stopping to inspect the glowing columns and the gemstones in the ground. *I must buy myself some time*, she thought.

"The only way in, yes, but there are many ways out." The wizard began to point around the cave. "There's an exit there, and there, and there, and there, and one over there, and two behind that column there." He turned his gleaming eyes to Mabel's, and she felt them pierce her soul. "Why? Are you in a hurry to leave?"

"Just…a little claustrophobic," Mabel said. And it wasn't a lie.

"Well, we can do a little something about that, can't we?" The wizard picked up his staff and cupped the gem with his left hand. He whispered some sort of spell to the stone, and the hall began to expand. The stone walls on all sides pushed themselves outward, and more stalactites and stalagmites sprouted from the new spaces in the ceiling and floor, forming a few dozen more columns. Mabel's heart sank as her exits retreated a bit, but at least she knew they were there. She crossed item number three off her mental list.

She had also hit upon a way to achieve item number one. *The staff is a source of power for him*, she thought. *If I can break his staff, I might have a chance.*

"Could I have a cup of tea?" Mabel asked suddenly, and, I think, rather shrewdly. If there was one thing she knew about grown-ups, it was that they were hopelessly tied to the expectations of proper society, and tea was a thing that could never be denied. Even a brute like the wizard would be expected to serve tea to a guest.

"Of course! Of course! Where are my manners? Things do get away from you a bit when you're secluded, you know. Give me a moment to put the kettle on." The wizard stood from his desk, stretched a bit so his back popped, and ambled over to one of the cavern walls. He plucked out a green stone, a pink stone, and a blue stone, and he put the blue stone where the pink stone had been, the pink stone where the green stone had been, and the green stone where the blue stone had been. Thus rearranged, the gems glowed even brighter, and Mabel heard a loud click from deep within the wall. The rock wall began to shake, and a piece of it broke free and slid open like a drawer, pushing the three gemstones along with it. Inside the open drawer stood a marble fountain filled with water. This, Mabel knew, was the wizard's brewpot.

The wizard picked out a yellow stone from the floor and dropped it into the basin. The water inside immediately began to bubble. "Make yourself comfortable," he said. "It won't be long."

The wizard went along the wall, rearranging stones and sliding open new drawers, looking for teacups and saucers. With his back turned to the desk, Mabel had her chance. She rushed forward and seized the staff from the desk. It was much heavier than it looked, but she was determined, and really rather strong for her age, and she heaved it over her head and brought it smashing down onto the floor. The gemstone shattered into pieces, and the wooden staff snapped in two. The stones situated around the room dimmed, as if in deference to their fallen comrade.

The wizard whirled around, his eyes wide with shock. He held two comically small pink teacups, one in each hand. "Why did you do that?" he asked.

"Because I don't want to be burned to a crisp, or frozen in a block of ice, or swallowed up by newts, or turned into stone, or whatever it is you have planned for me! I've already been made into stone once today, and that's plenty."

"Burn you to a crisp? Turn you into stone? Why in the world would I want to do any of that?" The wizard set the teacups down on the edge of the fountain and pressed his palms together. When he pulled them apart, a new wooden staff grew between them. It had an empty, cage-like knob near the top, and he picked out a purple gemstone from the wall and snapped it into place. The staff glowed with power, and the gems in the cave grew bright once again.

Mabel's heart burned with anger. She had come all this way, she had bested so many obstacles, she had made it all the way to the hall of the great wizard who swallowed the sun, and now he was teasing her. Given all she'd been through that day, it was an insult she couldn't bear. "Why would you do any of it? Because that's the sort of horrid thing you do to children! Because you're awful! Because you're evil! *Because you're the wizard who swallowed the sun!*"

Something clicked in Mabel's brain just then. She suddenly

remembered Zoumbrus' words for making his beaconstone shine. She reached into her pocket and pulled out the little green rock. She held it between two fingers, covered her eyes with her free hand, and said, "Beacon bright!"

The cave exploded with a powerful green flash. The beaconstone flamed white hot in her hand, and she dropped it with a cry of pain. The light sputtered out as the stone hit the floor, and Mabel could see nothing but the bright pink afterimage of the light. She fumbled down on the wizard's desk until she felt paper under her hands. She closed the book and turned to run, but she didn't see the stalagmite chair, and she smashed her shin into its hard edge. She cried out again and went sprawling across the cave floor. The book went skidding over the stone.

The wizard, meanwhile, appeared to be quite unaffected. Mabel didn't know this, dear reader, but I might as well tell you that light-based magic is the first type of magic you learn to counter when you begin wizard training. The old man looked down at the fallen Mabel, his eyesight completely unimpeded, and gave a heavy sigh. "I think you'd better drink your tea," he said. He reached into one of the open drawers and pulled out a little satchel filled with leaves and petals. He dropped it into the bubbling water in the fountain, and the smell of chamomile instantly filled the air. The wizard dipped both cups into the basin and set them on his desk. Then he went over and helped the young girl to her feet. "Mabel, do you know why you're here?"

Mabel pulled her arm from the wizard's clutches and clenched her hands into fists at her side. There was no use in cloak and dagger answers, not now. "I'm here to steal back *The Boneyard Compendium* and return it to Elder Alder."

"Ah!" The wizard clapped his hands together happily. He picked up the book from its place on the floor and set it down on the desk in front of Mabel. "That would be a great kindness. You'll save me a trip!"

Mabel's eyebrows arched so high, they threatened to pop right off her forehead. What sort of trickery could this be? "What are you doing?" she asked.

"Giving you the book," the wizard said pleasantly. "It's what you came for. Please give the elder my regards when you drop it off. And don't forget your remarkable stone." He plucked the beaconstone off the ground and set that before Mabel, too.

"Is this a trick?"

The wizard scoffed. "Certainly not!" He returned to his seat and sipped at his tea. "Do try yours, before it gets cold."

But Mabel could not focus on her tea. Something strange was afoot. She eyed the wizard suspiciously. "Have you already memorized all the worst spells?"

"Spells?" the wizard asked, blowing on his tea. "Is that what the elders told you the compendium is? A book of spells?" There was an unmistakable gleam in his eye.

Mabel frowned. "Isn't it?"

The wizard broke into a laugh. "Not in the slightest!" he said. "My dear girl, *The Boneyard Compendium* isn't a grimoire! It's a history book!"

Mabel blinked. Then she blinked again. "A history book?" she asked.

The wizard nodded. "See for yourself."

Mabel's head felt suddenly very fuzzy. She felt as if someone had just slipped inside her skull and wrapped her brain in cotton gauze. She reached down opened the book.

The Horrible Monster That Gobbled Up Children, read one title. She flipped to another page and found *The Teacher Who Always Wore Gloves*. Then she turned to yet another page and saw *The Boy Who Trucked with Crows*. The book was filled with stories; there wasn't a single line of a spell or a single potion ingredient to be found. She raised her wide eyes up to the wizard. "Are these fairy tales?" she asked, incredulous.

"Some would call them that, yes. But what are fairy tales but histories that we'd rather not fully believe in?" The wizard nodded at her chair. "I think you'd better sit down. We have a few things to discuss." He nodded at Mabel's teacup. "Do you take sugar?"

To be honest, Mabel didn't know if she took sugar or not. She'd never had tea before. In the orphanage, the closest thing the matrons ever served was tepid water. Tea was an adult drink, they said, and waifs and strays were most certainly not adults. But Mabel enjoyed sugar, as a general rule, so she nodded. The wizard's hand gave a little flourish, and a sugar bowl appeared next to Mabel's cup. She dropped in a spoonful and began to stir it absently. "Where are the spells?" she said aloud, though she said it more to herself than to the wizard.

"In some other book, I imagine," the wizard said. "You see, Mabel, things are not always what they seem, and truths are not always as they are told. The elder who told you this was a spell book… he also told you I planned on using it to destroy Brightsbane, no doubt. Or perhaps even the entire world." He gave a sly smile.

"He did," Mabel squeaked. Her throat was suddenly very tight. She felt a little dizzy, and for a moment she wondered if the wizard had slipped something noxious into her tea. But then she remembered that she hadn't drunk any yet.

The wizard nodded and took a thoughtful sip of his own tea. "Did you know that Brightsbane was not always a land of constant nighttime? Long ago—very, *very* long ago—we had a sun. Did you know that?"

Mabel nodded. "Everyone knows that," she said. "And everyone knows that—that—"

"That the evil wizard swallowed it up," the wizard finished. Mabel nodded, and the old man smiled. "It's a remarkable tale, isn't it? As remarkable as it is ridiculous."

"Ridiculous?" Mabel asked. "What do you mean?"

"I mean I can barely stomach mild prickle peppers, much less a burning hot sun!" he said with a chuckle. "And besides, the sun was actually quite large. Even if I could have eaten it, it would have taken ages and ages. I'd *still* be chomping away at the cursed thing."

Mabel couldn't take it anymore. This was all too much. She grabbed up her tea and drank down the whole cup. The chamomile burned down her throat and warmed her from the inside, making her feel a bit better—or a bit calmer, anyway. "If you didn't swallow the sun, why does everyone think that you did?"

"Ah! *That*, my young friend, is precisely the question. *That* is why I borrowed this book from Elder Alder," he said, tapping the compendium. "The answer is in here."

Mabel crossed her arms. "I don't believe you."

The wizard smiled. "See for yourself." He reached over and flipped through the pages until he found a story called *The Day the Sun Set*. "Give this one a read."

Mabel pulled the book closer and squinted her eyes in the gloom so she could read the tale. The words unfurled themselves sinisterly before her eyes, and with each sentence, her stomach dropped away a little more.

I shan't recite the story in its entirety here for you, dear reader, for it is a bit beyond the boundaries of our particular tale, but I can tell you this: the story Mabel read was one of vile betrayal. It was the story of a crime against Brightsbanians of astronomical consequences.

"This can't be true," she whispered when she'd finished reading.

"I dare say, I was surprised myself," the wizard admitted.

Mabel looked up and locked eyes with the sorcerer. "You didn't swallow the sun," she said.

"No. I did not." He tented his fingers on his chest and leaned back in his seat. "It would seem that it was traded away to a faraway land called Dimsdeath."

"Traded by the elders," Mabel said.

"Yes indeed. Not the elders we have today, of course. Their fathers' fathers' fathers. I remember them all, and very well. It's a curse and an embarrassment that I shouldn't have seen them for what they really were back then," he muttered.

Mabel's thoughts were scrambling about in her brain and elbowing each other for superior position. It all made quite a row deep within her skull. "I don't understand," she said, rubbing her temples. "Why would the elders trade the sun—*our* sun—to another village for…" She scanned the story until she found the bit about the barter. "For a potato?"

"The reasons are a part of the story you won't find in any compendium. You'll only find that bit up here," the wizard said, tapping his temple. "Of course, I have no idea what happened to the potato. But I can tell you precisely why they would give away our sun. It all makes perfect sense, and I'm an absolute fool for not seeing it centuries ago. You see, once upon a time, the elders were the largest landowners in all of Brightsbane. You know Farmer Parchrock's field, I'm sure."

"I was there earlier today," Mabel said.

"Ah! The first key, of course you were! Clever girl, clever girl. Yes, well, Farmer Parchrock's is the largest mudroot field in the entire village. But did you know that he does not *own* the field? He only rents it. Guess who holds the title to that particular piece of land."

"The elders?" Mabel said.

"Correct. And you see, mudroot only grows in moonlight. When Brightsbane had a sun, it simply wouldn't grow. Any crop that sprouted became gnarled and stunted. It wasn't until the sun was gone forever that the field became the foundation for a hearty, healthy mudroot crop. The value of that land rose through the roof, and the elders have charged the Parchrocks a pretty sum to work the fields ever since. The elders have grown quite rich off Farmer Parchrock's labors. If they hadn't done away with the sun, the ground would have remained completely worthless."

Mabel started. "The elders traded the sun for a potato because they wanted to make money on a mudroot field?" she asked, bewildered.

"It wasn't *just* the mudroot field. The Elders also oversee the Brightsbane River, and the sun used to dry it up so that in the summers it was little more than a damp rut in the ground. Now that the sun's been done away with, the river always flows, and the trade ships run through Brightsbane all year round. There's quite a bit of money in the trading of goods along the Brightsbane River, and the Elderary takes a hefty percentage of all of it. You may also know that the elders control of the moon pool, and eternal nighttime is much more profitable than a life chronologically bisected by sun's light. No one would pay to pull a miniature sun out of the fountain, it would burn right through their hands! But when the moon is always shining, ah! We get Luna Lamps! Business booms all night, and all day, too. And I'm sure there are more ways they benefit. Those are just the ones I know offhand."

"That's why Elder Alder sent me to track you down and reclaim the book. So you wouldn't put the pieces together," Mabel realized.

The wizard nodded. "I didn't know what I'd find in this book—and in fact, I didn't know that I'd find *anything* in this book. There are thirteen such historical compendiums hidden throughout Brightsbane, you know, and this is only the fourth I've been able to procure. I knew the truth must have been tucked away in one of them; I just didn't know which. But the Elders knew…they needed to prevent me from learning the truth, which is part of the reason I've been locked out of the Elderary all these years, so that I might not swoop in and spirit away their books. When Elder Alder's father passed, though, his protection magic passed with him, and I seized my chance."

Mabel couldn't believe her ears. She sank down in her chair and wondered idly if she could hide here under the mountain for the remainder of her life. "But the elders are good and gracious men," she said quietly. "The finest members of the Brightsbane community."

"Aye," said the wizard Croup, with a sparkle in his eye. "And who started that rumor, I wonder?"

Mabel didn't have to say the answer. It hung between them like a fog.

The elders, of course.

"But my Letter of High Station," she said sadly. Was Elder Alder lying about that, too?

"Is that how they got you to agree to this little errand?" the wizard chuckled. "Well, far be it from me to cost you your great reward. You've been remarkably brave and persistent, young Miss Gray. If you'll allow me…" He reached into his pointed hat, mumbled a secret word, and pulled out a small scroll. He handed it over to the girl.

"What's this?" she asked, her breath catching in her throat. She took the scroll carefully, as if it might be made of needles. She pulled open the red ribbon that held it tight and unrolled the paper.

"It's a Letter of High Station, made out in the name of one Mabel Gray, signed and sealed by all seven elders of Brightsbane."

Mabel gasped. "Is it real?" she asked.

"As real as any letter bearing their seals can be," said the wizard, somewhat cryptically.

Mabel wiped a tear from her eye. Here it was, at long, long last, after all her trials. Not just the ones she'd faced today, but the ones that had plagued her throughout her entire life. This, finally, was the turn of events that promised to change things forever. This was the key to the future she so hungered for, her ticket out of the orphanage and into the world, where she could rise through the social ranks, yes, but more importantly, where she could be free to explore the world and maybe, just maybe, satisfy herself to the truth about her parents once and for all. And now that the wizard had no desire to destroy the world, there would be plenty of time for her to seek out the truth. "Thank you," she whispered.

"You're welcome," said the wizard. "I daresay you've earned it."

Mabel scrubbed the tears from her eyes and wiped her nose on her sleeve. Her cheeks flushed red from having let a stranger see her become so emotional. She tucked the letter safely into the pocket of her shift and pressed against its shape from the outside, reassuring herself that the paper was real. "So," she said, sniffling herself dry and returning her focus to the issue at hand. "Why have you gone to all this trouble of seeking out the different compendiums and searching for the truth? If you're not going to destroy Brightsbane, what *are* you going to do?"

"Exactly the opposite," the wizard said with a sly grin. "Would you like to help?"

Mabel raised her eyebrows. "Me?"

The wizard leapt up from his chair and began pacing the floor of the hall. "Do you remember when you first entered my chambers, I said that I was hoping it would be you? No? Well, I'm sure you had much on your mind. You see, I was expecting *someone* tonight. I didn't know who, but I knew someone would come. I saw it in the stars."

"The matrons say that the stars cannot be read," Mabel said. "They say that the stars do not portend."

"Quite right! Quite right. Not the stars in the sky, anyway. If we relied on *those* stars to tell us our next move, we'd all head north and keep one eye open for the Warrior Dromedary, wouldn't we? I don't read *those* stars, child. I read *my* stars." He gestured toward his robe, and Mabel glanced over at the swirling, spinning points of light against the dark blue background.

"Surely they're not *real* stars!" she said.

"As real as any. Touch them, and they'll burn right through your hand. I read the stars each morning, and today, they told me that I would be joined by a young adventurer who would help me in my quest. That adventurer, it appears, is you."

Mabel couldn't exactly disagree with that assessment. This last day of her life had been nothing if not filled with adventure. "What quest?" she asked.

The wizard gave her a soft, almost sad little smile. "The most important quest in the history of Brightsbane," he said. "The quest to find the sun."

Now it was Mabel's turn to stand. "You want me to help you find the sun?" she cried, incredulous.

"Well, strictly speaking, I don't want you to *help* me find the sun. It would be more accurate to say that I want you to find it all on your own."

Mabel started. "You want to send me out to find it *on my own?*"

"Well, not necessarily on your own. I'm sure that great-great-granduncle of yours would be more than willing to keep you company." The wizard crossed the gap between them and took Mabel's hands in his own. "I must admit, the task is far more treacherous than any you've had up until this point. But the elders have a bit of their own magic, Mabel, and if I leave the village in search of Dimsdeath and the sun, I'll lose what's left of my hold on Brightsbane. The elders will lock me out with their magic, and I'll be forever banished. There used to be other wizards, you see; seven of us all together. There was one wizard for every elder, but one by one, the others were cast out or disappeared, all under extremely suspicious circumstances. I'm the only one left, and if I leave the village, I'll disappear, too. I must stay and do what I can to undermine the elders here, and there's no one else I can trust to go in my stead. Only you, young Mabel, who have proven your bravery, your intelligence, and your mettle. You bested many great obstacles to reach this point, and you managed to find my cave, which no one else has done in the history of Brightsbane. You were the only one clever enough to know where to go to find the compendium's keys when all the other orphans came here to Gallows Hill. You showed great perseverance, and great goodness as well...for even though you didn't kill Reginald to protect yourself, you felt awfully bad when you thought you had, and only a very good person feels guilty about possibly killing a child-eating dragon. Don't you see? The sun still exists, the elders have hidden it away, and you are the only one who can seek it out, restore it to our sky, and mend the greatest wrong in the history of Brightsbane." The wizard patted Mabel's hand and held her eyes in his gaze. "It is no paltry thing that I ask. But will you make a dangerous and ill-advised journey to Dimsdeath in search of the sun?"

Mabel's knees felt weak, and she commended herself on not

falling over, despite the fact that her entire world had just been tipped on its end. The elders were evil, and the wizard was good? The Elderary was the source of darkness, and the wizard's cave was the home of a brave and daring plan to bring back the light? It all ran absolutely contrary to everything she'd ever been taught, and yet, she knew these things to be true, on a very deep and irrefutable level, because, upon some reflection, life in Brightsbane had always felt a little bit anxious. The villagers in town were always just a little too curt. The walls of Devilden were always just a little too high. The annual pageantries in the square were always just a little too rehearsed. The entire village seemed perched on the delicate edge of a knife, where one wrong breath might send it tumbling over the brink.

And the elders—the calm, powerful elders—were the fulcrum.

Mabel had a thought, then. She thought that perhaps there were two kinds of light in the world. There was the type of light that was bright and warm and helped you see in the darkness, but there was also a type of light that was truth, helping you see things for what they really are. And she had an inkling that both types of light were of great and dire importance. Mabel had lived her entire life in the dark in both respects, and even if the wizard was lying, and even if the elders hadn't traded the sun for a potato, the idea that she would not know, she *could* not know, unless she ventured out and discovered the light of the truth for herself, well…now that she'd seen just a flicker of light in the darkness, that thought was too much to bear.

"I'll do it," she said, and the gemstones in the wizard's hall intensified, washing the cavern in color and light. "I'll go and seek out the sun."

The wizard smiled. "Excellent!" he cheered. "Bravo, Mabel. Bravo! Come, I shall pour us another cup of tea. We have much planning to do, young lady, and not very much time. The sooner your journey to Dimsdeath begins, the better."

And that, dear reader, is where our story, *Mabel Gray and the*

Wizard Who Swallowed the Sun, must end, for from this point on, he is no longer the wizard who swallowed the sun, but the wizard who was *wrongly accused* of swallowing the sun, which puts us on the trail to a quite a different and larger story. I hope you will not feel cheated, for we have covered quite a bit of ground in this tale, you and I. And if you have a strong stomach, and if you have not been put off by this first chapter in young Mabel's adventure, perhaps you will join us for the next installment, *Mabel Gray and the Ill-Advised Journey to Dimsdeath*.

For although our current tale has reached its limits, Mabel's quest for light is just beginning.

An Epilogue
That is Practically Dripping
with Danger

Elder Whip stood at the head of the table, his face tight, his mouth pressed into a line of iron. He shifted his sharp eyes around the room, taking measure of each human and creature in attendance. "Viceroy Abernathy," he said, his voice ringing like metal. "What is your grievance?"

"It's *Fullroy* Abernathy now," the little monster grumbled, rising from his chair, "and that is precisely why I'm here. One of your youths of Brightsbane agreed to retrieve a selection of moffat mushrooms from Briarbranch Woods and hand them over to me so that I might assuage the previous Fullroy's terrible toothache, the one that caused him to step down from his office in the end." The little yellow monster glowed with anger. "I traded temporary custody of a very powerful reflectoken to this young girl for services promised, but those services were not rendered. I would like my reflectoken back, and I would like to see the girl punished."

Elder Whip clasped his hands behind his back. "How long ago was this?" he asked.

"One full week last night," the Fullroy said. "I demand satisfaction!"

"Remember where you are," the elder said curtly, his voice frosting over. Fullroy Abernathy blushed, then awkwardly lowered himself back down into his chair.

"One week ago is *precisely* when our sister disappeared!" the Good Witch cried from the corner of the room. She was too upset to sit, and so instead she paced the back wall of the chamber.

"Devilden sends a mischievous girl into the Briarbranch

Woods, and that same night, Belinda disappears?" said the Witch of Neutral Position from her seat at the table, picking a struggling gnat from beneath her fingernail. "The two are certainly connected."

"Not necessarily," Elder Alder threw in. A thin sheen of sweat dampened his forehead. "The idea of a young girl besting the Bad Witch is…well, it's really quite unbelievable."

"We spoke with the statues at the bottom of Belinda's enchanted well!" the Good Witch wailed. "They saw the girl that night and swear she was hoisted from the water by our sister herself!"

"Mmm," Elder Whip said. His eyes bored into Elder Alder's. "Perhaps not so unconnected after all."

Elder Alder wiped a bit of sweat from the palms of his hands.

"What is the rumbling from the Boneyard?" Elder Whip demanded. A small skull launched itself up onto the table and rolled lopsidedly along until it came to a rest before the elder.

"The Warden bade me tell you that one week ago yesterday morning, he recited the Skeleton Key riddles for a young girl who was possessed of quite a bit of bluster. She had dark hair and large eyes, and she seemed like a great nuisance."

"Yes, yes! That's the girl exactly!" Fullroy Abernathy cried.

Elder Whip silenced the monster with a wave of his hand. "And why, pray tell, did the Warden of the Boneyard divulge these secret rhymes to one such as she?"

The skull coughed a bit, and fidgeted its jaw. "He…he would rather not say," it finally said, sounding a little embarrassed.

Elder Whip lifted his eyes to Matron Marble, who sat at the far end of the table. "Shall I presume this girl is one of your many escaped children?" he asked sharply.

Matron Marble sat up straight in her chair and folded her hands crisply on the table. "We have recovered nearly 90% of the children from the desert," she said primly, though the pallor of her face suggested an underlying discomfort. "The only girl we haven't yet recovered is young Mabel Gray. It is theoretically *possible* that she may be the girl in question."

Elder Alder flinched a little at the mention of Mabel's name. It did not go unnoticed by the head of his order.

"Elder Alder," the older elder said, "what do you have to say about all this?"

Elder Alder opened his mouth, but no words came out. What little color was left in his face drained away, and the sweat started running down his cheeks in droplets. "I—I—"

"There is no need for you to say anything," Elder Whip said. "The fact of the matter is this; *The Boneyard Compendium*, which was entrusted to your care, disappeared from your shelves one week and one day ago. We divined the magical records, with the help of our friends the witches." The Good Witch and the Witch of Neutral Position inclined their heads graciously. "It seems your library was without magical protection for almost one full day. Is that correct?"

"It—it is," Elder Alder admitted.

"And in that time, the compendium was stolen from your shelves. Is that, too, correct?" Elder Alder nodded. "So. The wizard broke into your office, stole the compendium, and you did not think to tell me?"

"I—I—thought I could get it back."

Elder Whip's teeth formed themselves into a little sneer. "Did you, now? All by yourself?"

"Yes," Elder Alder said quickly. "All by myself."

Elder Whip cleared his throat. The door to the room swung open, and a small, hunched figure shuffled into the room. Elder Alder's heart sank when he saw who it was: the blind seamstress. "Mrs. Pucklebuck," Elder Whip said, looking directly at the younger elder, "perhaps you could give us your account."

The old woman smiled wickedly, and she plucked up a small feather from the folds of her smock. She stuck the feather into her mouth, swished it around a bit, then spat it onto the table. Those seated nearby shrank away in disgust.

"What an abominable way to act!" Fullroy Abernathy declared.

Elder Whip raised his hand for silence. Slowly, the feather began to rise so that it stood straight up, with its quill touching the table. Thus situated, it began to scribble out words on the wooden surface. The assembled creatures gathered around and read what the quill wrote, which was a perfect record of the scene that transpired in Elder Alder's chambers while Mrs. Pucklebuck sewed up the disjointed Zoumbrus Gray.

"Thank you, Mrs. Pucklebuck," Elder Whip said when the feather had written its final word. "That will be all." The old woman snatched up her feather and stuffed it back into her smock. She flashed her wicked smile at Elder Alder, then shuffled back out of the room. The door closed behind her.

"Well, Elder Alder," Elder Whip said, placing his hands on the table and leaning forward. "What do you have to say for yourself?"

The younger elder closed his eyes. He was caught, and there was no way around it. A ward of the village had come to him and, at his request, had made quite a mess of the village. She had not returned since she left with Zoumbrus to find the Babbling Brook, and the elder knew not where she had ended up. For all he knew, the girl was dead. If she was not, she would soon find the might of the Brightsbane elders crashed down upon her head.

As Elder Alder wondered how to word his response to Elder Whip, there was one thought that rang quite clearly, and quite loudly, in his mind:

Mabel, if you are still alive...run!

For more Mabel, Brightsbane, wizards, and magic, join Clayton's newsletter at:

WWW.STATEOFCLAYTON.COM

Acknowledgements

It took quite a bit of wizardry and magic to bring Mabel Gray into existence. I'd like to thank my wife, Paula, who is a Terribly Good Witch, for helping me shape Mabel's story from the get-go. She helped turn little Mabel from a mild-mannered child into a friendless orphan on a mission. Which...doesn't sound so nice when you put it like that, but trust me. It's a good thing.

Paula also used her magical proofreading powers to do a wonderful last-minute tidying of this tale. Thanks for making me look good, darling. As always.

A very tremendous thanks also goes out to Steven Luna, who is so immensely talented in so many ways that there's no way he's not a Wizard First Class. Steven played many roles in the creation of this book, including, but not limited to, developmental editor, copy editor, sounding board, cheerleader, character name generator, dragon wrangler, and riddlemeister. Oh, and you may have noticed that this book has a cover. *Steven created that from nothing.* He drew and painted the illustration and managed the complete cover design. His talent just explodes way beyond where any talent has any right to go.

He's definitely a wizard, and one I'm glad to have on my side.

I'd also like to thank my trio of beta readers, David Bloom, Jenna Miller, and Alex Kimmell. A wise man once said, "The smallest of adjustments can make a world of difference." That man was probably a chiropractor. But it also holds true for books. Thank you for your invaluable input!

I'd also like to thank Grant Faulkner and the rest of the folks at the Office of Letters and Light. This book was my National Novel Writing Month novel in 2014, and without the annual prompting of the OLL, this book simply wouldn't exist.

And thank *you*, dear reader, for supporting indie authors!

About the Author

Photo by Emily Rose Studios

Clayton Smith is a writer, teacher, ghost, and frost giant who lives in the Shadowlands outside of Chicago. When he's not writing, teaching, haunting, or smashing things up with his ice mallet, he is usually hard at work learning new potions. In fact, he recently mastered a potion that turns your nose inside-out. (Practical applications are still being examined.)

Clayton hopes to write down all the Brightsbane tales he knows before the goblins break through the magical barrier and drag him off to their secret and poorly-tended lair beneath the Stones of Accidental Misplacement, but if he doesn't manage it, just know this: They all lived happily ever after.*

*Maybe.

WWW.STATEOFCLAYTON.COM

Made in the USA
Lexington, KY
24 March 2015